D0478935

*It began with Dylan. It was the way he had of charming everyone, drawing them into another world where anything was possible. When you felt the walls that held you prisoner fall away, glimpsed the glittering horizons of his world, you couldn't go back. Not ever.*

*Hollie didn't have a chance. She was too fragile, too easily mesmerized by his promises. There was so much people never knew about Hollie. How her mind had found a way to twist her past, until she'd turned it into something that made sense to her. The blameless mother who screwed her up, then killed herself; the father who didn't have time for her; the stepmother who wanted to love her, but couldn't.*

*It seemed inevitable that Hollie and Dylan would fall in love. For a while, it was glorious. They were a common sight around the village—hand in hand, his ⸺ ⸺ towering above hers, dressed in th⸺ ⸺ zed coats. Bu⸺ ⸺ ⸺hing else w⸺ ⸺ ⸺ urgency seemed to fill the ⸺ ⸺ was running out and they had to make the most of every second. Run faster, speak louder, cram more into each day, while they still could . . .*

*Until on a day of yellow sky and wild winds, it all stopped.*

Also by Debbie Howells

*The Bones of You*
*The Beauty of the End*
*Part of the Silence*
*Her Sister's Lie*

# THE
# STEPDAUGHTER

## DEBBIE
## HOWELLS

KENSINGTON BOOKS
www.kensingtonbooks.com

This book is a work of fiction. Names, characters, and incidents either are products of the author's imagination or are used fictitiously. Any resemblance to actual persons living or dead, or events, is entirely coincidental.

KENSINGTON BOOKS are published by

Kensington Publishing Corp.
119 West 40th Street
New York, NY 10018

Copyright © 2020 by Debbie Howells

All rights reserved. No part of this book may be reproduced in any form or by any means without the prior written consent of the Publisher, excepting brief quotes used in reviews.

To the extent that the image or images on the cover of this book depict a person or persons, such person or persons are merely models, and are not intended to portray any character or characters featured in the book.

All Kensington titles, imprints, and distributed lines are available at special quantity discounts for bulk purchases for sales promotion, premiums, fund-raising, educational, or institutional use. Special book excerpts or customized printings can also be created to fit specific needs. For details, write or phone the office of the Kensington Sales Manager: Kensington Publishing Corp., 119 West 40th Street, New York, NY 10018. Attn. Sales Department. Phone: 1-800-221-2647.

Kensington and the K logo Reg. U.S. Pat. & TM Off.

ISBN-13: 978-1-4967-0696-6 (ebook)
ISBN-10: 1-4967-0696-X (ebook)

ISBN-13: 978-1-4967-1875-4
ISBN-10: 1-4967-1875-5

First Kensington Trade Paperback Printing: July 2020

10 9 8 7 6 5 4 3 2 1

Printed in the United States of America

*For my sisters*
*Sarah, Anna, and Freddie*

# 1

# Elise

As the aircraft accelerates down the runway and takes off for London, from my crew seat I watch the woman in front of me. Her blond hair is shoulder length, her eye makeup minimal, her lips red. I envy the biker jacket over the green dress she's wearing, as I'm drawn to a line on the cover of the magazine she's reading. *Only ten percent of people are good.* Ten percent . . . It's a small number. I frown, trying to work out if I'm one of them.

The ground falls away and I glance through the window as the world shrinks and snowcapped mountains come into view. Then the seat belt sign goes out and I get up, glancing for a moment down the length of the aircraft. One hundred and twenty-three faces seeing my neatly pinned-back hair and mask of immaculate makeup, my navy uniform dress and smart shoes. One hundred and twenty-three lives I know nothing about, just as they know nothing about mine.

As I set up the drinks trolley, the statistic on the magazine cover stays with me, and I think about how many people cause suffering to others. I used to believe that extreme behavior could be explained by abusive childhoods or desperation or personality disorders—and sometimes it can. But that was before I realized people have choices; make decisions. That innate brutality exists.

The passengers are mostly students in big coats and running shoes; blank-looking business travelers; wealthy Italians in designer wear. As I serve cups of tea, I'd usually imagine them as parents, families, friends, vacationers. But today, as I look at their faces, I'm wondering which of them are in the ten percent. It's impossible to tell. None of us know what we're capable of in extreme circumstances.

Now and then, I glance through a window to take in the bird's-eye view I never tire of, a world that's endlessly beautiful. Beneath a pale blue sky, mountains have given way to a sea of snowfields, broken here and there by a circular town or a spider's web of serpentine roads; by monolith chimneys from which vertical smoke rises, scored into the whiteness. Over northern France, the snow reduces to an icing-sugar dusting. Then as we start our approach into London, as the clouds thicken, the reality of my life comes flooding back.

While the passengers disembark; on the crew bus to the crew room; on another bus that takes me to the parking lot, I wear the mask. Only when I'm alone in my car does it slip. As I leave the airport perimeter road, I open the window and light a cigarette, suspending my reality for as long as I can: of the neighbors who think they know me; my cheating husband whose patients think he's God; my changeling daughter, who lives in her own world; our family life tenuously held together by my silent promise.

Abingworth is a thirty-minute drive from the airport. As I turn off the main road, I light another cigarette, my eyes narrowing when I think of Andrew, wondering who *she* is; grateful for small mercies. As far as I know, this is his fourth, though

I've no reason to believe there haven't been more. So far, she's been discreet. The humiliation of not being enough for your husband is multiplied a hundredfold when everyone else knows.

Slowing down as I reach the village, I pass the sign reading ABINGWORTH. When we moved here five years ago, it was with a tacit agreement that this was a chance for a new start. But under no illusions, I made another silent promise, to myself. If Andrew cheated on me once more, I'd make him pay.

Now, as I drive toward our house, I try to remember the feeling I had back then. Hope, weighted with mistrust, a jaded anger with my husband, a need to protect my family. It isn't Niamh's fault her parents' marriage is a mess. I've learned the hard way not to trust Andrew; that the most practiced liars hide behind blank eyes and cold smiles; wield blame, criticism, and belittlement to mold their world and everyone in it.

Slowing down, I turn into our lane, then through tall gateposts into our driveway, feeling my tension ease. The garden is surrounded by flint walls, the cedar trees in front of the house giving it seclusion, privacy. There's no sign of Andrew's car. My relief that I'm alone is instantly squashed by the thought that's never far from my mind. *He could be with her.*

At one time, I would have phoned his practice, desperate, cobbling together an excuse for calling when I didn't need to, but I no longer care enough. Today, I park by the back door and take my crew bag inside, thinking about the three days off I have, imagining tidying the house and going for a run; catching up with one or two friends before next week's flight schedule starts. Maybe I'll take Niamh shopping and get her out of those awful velour leggings she lives in. *Maybe Andrew will dump his lover. Actually see me properly. See Niamh. See anyone but that fucking bitch he's sleeping with.* But even if he did, I'm not sure I'd want him. Swallowing hard, I blink away the hot tears filling my eyes, hating how the thought of him makes me feel.

In the kitchen, my heart skips a beat as I see the light flashing on the house phone. I leave it until I've showered and changed, until I've made myself a cup of coffee. Putting it off until I can't. When I play the message, there are no distinguishable words, just a faint crackle. After it plays through, I delete it, then retrieve the caller's number, my blood like ice in my veins. I write it down with shaking hands, knowing it's his most recent lover. *It's what always happens. It's just a question of when.*

There is no escape from my husband's betrayal. Even in my home, I'm surrounded by the ghosts of his lovers leaving their silent messages of possession. Most women would have left, but I haven't. Not yet. But I will. The only way through this is to wear the mask. Hide the truth from Niamh, let Andrew do what he wants to do, knowing the day will come, one way or another, when it ends for good. Picking up my mug, I sip my coffee, finding it cold, bitter. My hands still trembling, I hurl it at the wall.

# Niamh

$A$s I get off the school bus, cold air rustles the leaves and blows my hair across my face; I feel the first spots of rain. While I walk up the lane, no traffic passes by. I live in a village of tall trees and stone walls, on a road to nowhere; a place of cold hearts and secrets. My stop's the last. No one gets off with me.

"Hey, Cat." Each day, the cat waits, a motionless sentry perched on the wall at the side of the road, his yellow eyes unblinking, his black head battle-scarred. His presence is an honor, rather than a given. A cat belongs to no one but himself.

By the time I turn into our drive, he's vanished. Gravel crunches under my feet as I walk toward the house. It's gray, austere, softened only by the wisteria that, in spring, is covered with racemes of lilac.

As I walk around the side to the back door, music from the radio drifts outside. In the kitchen, my mother's wearing jeans and a wide-necked sweater that slides off one of her tanned shoulders.

"I need some money for the science trip," I tell her, putting down my school bag and getting juice from the fridge, before *going to the pantry for a bag of potato chips. Opening it, I take a handful, watching her leaf through today's mail; her hand pausing on a letter, her intake of breath; the perceptible paling of her skin.*

*"It'll have to wait, Niamh. I don't have any cash." She adds, "Don't eat all of those."*

*Taking another handful, I ignore her. "Whatever. You can pay online. Probably easier." I shrug as her phone buzzes, her face closing over as she picks it up and glances at the screen.*

*"Remind me later, honey. I have to get this." There's a catch in her voice.*

*I stare at her. "Who is it?"*

*In the time it takes her to respond, the hairs on the back of my neck prickle. "No one you know. A friend." As she glances in my direction, I notice the semitone rise in sharpness in her voice, the five seconds of fake brightness in her smile. Turning her back, only when she's out of earshot does she start talking.*

*That's when I know it's another of her lies. She'll tell herself I haven't noticed anything wrong, then forget all about it. My mother sees what she wants to see. But I know the password on her phone. I can find out who's called if I want to.*

*Taking the chips, I go outside, shaking off my uneasiness as I wander down to the end of the garden that borders the road, wondering if all families lie to each other. Pulling myself up onto the same flint wall where the cat was waiting for me just minutes ago, I envy the simplicity of his life, his past forgotten, his future uncontemplated; his only concern the eternal present.*

*As cars pass, I watch the people inside them, just as I watch everyone, see unreadable faces, imagine sunlight bouncing off their armor. Like my father in his doctor's office, my mother in her airline uniform, all of them are practiced, unemotional, closed.*

*From under the shadow of the eucalyptus tree, I look across the lane into the Addisons' garden. Through the branches, I can just about make out dimly lit windows, hear faint strains of violin concerto drift across the lawn.*

*The breeze picks up and I shiver. Slipping down, I cross the road, wandering past their drive toward the next, registering the absence of cars parked there, the closed curtains in the windows. It's the kind of house I'd like to live in one day, with sharp lines and a modern glass extension, sparsely planted with spiky plants and grasses.*

*The Enfields, who live here, are away in their vacation home in Marbella. I make my way across their garden, hidden from next door by the fringe of silver birch trees that separate their drives. At the back of the house, no one sees me peer in through the window at the bland interior with white sofas and no photographs. It's a house without an identity, not a home.*

*It's dark when Hollie appears in my bedroom doorway. Her hair is windswept. I can tell from her eyes she's been crying. Staring at her face, I know before she tells me what's wrong.*

*"Your dad?" I ask. He's the only person Hollie cares about. She nods, words, tears, snot, pouring out of her as she starts to blubber. I watch, fascinated. I've never seen anyone cry like Hollie does.*

*"He was talking to someone on his phone." Her hair gets in the way as she breaks off to wipe her face on her sleeve. "Whoever it was, they're a bastard." There's hatred in her voice. Not wanting my mother to hear, I glance toward the open door.*

*I lean toward her, curious. "What were they talking about?"*

*Her lip wobbles. "I can't tell you." Then her shoulders start to shake. "I can't tell anyone! Do you know how that feels? To know something no one else will ever believe?"*

*I stare at her, appalled. I've no idea what she's talking about. "You can tell me, Hollie."*

*She shakes her head. "I can't. You're too young." Coming over, she awkwardly strokes my hair, before perching on the end of my bed as she tries to get control over herself. When she turns to look at me, her face is tearstained. "Have you ever found out something really shocking?"*

*I frown. "Like when someone dies, you mean?"*

*"Worse." She whispers it, her eyes huge. There's a silence before she takes a deep breath. "There's someone I thought I could trust. With anything. With my life. And now . . ." She breaks off again, her body shaking with silent sobs, while I wait for her to stop.*

*"It's happening again." Her eyes are wild as she stares at me. "I don't know what to do, Niamh. I can't tell anyone."*

# 2

# Elise

The new message on the house phone unsettles me. I have an hour or so before Niamh's bus gets back. The sky threatens rain but I pull on running clothes and shoes, needing to shift the sense of unease hanging over me.

Slipping the back-door key into a zip pocket, I pull up my collar and walk briskly down the drive onto the lane, breaking into a run as I reach the main road, the cold clinging to my hands, my cheeks; running harder, feeling the slow spread of heat thaw them.

Through the village, I see no one. Windows are closed and dark, drives are empty. Only as I pass Ida Jones's house are there signs of life: the warm glow from her downstairs windows, the wood smoke spiraling from her chimney. The thought comes to me. Ida knows everyone around here. Maybe she knows who *she* is.

I could ask her, but not today. Without stopping, I carry on past the last houses, where a footpath slopes down through woods and across a stream, then up the other side to the village church. Under the trees, the path is dark and muddy, fallen leaves making it slippery underfoot, and I pick my way carefully, winding my way down, then over the narrow bridge, before coming out of the trees into the churchyard. Here, amongst the dead, I stop.

The graves have become familiar to me. My eyes pass over their inscriptions as I walk through them, always pausing in the same place to read words I know by heart about a life that ended too soon. *Never forgotten.* Most days, I find a sense of peace here, but today, I'm thinking of the magazine statistic again. Only ten percent of people are good. The rest are like Andrew—they do what they want, or whatever it takes to sate blind ambition, to slake lust.

As I stand there, a desperate sense of hopelessness washes over me. Instead of fighting my tears, I let them stream down my cheeks. I used to have hopes and dreams, but nothing in my life has worked out as I'd imagined it would. Now, I'm driven by Niamh's future. It's the only thing in my pointless world that's important to me.

"You haven't forgotten tonight, have you?" Without explaining why he's late, Andrew hangs up his coat and walks into the kitchen to put the kettle on, but he never justifies anything. Even off duty, his characteristic air of authority never leaves him.

My heart sinks as I remember. He's talking about the end of January drinks in the pub—a village tradition, after a month off alcohol. I had forgotten. If I hadn't, I'd have invented an excuse, but it's too late for that. "I had, actually." I pause, wanting to say I'm too tired. It's true—I had an early start this morning. Instead, I glance at the clock. It's seven thirty. "What time is everyone meeting?"

"Eight." Changing his mind, Andrew switches off the kettle and uncorks a bottle of red wine.

"Fine." My mind is restless. I'm thinking, if I'm right, if *she* lives locally, the chances are she'll be there. Right now, it's too good an opportunity to miss. "I'll just change."

Pulling on a black tunic over my jeans, I knot a pale scarf over it, then brush my hair and touch up my makeup. The spritz of perfume is defiant, reflecting my mood. As I go downstairs, there's music coming from the sitting room. I push the door open enough to see Niamh slumped on the sofa, and Hollie sprawled on the rug in front of the fire. Neither of them looks at me.

"We're just going out, girls. We won't be late." My voice is intentionally light, painting a picture that Andrew and I are off on a cozy evening out.

Niamh turns briefly, hair the color of flax falling across her face. "OK, Mum." Her words are expressionless, her eyes blank, as they mirror mine. Not for the first time I berate myself for not being the kind of mother who hugs, laughs, jokes. Hideous guilt paralyzes me for not being able to make everything right in her world.

I look at Hollie. "Are you staying, Hollie?"

Hollie Hampton lives at the other end of the village from us. At sixteen, she's two years older than Niamh, but they're kindred spirits somehow, probably because of shared pain. Riveted to the television, Hollie nods imperceptibly, pulling her long dark hair over one of her thin shoulders. Elfin-faced, with her translucent skin, frayed jeans under a pale silver dress, she's diaphanous.

"Are your parents going to the pub?"

This time, she doesn't speak, just shrugs.

"There are snacks in the cupboard if you're hungry," I remind them. "See you later, girls."

Pushing the door closed behind me, I go to find Andrew. In the hallway, he's already wearing his coat. He barely glances at me. "Ready?"

His tone is brusque. I nod, pulling on a jacket and knitted hat, trying to remember the last time my husband was affectionate toward me.

*   *   *

We walk to the pub in silence. The air is damp, the drops of rain from earlier yet to turn into anything more. For some reason, Hollie's on my mind. Her father, James, is a writer; her stepmother, Stephanie, is a florist. But in the last couple of years, Hollie's seemed troubled. I've seen it when she appears at the door, uninvited, as if she has nowhere else to go; the way sometimes she's quiet as if her mind is far away, while other days emotions race across her face like clouds across a sky. I've seen her running through the fields, her hair flowing behind her, almost a romantic figure, until you see the angst in her eyes.

Hands in my pockets, I hurry through the darkness, trying to keep up with Andrew's brisk, staccato steps, like everything about him, deliberate, purposeful. I wonder if he's thinking of *her.* When he speaks, it takes me by surprise.

"We should plan a holiday, Elise. I'm thinking about Dubai."

For the second time today, I'm hit by shock. I should be delighted, but instead, I'm outraged, upset, cynical; smothering the urge to flail my fists into the softness of his overcoat, to scream at him, *Why this pretense, when we both know you want to be with her?* It's replaced by numbness. There's no point in my outrage. He's playing a game with me, goading me. He doesn't want me. There's no going back to how we used to be.

I put my hands in my pockets. "Let's see, shall we?" I know my cool response won't be what he's expecting.

"You're always saying you want me to make more effort," he says through gritted teeth. "But the trouble with you, Elise, is that it's always one bloody way—your way."

Angst rises inside me. It's so far from the truth, but he never listens to what I say. But this is what Andrew does. Twists everything, until black is white, light is dark. Words fill my head, words I stuff down unspoken, because there's no point when he stores away everything I say to use against me.

# Niamh

*From the moment I first met Hollie, I knew she was different. She was in the churchyard, standing with her back to me. I noticed her long dark hair, her pale skin as she turned around when a twig cracked under my foot.*

*I stared at her for a moment. In her thin white dress, she looked delicate, as though the wind could blow her away. "I'm Niamh."*

*Her wide eyes darted around before settling on mine. "I'm Hollie."*

*"I know." Imagining Hollie as a ghost surrounded by the silent graves between us, I felt myself shiver. I was about to walk away, but curiosity got the better of me. "Are you OK?"*

*As she nodded, I saw loneliness in her eyes. The first raindrop fell on my skin. Then as more started to fall, I glanced up at the sky just as the heavens opened.*

*Hollie nodded toward the church. "Maybe we should go in."*

*I nodded, following her toward the wooden door, which creaked open as she lifted the heavy latch. In the doorway watching the deluge, neither of us spoke for a moment.*

*"I like your dress." My words were almost drowned out by the rain falling on the tiled roof as I gazed at her, her dress translucent where the rain had caught it.*

*She didn't reply. Instead, I watched her shiver. "You can feel them, can't you?" she asked, her arms tightly hugging herself. I could tell from the way her eyes roamed across the churchyard, she was talking about the souls of the dead.*

*I nodded, imagining the heartbreak of their families lingering in the air, wondering if after enough time passed, the rain washed it away.*

*"Do you ever think about all the people who've come here? The christenings, weddings, funerals..." Her words echoed through the church as she fell silent. "My mum died. I was ten. I wasn't allowed to go to her funeral." Her voice was small, choked with tears.*

*The crash of thunder overhead startled me. I thought of my father, spending another Sunday in a fug of red wine and temper; how my mother was never happy. Without thinking, my hand reached for hers.*

*At first, she didn't respond. Then she muttered, "They think she killed herself." Her eyes were blank as she stared outside at the rain. For the first time, she raised her head to look at me; then her eyes widened. "They're wrong. I know they are. She wouldn't have done that." She sounded angry. "But no one believes me." She broke off.*

*I didn't know what to say. In the streak of lightning that lit the church, I saw the emotion flashing through her eyes. In those few minutes, I was under her spell, just as Dylan was.*

# 3

# Elise

When we reach the pub, I hover outside, thinking of the charade ahead of me on the other side of the door.

"What's wrong with you?" Andrew is unsympathetic.

"Absolutely nothing," I tell him. "I just remembered something." I'm putting off the moment, when the last thing I want to do is go inside. But I've long stopped caring about lying to him because Andrew's entire life is a lie. There's the amiable doctor, the caring father, the solicitous husband, the solid neighbor making his entrance into the pub, when the real Andrew is a cruel, manipulative liar.

"It's too cold to stand around out here." He sounds impatient.

"Then don't." I say it through gritted teeth. Then instead of turning around and walking home, I push past him and open the door, latching on to the first familiar face I see inside, feeling my heart sink. "Julian!" Unbuttoning my jacket, I pin on a smile. "How lovely to see you! Is Sophie with you? How was Goa?"

"Hot." As he kisses my cheek, the smell of his aftershave is cloying. "She's over there."

Across the pub, Sophie raises her hand, looking anxious. Craning my neck, I see she's been snared by Christian. I pull a sympathetic face at her, before turning away.

"Drink, Elise?" Andrew's voice comes from behind me.

"Vodka and tonic. I've never been." I'm talking about Goa.

"Julian . . . good to see you. Can I get you another?"

After he comes back with my drink, I leave him and Julian, before drifting in the direction of Sophie, who's the only person I'm remotely interested in talking to, waiting while she extricates herself from Christian's lengthy monologue.

Looking around, I see James and Stephanie Hampton, Hollie's parents. As I catch Stephanie's eye, a look of recognition flickers across her face. It occurs to me to bring up my concerns about Hollie. But then Sophie comes over. "Bloody circus, isn't it?" She kisses me on both cheeks. "I don't know why we put ourselves through this."

"You know as well as I do. So that we can gloat over our successes and crow over each other's failures. You look great, Sophie." Her hair is lighter, her skin sun-kissed. But the Calders are often away somewhere hot.

"After two weeks in Goa, I ought to have a tan . . . It won't last around here in this god-awful weather. Luckily we're off to Barbados for a fortnight. Are you going anywhere?"

"Apparently Andrew wants to go to Dubai." My words are expressionless. I've still no idea why he even mentioned it, unless it's lip service to his role as dutiful husband. "I won't be going with him."

There's an odd look on Sophie's face. "Have you told him?"

I shake my head. "Not yet." It'll cause another fight I don't have the energy for; like everything else to do with Andrew, it would be pointless.

She frowns at me. "Are you alright?"

"Fine." I sip my drink, unable to taste the vodka, putting it down. Then I close my eyes for a moment. "Actually, I'm not.

My vision's gone blurry." Sophie knows I get migraines. I search my bag for my pills. "I can't believe it. They're in my other bag." I glance around, noticing Andrew deep in conversation, on the other side of the room. "Do me a favor and tell him, would you? I should go home and take a pill before it gets any worse. Can we catch up another time? I want to hear about Goa."

Sophie's concern is genuine. "He should take you home. I'll get him."

I'm shaking my head. "Please, don't. We've only just got here. I'll be fine on my own."

"You're sure? Would you like me to walk with you?"

I shake my head. "If you could just tell Andrew . . ."

Slipping outside unnoticed, I take a deep breath. I have no migraine, just an intolerance for an evening wasted with people I don't want to see. I'd rather be alone. As I walk home, I know Andrew won't come after me, or even call me to check if I'm alright. I have no guilty conscience about the lie. In a life that's full of them, one more makes no difference. I think of the expression on Sophie's face when I told her I wasn't going away with Andrew, and it creeps into my mind that she could be his latest. But she's been in Goa, I remember, relieved, because Sophie's the only person around here that I actually like.

Through the darkness, the sound of an owl reaches me. When we moved here, I thought I'd grow to love the countryside and the changes of the seasons, but I haven't. Instead, it suffocates me. In a small village, there is no privacy. Everyone sees you. I wonder how much longer I can keep up the pretense that Andrew and I have a functioning marriage, just as I wonder how many people already know we don't.

Just before I reach our drive, I hear the unmistakable sound of footsteps running on gravel, then Hollie springs through the open gate, her hair caught in the dim glow from the lamps on top of the gateposts. Without looking round, she carries on up the lane, and I hear her sobbing. Hollie's always been melodramatic, but lately . . . I shake my head. There's something different about her. But the trouble with Hollie is her hype. When nothing small ever happens to her, it's impossible to know what to believe.

Inside, I linger in the kitchen. Upstairs, I can hear Niamh moving around; then she comes downstairs, no doubt checking why I'm back so soon. If she's surprised to see me, I can't tell.

"I have one of my migraines," I explain. "Have you eaten?" Niamh's face is blank as she looks at me. "We had pizza."

Out of the corner of my eye I see the empty box on the side. "Was Hollie OK?"

"She's fine." But Niamh's answer is too quick.

"I passed her just now." Hollie clearly wasn't fine. I wonder if something happened between them in the hour I was out. "She came running out just as I got back. She seemed upset about something."

As Niamh shrugs, I know she isn't going to tell me anything. Then she wanders out of the kitchen and I hear her light footsteps on the stairs. Fetching a glass, I make myself another drink—full strength this time, not like the insipid version the pub serves—then go over to the sofa at the far end of the kitchen, flicking the TV on.

The kitchen is my favorite room—calm, light yet cozy. Looking around, I imagine Andrew in the pub, no doubt smugly holding forth to anyone who'll listen. I allow self-pity to wash over me, but only fleetingly. Sipping my drink, I remind myself, I chose this life, just as I choose to stay, not because I love this lifestyle or this house, because I don't. It's for Niamh. It won't last forever.

By the time Andrew gets home, I'm in a vodka-induced slumber, which absolves me of having to talk to him and from which I awake late the following morning to find the bed empty. As I lie there, the sound of Andrew crashing around the kitchen reaches my ears, then the quieter sound of Niamh's bedroom door opening, her footsteps fainter as she goes downstairs.

Closing my eyes, I think about staying in bed. I'm often on an early flight—the two of them are used to mornings without me. But propelled by a sense of maternal duty, I force myself to get up.

"Are you better?" Andrew barely looks at me as I walk into the kitchen.

He misses my nod as he grabs his keys. "I'll be late," he says abruptly. "I have a meeting."

"Fine." Then I look at Niamh, her face implacable as she watches him. For her sake, I add, "I hope it goes well," making my voice sound caring, trying to counteract that his is anything but.

"See you tonight." Grabbing his jacket, he marches outside. Niamh glances at the clock and pulls on her coat.

"Have a good day, Niamh."

"Bye." I watch her walk outside, then push the door closed behind her. Her face is paler than usual, bleached by the negativity between me and Andrew, a storm cloud she can't escape from. I wait for the sound of his car starting, but instead I hear him swear loudly. Then he marches back inside. "Some little shit's been at my car."

"What?" I'm incredulous. Nothing like that happens around here. "What's happened to it?"

"The fucking tires have been slashed." Andrew's face is white with fury. "I'll have to take yours."

I frown, wondering when it happened, how none of us heard. "You should tell the police. Just a moment . . ." As his eyes search the kitchen, I reach for my keys before he sees them. "You're not helping yourself to my car, Andrew. I have plans."

"You can change your so-called plans," he says nastily. "You have a day off, don't you? Whereas I don't. I have a job to go

to, patients waiting to see me . . . I'd say that's far more important than anything you might be doing today."

His arrogance renders me speechless. He has absolutely no
idea what I'm doing. And I wouldn't mind betting it isn't his
patients on his mind, more the so-called meeting he has after
work, probably with *her*.

"No." My fingers close around my keys.

"For Christ's sake, Elise."

"Call a taxi, Andrew." Slipping the keys into the pocket of
my pajamas, I turn around and go upstairs.

# 4

# Elise

I could have offered to run Andrew into work, or to arrange for someone to come here and fit new tires, so as to save him the trouble, but I don't, nor do I give in to his demands. In a marriage based on lies, on infidelity, there is no kindness. Instead, I wait upstairs until I hear a taxi arrive to take him to the medical practice, then change into running clothes.

It's another chilly February morning as I set off down the drive, pausing beside clumps of pinprick green shoots pushing up through the grass. They're the first snowdrops, their subtle green and white a prelude to the soft yellow of the wild daffodils that have colonized under the oldest trees. A desire to fill the house with flowers grips me. I want beauty, color, fragrance to neutralize the odor of my marriage. Breaking into a jog, I think of Stephanie Hampton's small florist shop in the next village.

As my body loosens up, I run harder, heading through the village along the narrow strip of pavement, which is all that's left where the grass verge has encroached, passing the first of the footpaths to the church, before turning up Furze Lane. Half a mile along, I take a path that leads into an area of woodland and for several minutes I run hard, my feet cushioned by fallen leaves. Then I take the rough steps hewn into the earth leading downhill, before the path slopes uphill again, opening out on the farthest side of the churchyard.

At this time of day, I rarely see anyone, but this morning, as I slow down, I see a slight figure leaning against one of the tallest oaks. It's Hollie. If it's possible for her to look any smaller or more fragile, when she sees me looking at her, she seems to shrink.

"Hey." I come to a stop in front of her. "Are you OK?" Agitated, she's standing amongst the oldest gravestones, clutching her hands, white knuckles protruding from bunched-up, too-long sleeves.

At first, she doesn't speak, just continues to stare at her hands.

I feel myself frown. "Shouldn't you be at school, Hollie?"

"Does it matter?" Her eyes darting around, she doesn't look at me. "I mean, actually . . . does it?"

"Well, yes." I'm trying to sound reasonable. "You have exams to think about. You don't want to miss too many lessons." Then I frown, wondering why she's irritated with me.

"I can't think about school," she mumbles. "Not now. There's too much going on."

The look on her face makes my blood run cold. "Such as what?"

This time, she stares right at me, tears blurring her eyes. "I can hardly tell you." She turns away. "Anyway, you'd be like everyone else. No one believes anything I tell them."

"I'm sure that's not true." Knowing she's prone to over-dramatizing things, I try to sound conciliatory. "James—I mean your dad . . . you have a good relationship, don't you?" But as I mention his name, a stricken look washes across her face.

She shakes her head. "Please don't . . . Please. I mean it. It won't do any good."

Frowning, I take a step closer. "Has something happened, Hollie? If it has, if you want to talk to—"

But she interrupts me. "Go away." Her eyes blaze but her voice is desperate. "You have no idea. You can't help me. No one can."

It isn't my place to interfere. But I'm not prepared for her to speak to me like this. "Fine. It's your life. You need to think about it, Hollie. You can't just take time out from school." It comes out more sharply than I intended.

"You can't stop me."

I frown at her. It's as though she's challenging me, pushing me, as if she wants something from me. "No." I pause. "I can't. But this isn't about me."

Out of the corner of my eyes, I see Ida Jones appear from under the trees. As she walks toward us, a look of panic crosses Hollie's face. "Don't tell her. Please . . ."

I don't have time to ask what I'm not supposed to tell her, before I hear Ida's gentle voice. "How are you, my dears?" Then turning to Hollie, she adds, "I didn't know it was the holidays."

"No." I'm acutely aware of Hollie's eyes on me. "Hollie wasn't feeling so well this morning. We just happened to bump into each other." The lie slips out. I've no idea where the need to justify why we're here together comes from.

"Oh dear . . ." Ida scrutinizes Hollie's face. "You do look pale, dear. Are you feeling poorly?"

"How's your granddaughter, Ida?" Glancing at Hollie, I change the subject.

"She's very well." A wistful smile spreads across her face, then as her phone buzzes, she fumbles in one of her pockets. "I'm so sorry, but it's my daughter. Would you excuse me?"

As she turns away to talk, I ask Hollie directly. "What are you hiding?"

She starts. "Nothing . . ." She pauses, but from the flush of color on her pale cheeks, I know she's lying.

*    *    *

For the rest of my run, then while I shower and change, Hollie fills my head. I try to imagine what's distressing her as well as what she's hiding, feeling an obligation to tell her father about our conversation. It gives me a dual reason to go and buy flowers this morning.

It's a ten-minute drive to the next village. Stephanie's shop is on the outskirts, one of a number of small businesses that have premises within a range of stylishly converted farm buildings. Turning into the yard, I park in one of the cobbled spaces just outside her window.

Pausing for a moment, I look through the window, where inside, Stephanie's talking on her phone. I watch her for a moment. She's attractive in a deliberate sort of way, with angular features and a hardness that even too much makeup doesn't hide. Today, she's clearly agitated, her face flustered as she speaks on her phone. As she ends the call, she stands in the window, not moving for a moment. Then, seeing my car, she seems to obviously compose herself.

I recognize the scent of eucalyptus as I open the door. Stephanie's behind her desk, going through what looks like a list of orders. "Hello." I watch her guardedly.

"Elise . . . I won't be a moment. How are you?" There's no trace of the agitation I witnessed earlier. As always, her every movement is measured.

"Fine, thank you. I was hoping for some spring flowers to brighten the house." As I speak, I'm thinking it isn't just the house, it's my life that needs a facelift. "This weather being so gray . . ." I gesture toward the window.

"It's a terrible winter." Putting down her book, she looks up. "But at least you get to see the sun."

"Not so much at the moment. I haven't had any long-haul trips for ages." On a good day, I still get a blast of sunlight through the aircraft windows as we break through the clouds, but not always. "Can I see what you have?"

"Have a look. I had a delivery this morning." She gestures toward the far end of the shop, which is where she sets out buckets of flowers. "Let me know if I can help."

Wandering over, for a few minutes I lose myself in the array of flowers, before pulling out bunches of narcissi, iris, ranunculus and carrying them over to her counter. Stephanie eyes me curiously. "Is there an occasion?"

I shake my head. She's probably itching to know if there's a party she isn't invited to. "Pure self-indulgence." I pause. "I saw Hollie this morning."

I watch a flicker of something cross her face. But whatever it is stays locked inside. "Is everything OK? She seemed upset."

This time Stephanie looks at me. "Oh, everything's more than OK." Her voice is bitter, her words sarcastic. "Hollie has James exactly where she wants him."

"It can't be easy." Not wanting to be drawn into Stephanie's family politics, I glance around, looking for a way to change the subject, my eyes alighting on a row of plants with dark green fernlike leaves, arranged on a shelf. "Those are unusual."

"Yes." Without looking up, she carries on wrapping my flowers. By the time she's finished, her face is flushed. "That will be sixty-eight pounds." Then as I hand over my credit card, she sighs. "Look, you may as well know, things are not alright. Hollie's determined to create a rift between me and James. I won't bore you with the details. I was talking to the school—just before you came in? She's missing too many classes. James needs to be firmer with her, but he won't." She breaks off. "Anyway, I'm not sure why I'm boring you with this. Everyone has their own problems."

As her eyes hold mine, I can tell she knows Andrew's having an affair. Is it with her? I stare at her, trying to imagine them together, then snap myself out of it. "Thanks." Gathering up my flowers, I can't get out of there fast enough. She's right. I have more than enough of my own problems, without taking on hers.

# Niamh

*Hollie was friends with Dylan first. But now that he's gone, she has me.*

*"People are so horrible, Niamh . . ." She was sobbing. It took ages for me to get the truth out of her, that one of her teachers had phoned her father, because the school is worried about her.*

*"The teacher said I wasn't eating. They think I'm anorexic. I don't eat because I can't," she added theatrically. I could understand her being upset about a teacher poking her nose in, but her hysteria left me mystified.*

*But as I found out, it was always the same. Like her clothes, Hollie's defenses are paper-thin. Every barbed word pierces her skin, is personal. She has no armor against a world she believes is set against her.*

*The day after my parents went to the pub with everyone else, when I come back from school, before the bus stops, Hollie's sitting on the wall, waiting for me, her eyes red, as if she's been crying. As the bus slows and I get off, she falls into step beside me. Even before she speaks, I feel her restlessness radiate into me. "I hate this place," she tells me, meaning the village. "Is your mum home?"*

*"I don't know." I lose track of when she's flying. Every week, my mother's roster is different. "You can come in if you like." Hollie looks wary. "Not if she's there."*

*I frown at her. Hollie doesn't usually mind my mum. "Why not?"*

*"I just don't want to see her. OK?" Her voice is fierce.*

*At the bottom of the drive, I glance toward the house. My father's car is there, which is odd. "She's out. That's my dad's car." I look at Hollie. "Are you coming in?"*

*She hesitates. But she knows we won't see him. "OK. But if she comes back I'm going . . ." There's an odd look on her face.*

*Whatever it is that's on her mind, I know she'll tell me. It's the reason she comes here. She doesn't have anyone else. I try the back door, finding it locked. "He must be out." I unlock the back door, and Hollie follows me in. I sling my bag on the floor, while Hollie goes over to the huge vase on the table. Usually empty, today it's filled with all kinds of flowers.*

*"D'you want a drink?" As I look at her, it's like she's inhaling them.*

*Then she looks up at me. "What is there?"*

*Shrugging, I go to the fridge, frowning as I pass the sink filled with several more bunches. What is it with my mother and all these flowers? "Orange juice, milk, Coke . . ."*

*"Is it diet?"*

*Hollie's skinny. That her teacher phoned her dad didn't surprise me—I hardly ever see her eat, but when she does, she wolfs down food as though she's been starved for a month. Checking the can, I nod, passing it to her, getting another for myself, before going to the pantry for a bag of chips.*

*"Let's go to your room." Hollie's more on edge than usual, constantly glancing through doorways and windows, as if expecting someone to appear.*

*"Yeah." But she runs ahead as I pick up my bag and walk upstairs.*

*In my room, Hollie collapses on my bed, gazing at the ceiling.*

*"God. This is the only place I feel safe." It's the kind of thing she often says, overly dramatic. "No one asks questions or expects anything from me here."*

*I half listen, wondering why she's avoiding my mum. Then suddenly she sits up. "You want to know, don't you? I saw her this morning. Your mum . . . I bunked school."*

*I'd guessed that already; otherwise she wouldn't have been waiting for me at the bus stop.*

*"She gave me one of those talks about not missing school. I thought she was different but she's just like everyone else. I used to imagine I could talk to her." Hollie sounds tearful. "No one knows how I'm feeling, Niamh."*

*Suddenly I'm irritated. It's like last night all over again. Hollie tells me something terrible is going on, something she can't talk about, and I'm supposed to just let her lie on my bed and wallow. Folding my arms, I stare at her. "I can't help if you don't tell me what's happened."*

*Before she can reply, there's the scrunch of car tires on gravel. Hollie leaps up and runs to the landing window. I follow more slowly.*

*"She's back. I have to go. Shit." She sounds hysterical again. "I don't want to see her."*

*Running back to my room, she goes to the window and opens it. It's the craziest overreaction. My window is too high for her to jump from. I put my hand on her arm. "Wait. She might go into the garden or to the bathroom or something."*

*From my bedroom, I hear the back door open as my mother goes into the kitchen, then cupboards opening and closing, before she runs the tap and turns on the kettle. Then I hear her boots on the wooden floor as she comes to the bottom of the stairs.*

*"Are you up there, Niamh?" At the sound of my mother's voice, behind me, Hollie shrinks back.*

*"Yeah."*

"I've put the kettle on. Would you like tea?"

"No. Thanks. I'm doing homework."

As I turn to go back into my room, Hollie's distraught, cowering behind my door. "Why are you so upset? Does it matter that you're here?"

"Shhh . . ." Hollie's eyes are wide as she shakes her head. "She'll know you're talking to someone. You have to help me. I have to get out."

Just then, I hear my mother coming up the stairs. Holding my breath, I glance at Hollie, then I hear the door to my parents' bedroom open, then another door inside to the en suite.

"Now," I tell Hollie urgently. "She's in the bathroom. Just be really quiet."

Without speaking, Hollie flies down the stairs. I don't hear the back door open, just glimpse her from an upstairs window, running across the grass, before I go back to my room and get my homework out. Five minutes later, there's a knock on my door, and my mother pushes it open.

"I just saw Hollie running across the garden."

I look away. "Yeah. She suddenly remembered something she had to do."

My mother gives me an odd look. "Be careful, Niamh. I know you and Hollie are close, but there's something going on. I'm worried about her."

My mother is now an expert on Hollie? I don't think so. I raise my eyebrows at her. "I have homework," I say pointedly.

Heat rises in my cheeks as she glances toward my unopened schoolbooks. "No doubt you do." Her voice is cool. "In that case, I'll let you get on."

# 5

# Elise

In this house of charades, Niamh pretends to do her homework, while I arrange the rest of the flowers, then start dinner for my disunited family. On the outside looking in, there's nothing to set us apart from anyone else: Soft gray curtains are drawn against the darkness; the smell of caramelizing onions filling the house; the serene sound of Classic FM floating in the air; the teenage daughter reluctantly studying in her bedroom; the wife cooking dinner for the doctor husband, who'll soon be home after another day of healing people. Ludicrous façades, when underneath, we barely know each other. For a moment I imagine a different kind of life—one with honesty, laughter, lightness; where love is demonstrated, not withheld or wielded with intent.

My daydream is interrupted by the sound of a car outside. It pauses while a door slams; then as footsteps on gravel come nearer, it drives away. When the back door opens, it's clear the day hasn't improved Andrew's mood. If anything, it's worse.

"You're early." I'm icily polite, imagining he's been stood up by his lover. Otherwise he wouldn't be here.

"Hardly," he snaps. "But I might have been, if I hadn't had to sort the car out."

"Is it fixed?"

"For Christ's sake!" he bellows. "Didn't you see it when you came in? You don't give a shit, Elise." He looks around in disgust. "Why are there flowers everywhere?"

*Because there is more to life than vile deception and anger. Remember beauty, Andrew? How it feels to be touched gently? To be loved?*

"I wanted to cheer up the house. You know I hate winter. Dinner will be about twenty minutes." Speaking as calmly as I can, I go to the fridge and pour a glass of white wine. But he's already storming through to the living room. Seconds later he comes back, slamming something down on the counter behind me; I hear the splintering of glass.

"Can't we have one fucking room without fucking flowers?" As he marches out, I turn to see a vase that used to belong to my grandmother, its crystal dulled by age. There's a jagged crack down one side, from which water's seeping, pooling on the counter, then dripping onto the floor.

Ripping out the flowers I arranged only a little while ago, I drop them on the worktop, then empty the vase and throw it away. The flowers are still scattered there when Niamh comes downstairs, her cool eyes skimming over them before settling on me. Her gaze is impenetrable. I wonder if she heard the way Andrew spoke to me just now, or the shattering of glass, before telling myself, *of course she did.* How could she possibly not have?

"Can you lay the table, honey?" My tone is light.

Without speaking, Niamh sets three places at the kitchen table, then fetches the peppermill and water glasses.

"Do you have much homework?"

"Not really." Niamh's voice is expressionless, as she comes over and peers into the pan I'm stirring.

"Pork," I tell her, suddenly aching for connection, for a joking aside, an affectionate exchange, but Niamh and I are not like that. What we share can only be described as a detached coldness. "Would you like to tell him it's ready?"

Without speaking, Niamh wanders out and I start serving food onto plates. I wonder what's going through her mind, but then she comes back, followed by Andrew. After pouring himself a glass of wine, he picks up a plate and a fork and goes back to the sitting room.

It's a pattern I've grown used to, but today, rage flares inside me at his deliberate contempt. Stifling the urge to tell him what I think, I take the two remaining plates over to the table as Niamh joins me. Sitting there, I watch her eat, picking at my food, filled with resentment that Andrew's behavior overrides everything else in this house—including Niamh. He doesn't care what she hears. He doesn't care about either of us.

For too long, I've forced myself to tolerate his behavior, while I hold our marriage together, no matter what, for Niamh's sake, ignoring the truth—that Andrew and I are toxic. He's bullied away what love there was and shattered my trust. There is no honesty between us. Whatever his reasons for wanting me here, he doesn't care about our marriage any more than I do.

After we've eaten, I wait for Niamh to go up to her bedroom, for the sound of her TV filtering through her cracked-open door, before I go to find Andrew in the living room. It's a large, high-ceilinged room, with a plush carpet and a pair of expensive leather sofas, behind which a series of tall sash windows look out onto the garden. Slouched on one of the sofas, his empty plate is on the coffee table, his shoes kicked off, his attention focused on his phone. In the home we share, having eaten the meal I cooked for him, he's blatantly texting *her*.

Pushing the door closed behind me, I walk over and stand in front of him.

"Not now," he says sharply.

"Yes, now." I don't budge. "For fuck's sake, Andrew. Why are we doing this?"

As he laughs cynically, I stare at him, trying to discern even the faintest trace of the man I fell in love with eighteen years ago. But he doesn't exist anymore. "Oh, I think you know the answer to that."

Leaning down, I snatch his phone away. "The very least you could do is show me some respect," I hiss, keeping my voice low to prevent Niamh from hearing. "I know you don't care about me, but Niamh sees the way you treat me. She sees everything. You could make an effort for once, instead of texting one of your sluts."

The word is unfamiliar on my tongue, but I'm driven by a need to confront him. Standing up, he twists his phone out of my hand, but not before I glimpse the screen, taking in the image on it, frozen with shock as it registers. Then my stomach lurches, and I feel my heart race out of control as I realize what this means. "You disgust me," I say with all the contempt I can muster.

Turning around, I walk back out to the kitchen, glimpsing a movement at the top of the stairs. Looking up, I catch the back of Niamh's head before she closes her bedroom door. If there was any closeness between us, I would go up there and talk to her, reassure her that everything's fine, that Andrew's still cross about what happened to the car tires this morning. Laugh about it—a shared moment between a mother and her daughter. *You know what he's like.*

But I can't lie to her; can't tell her platitudes that neither of us believes, because Niamh would see through it. She knows what's going on, but we're too distanced to talk about it. Far easier for both of us to say nothing.

# Niamh

*My parents' marriage falls another step toward ruin, and I wonder why they stay together; but as always, it's easier for my mother to say nothing.*

*I don't see Hollie until the following weekend. She comes over while my mother is working and my father's playing golf. Her eyes hold mine, open yet closed; making contact yet telling me nothing.*

*"I don't know what to do." For once, she isn't theatrical. "Too many things are wrong."*

*Not sure what to say, I watch her.*

*"Do you really know your dad?" Her eyes are huge. "Or your mum? Do you ever think like they're this person with stuff in their life you know nothing about?"*

*I frown at her, not sure what she's getting at. I know my parents aren't happy, but only because it's obvious. They don't ever tell me anything. "Like what?"*

*"If I tell you ..." Her bottom lip wobbles. "You have to swear, Niamh. On your life. You can't tell anyone. Not ever."*

*"I swear."*

*Hollie's eyes dart around, and then she blurts out, "I've found something out about my dad."*

*Hollie's dad wrote a couple of books a few years ago. For a moment, I imagine one of them being made into a movie. But Hollie would be excited about that, not upset. "What about him?"*

*"He's into something. He knows bad people, Niamh." Then she breaks off. "I can't talk about it."*

*"But you've started. You have to tell me." It's typical of Hollie to do this.*

*She jumps up. "Let's get out of here."*

*"Hollie, it's raining. And there isn't anywhere."*

*"I know somewhere." As she pulls on her jacket and does up her boots, I know she's crazy, because there isn't anywhere around here, just scattered big houses behind garden walls and a village church. But under her spell, I follow her.*

*There's a rawness in the air as we step outside, where Hollie's introspective mood is replaced by recklessness as she runs across the garden into the lane.*

*"Wait . . ." Zipping up my jacket, I run after her. "Where are we going?"*

*"Deeprose House."*

*Deeprose House has high hedges and heavy locked gates. "We can't, Hollie. It belongs to someone."*

*"Of course we can. We can do whatever we like. It's empty—it's been empty for weeks. The Penns are away. They're not back until March."*

*At her side, I jog to keep up. "How do you know?"*

*She's silent for a moment. "I just do. Oh God . . . Ida Jones has seen us. Run!"*

*As I glance at Ida's window, she seems to be beckoning me. I pause, momentarily torn between finding out what she wants and Hollie's retreating back, then break into a run.*

*Side by side, we turn up Furze Lane, past the row of terraced flint cottages, their small windows dimly lit, coils of wood smoke coming from two of the chimneys. Then beneath the trees on either side, the lane narrows. Deeprose House is still a few yards ahead, but Hollie stops suddenly.*

*"We'll go this way." She points toward a metal farm gate, the top bar of which is wrapped in barbed wire. Undeterred, she climbs over into a field of thick grass, waiting for me to join her, before heading toward the middle of it. "There's a back way."*

*My head fills with questions, but I don't ask any of them. Being with Hollie is how it was with Dylan. It's an escape into a world so different from mine that at times like now, I don't question her, just allow myself to be swept along for the ride.*

*At the other side of the field, there's a post and rail fence, which we slip through.*

*"This way." Hollie skips through an orchard where last year's apples lie mostly unused, rotting underfoot. As we reach the other side, she stops and gestures dramatically at the stark hedges, beyond which a sweep of lawn slopes uphill toward the house. "Crazy, isn't it." She shakes her head. "I mean the Penns . . . They have a place like this, but half the time, they're not even here."*

*If I had a house like this, I'd never want to leave it, but right now, the gardens have a wildness about them, from being untouched. There are dead flowers and fallen leaves everywhere I look. As I glance toward the house, taking in its cold walls and dark windows, I shiver. "We shouldn't be here, Hollie." Then, in one of the windows, I think a light flickers. I clutch at Hollie's arm, pointing to it. "Look."*

*For a moment she stares, then she says, "There's nothing there."*

*"It's gone off now," I persist. "But I'm sure I saw something. There must be someone in the house."*

*"There isn't," she flashes, raising her voice. "I told you, Niamh. They're away."*

*For a moment, I imagine a face in one of the windows, watching us. "We should go," I tell her, suddenly uneasy.*

*But she ignores me. "Come on! I want to show you something!" She starts marching toward a gap in the hedge. Reluctantly, I follow her through into a rectangular area, surrounded by tall hedges and carpeted in fallen leaves. Bending down to pick something up, Hollie grabs my arm. "Listen."*

*She throws something into the middle of the leaves. After a couple of seconds, there's a loud splash as it hits water. "The pool," Hollie says casually.*

*I shrink back against the hedge. With all the leaves, it's impossible to tell where the ground ends and the water starts. Suddenly I'm freaked out. "Why have we come here?"*

*It's as if someone's walked over her grave. There's a look of desolation on Hollie's face. "Let's go," she mumbles.*

*Spooked by the dark house and the invisible pool under the leaves, I've no desire to change her mind. But when we get home, my father's car is in the drive and Hollie refuses to come in.*

*"I gave Ida Jones a lift earlier." Still wearing her airline uniform, my mother's slipped off her shoes and undone her hair so that it hangs down past her shoulders. "I need to change." Picking up her shoes, she's halfway out of the kitchen when she pauses. "She said she saw you and Hollie walking together."*

*She tries to make it sound light, conversational, but I know what she's going to ask.*

*"Where did you go?"*

*I shrug. "Just for a walk."*

*My mother frowns slightly. "Ida said someone saw you in Furze Lane."*

*Irritation flares in me. "So?"*

*"You weren't just walking, were you, Niamh? You were seen climbing over a gate. You can't go onto other people's private property like that." She sounds annoyed.*

*I frown at her, trying to imagine what kind of small-minded gossiping villager told Ida exactly where we were. "We went for a walk, that's all. It was a mistake. It's not like there's anything else to do around here."*

*"It's no excuse," she snaps.*

*I stare at her, wondering why she's so angry with me. Flinching as her anger ricochets off the walls at me; stings.*

# 6

# Elise

As days pass, there seems no end to this dismal winter. Ice and snow disrupt flights, while the tension between me and Andrew escalates as my schedule changes at short notice. On the third day, my flight is canceled. That I am at home instead of conveniently out of his way at thirty-five thousand feet has implications for Andrew's love life.

"I thought you were in Zurich tonight." Not expecting me to be here, he doesn't attempt to hide his irritation. As always, he gives no thought to Niamh. Home early, he'd planned to shower and change before going out again, leaving her here alone.

"The flight was canceled. Does it make any difference to anything?" It's an innocent enough question he chooses not to answer, instead storming upstairs, reappearing ten minutes later wearing different clothes, before grabbing his jacket and walking out without speaking to me. Minutes later, when I hear a car pull up outside, my heart sinks. I imagine Andrew coming back for something, preparing myself for another verbal onslaught, but instead, there's a knock at the door. When I open it, James is there.

"James." His face is pale, his eyes flitting about nervously.

"Is something wrong? Would you like to come in?"

"I won't stop, Elise. I just wanted to ask if you've seen Hollie."

"Not since . . ." I think back, remembering seeing Hollie run across the garden, from an upstairs window. "Well, she was here one evening last week, but I didn't talk to her. I have a feeling she was avoiding me."

His face wrinkles into a frown. "Why would you say that?"

"Oh . . ." I try to remember our conversation. "To be honest, I think she'd skipped school that day. I made some comment about it being important that she didn't get behind."

James nods. "They called me a while ago. Seems she's skipped quite a few days recently." He doesn't say how many. "Do you know if Niamh's seen her?"

It's in line with what Stephanie told me, but warning bells are ringing. "I don't think so, but if you wait, I'll go upstairs and ask her."

Leaving him alone, I go to find Niamh. "Niamh?" When I push her door open, she's engrossed in one of her schoolbooks. "Have you seen Hollie at all the last couple of days?"

Her face is blank as she shakes her head. "Why?"

"Her dad wondered, that's all. I'll tell him." Not wanting her to worry unnecessarily, I go back down to tell James. "She hasn't seen her. Is Hollie OK, James?"

He freezes. "To be honest, I don't know. We've been in touch with the police. Look, I need to get going. I'm trying to talk to everyone in the village before it gets too late."

"Let me know?" At the thought that something might have happened to Hollie, my heart is thudding in my chest. "When she comes back?"

He nods, before turning to walk away. I close the door and seconds later hear his car start, then its tires on the gravel before the sound gradually fades away.

Niamh's voice from the doorway startles me. "Why was he here?"

"Hollie's missing." I pause. "Do you remember the last time you heard from her?"

Niamh's eyes hold mine as she shakes her head. "There was that day Ida Jones saw us. I can't really remember."

"Would you have any idea where she might be?"

"No." Niamh's voice is clear, light, as I fight off unwanted emotions, imagining how I'd feel if my daughter had gone out one day and hadn't come back.

"If you hear from her, can you let me know? Even if she doesn't want James to know where she is, he needs to know she's OK."

Niamh nods slowly; then fear crosses her face. "What if she's not?"

I feel an unfamiliar urge to protect my daughter from the horrific possibility that something could have happened to Hollie. "I'm sure she's fine, Niamh . . . We both know she's a little bit unpredictable. Maybe she had an argument with James and she's punishing him."

But from the way Niamh stands there, I know she isn't convinced.

"Try not to worry. I'll call James later—just to see if there's any news."

That seems to satisfy Niamh for now and she goes back upstairs. Seconds later, I hear her door close, then music drifting through the gap underneath it. Not the usual upbeat tracks she plays, but a haunting instrumental that tells me what my daughter can't put into words.

She's frightened.

I leave it until just before I go to bed to call James. "I'm sorry to call so late. I was just wondering if you'd heard from Hollie."

"No. No one's seen her." He sounds worried sick—and defeated. "I've spoken to the police again and they're on their way round here. They may well call in on you tomorrow."

"Tomorrow?" I'm thinking on my feet. "I'm working, James. I have to go out early."

"Can I give them your mobile number? Hollie's spent so much time at your place. I'm sure they'll want to talk to you—and Niamh."

"Of course." Uneasiness fills me. "But let's hope it doesn't come to that."

For an hour, I lie in bed awake, angry that Andrew hasn't returned, envisaging him in bed with *her*, before my thoughts turn back to Hollie, as I try to imagine what could have happened to her. Losing her mother when she did, then having to come to terms with James marrying Stephanie so soon after, Hollie's had enough difficulties to deal with in her life. It seems incomprehensible that anyone would wish her harm. But I can't shake the feeling of foreboding that hangs over me. It was in James's voice, his face when he came here. He's used to Hollie's comings and goings, but even so, he's clearly worried.

I'm drifting off to sleep when the sound of Andrew's car pulling up in the drive stirs me. Rolling over so that my back is to him, I feign sleep when he comes in and gets undressed. After getting into bed, he starts to snore almost immediately. I wonder if he knows that Hollie is missing, and for some reason I'm reminded of the photo I intercepted on his phone. Suddenly, I'm wide awake.

# Nicki

I think about letting the phone ring. It's late, the end of a long first day back at work. After a month's compassionate leave—supposedly to get over my husband walking out, I imagine some naïve psychologist calculating the number of days before shock subsides, grief levels out, before the new normality of being left starts to settle, getting it massively wrong, because after ten years of marriage, anyone can tell you a month is nothing.

But habit wins out. "Nicola May." I listen to the district inspector's voice at the other end, my stomach suddenly lurching when he tells me that a teenage girl has disappeared in Abingworth village, not far from here. I dread the idea of facing distraught parents, now, when my own emotions are still raw. "Look, I wouldn't normally ask, sir, but isn't there someone else who could do this?"

He hesitates. "I need someone good. And you know what's going on. This is the perfect opportunity to get someone into the village without suspicions being aroused." He pauses again. "But I understand. I'll see if Robson's around."

I pause, knowing he's referring to a porn ring that's been

linked to the area. There have been accounts of photographs of abducted teenagers appearing online, weeks after they've disappeared. Most of them have never been found. But I know that if I'm back at work, I have to be able to rise to the challenge. The sooner I get over to Abingworth, the better.

"It's fine, sir. I'll do it."

"You're sure? Thank you, Nicki." The DI sounds relieved. "We really need you in there."

I've never heard him use my given name before. After he hangs up, I take a deep breath. Minutes ago, I thought I was on my way home. But with a teenage girl missing, I can't afford to waste time.

Though the roads are mostly clear, the drive to Abingworth takes longer than I'd expected, slowed by an accident that's closed one of the lanes on the two-lane highway. When I take the turnoff too fast, my car skids briefly on black ice, and I drive more slowly, using the time to think.

All I know is that Hollie Hampton went missing two days ago. That her father didn't call us straightaway, that he's used to her disappearing now and then, is already setting off alarm bells. Hollie is sixteen and pretty. The DI emailed her photo to me. If she were my daughter, I wouldn't have waited.

Following my GPS, I turn into a narrow lane without road markings, edged with grass coated in frost. A row of cottages comes into view before I pass a number of bigger houses set back behind flint walls, slowing down as the lane bends sharply left. A hundred yards ahead, through the trees, a flashing blue light alerts me to the Hamptons' house.

As far as I can tell in the darkness, it's a long, rambling place. Pulling over, I park on the sloping drive, then get out and take the rough steps down to what looks like the front door. When I knock, it's opened straightaway by a man who I imagine is Hollie's father. He looks as though he hasn't slept for a week.

"Mr. Hampton? I'm DS May. Can I come in?"

"Yes. Of course." After closing the door behind me, he says, "They're in here."

I assume he's talking about the local police. "You still haven't heard anything from your daughter?"

"No," he mutters, his head down as he leads the way.

Now that I'm inside, it's obvious the house is old, with wide, uneven floorboards, here and there the timber frame and old bricks exposed. In the small sitting room that James Hampton takes me to, I recognize one of my colleagues, Sarah Collins. She's with another uniformed policewoman and a fair-haired woman who's clearly been crying. I assume she must be Hollie's mother. "Mrs. Hampton? I'm Detective Sergeant May. I'm just going to ask Sergeant Collins to update me. Then I'd like to talk to you and your husband. Can you give us five minutes?"

Fear, uncertainty, dread hang in the air, a feeling I remember from the last time I worked on a missing teenager's case, where every question, every phone call, has the potential to reveal a truth no one wants to hear. She nods, getting up and going over to her husband. "Can I make you all a cup of tea?"

"Yes, please." I nod. Her offer has the added bonus of getting them out of the room so that we can talk more openly. As they leave, I turn to Sarah Collins. "Tell me what you've got."

She glances at her notes. "Not much. Hollie was last here two days ago. Her parents—it's worth mentioning that Mrs. Hampton is her stepmother—anyway, they both say that it isn't unheard-of for Hollie to disappear for a night without telling them, but never longer than that. Also, they've always been able to get hold of her at some point by phone, but this time, they haven't been able to."

"You have her number?"

Sarah Collins nods. "We're already checking it out. We have the contact details for her school. According to Hollie's father, they called him recently. Apparently she's missed quite a bit of school lately. He seemed to think it wasn't anything unusual.

We've also got contact details for her friend, Niamh Buckley, and Niamh's mother, Elise. Mr. Hampton called round to see them earlier, but neither Niamh nor her mother had seen or heard from Hollie for a couple of days."

I look at her. "Is there anything else I should know?"

As Sarah shakes her head, I realize we really are starting with nothing. There's no time to waste. In this extreme cold, too much time has already gone by. "I'll go and talk to her parents."

Just then, the Hamptons come back in with a tray of mugs. "Thank you." I take one of them. "If you don't mind, I'd like to ask you about Hollie."

Under makeup streaked by her tears, Mrs. Hampton's face is white as a sheet. Her hands are shaking as she places the tray on the coffee table. "Won't you sit down?"

While they pull up chairs, I get out my notebook and pen. Looking up at them, I do my best to reassure them. "We'll be starting a search at dawn tomorrow. It'll be centered on the village, but we'll widen the search until we find her. Unless there's anywhere specific you think she might be?"

When they shake their heads, I go on. "Can you tell me about Hollie? Do you have a photograph I could take?" As I speak, Sarah Collins passes me a six-by-four color photo. "It was taken six months ago."

"Great." I pause, taking in Hollie's huge eyes and long dark hair, which look so much more striking than in the small photo the DI sent me. She's a beautiful girl—and slightly ethereal looking. "When she wasn't at school, was there anywhere she went, any friends she saw, any clubs she took part in?"

I watch their faces carefully as James speaks. "As we've told your colleagues, she's friends with Niamh Buckley in the village. We don't really know her school friends. She doesn't bring them back here."

It's not unusual when teenagers reach a certain age, though I can't help thinking that sometimes there's a reason why they keep their friends from their parents. "How would you describe her?" Knowing as I voice the question, the answer depends on whom you ask. Parents are not always entirely objective. But maybe because Hollie isn't her birth daughter, Stephanie Hampton's assessment sounds believable. "She's spirited and very clever, but she has demons. Hollie's fragile—her mother died six years ago. I don't think she's ever come to terms with the loss. I think that knowing her for such a short time, I see her a little differently from James." She glances at her husband. "I'd describe her as ferociously loyal, artistic, given to drama . . . but in short, she's a tortured soul."

I turn to James Hampton. "You think that's a fair description? Would you like to add anything?"

He shakes his head slowly. "Not really."

I turn back to Stephanie. "As her stepmother, did you get on well? I'm sure it isn't always easy."

"It wasn't—not at first. I knew I couldn't replace Kathryn—James's first wife—but I thought that if I was someone Hollie knew she could rely on, it would be the best basis for a relationship with her. That's what I've tried to be."

It sounds a sensible enough approach to the minefield of stepparenting. "Has Hollie seemed upset lately? Or different in any way?"

"Not really." As Stephanie looks at James, something flickers between them. "I'd say she was the same."

James looks haunted. "Hollie's always been a bit of a drama queen. It's the way she's made."

I move on to the facts. "You last saw her when?"

"Tuesday." Stephanie's voice is sharp.

It's now Thursday. "Was that Tuesday night?"

Stephanie nods. "Yes, at tea. We assume she spent the night here. Neither of us saw her on Wednesday morning. When it got to breakfast time, James went to wake her, but her bed was empty. It looked as though she'd slept in it, though."

"So she left here sometime between Tuesday night and early Wednesday morning. What time do you get up?"

"I'm usually up around seven." Stephanie glances at her husband. "James is later, as a rule."

"So it's reasonable to assume that Hollie had gone by then?"

Stephanie nods. "She could have slipped out while I was getting up, without me noticing, but it's unlikely. Usually I hear her."

But not impossible . . . I make a note. "So that morning, when you went to wake her for breakfast, you wouldn't have been concerned that she wasn't in her room?"

"No." James Hampton frowns at me. "I really don't see how this is helping anything."

I hesitate, looking at both of them. "It may seem trivial, but I need to establish what Hollie's routine usually was—what was and wasn't normal. When did you think about calling the police?"

"I wanted to call that first night." When Stephanie sounds resentful, my ears prick up. "James thought we should wait. He thought Hollie was probably at a friend's house. On Thursday, we gave her until the end of the school day, but when she didn't come home, we couldn't wait any longer."

"Would you have any idea from clothes that are missing, what she may have been wearing?"

Again, it's Stephanie who speaks. "Probably jeans. There's a pair I can't find. Her jacket is missing—it's green with a fur-lined hood."

It's more detail than I'd expected. "Would you mind if I had a look in her bedroom?"

James is tight-lipped as he gets up and heads toward the stairs. At the top, I follow him along the landing until he stops outside a half-open door. Feeling inside for the light switch, I turn it on. At first glance, it's a typical teenage girl's room—messy, items of clothing strewn here and there, drawers not closed properly, the doors to the wardrobe left ajar. A white metal-framed bed is along one wall, its pale pink covers disturbed, almost as though she's just got out of it.

But this is the one part of this house that's Hollie's. The smallest clue could help find her. Without moving anything, my eyes scan bits of paper left on the pine desk where her laptop is, then a few that she's stuck to the wall, photos and quotes alongside reminders to herself about homework.

I turn to James. "Do you know if Hollie keeps a diary?"

When he shakes his head, I ask, "Does she have a boyfriend?" Hollie's a pretty girl. It would be more surprising if she didn't.

"No."

My eyes linger on the laptop. "It might help if we were to take this. Is that OK?" Not that it's optional. If Hollie's in danger, we need all the help we can get.

"Fine." James speaks abruptly. Then he adds, "I don't have her phone. We think she must have it with her."

"So I understand." I pick up the laptop. "Thank you. I think that's all—at least, for now."

After reassuring the Hamptons that we'll be in touch, we walk outside. In the time I've been in the house, frost has covered my car and as I get in and drive away, I feel myself shiver. I think about how James was on edge, haunted, stressed, while Stephanie was brittle. Judging from the size of the house, they clearly have a lot of money. Then I think about the dynamic between them. They were at odds over something—and in spite of what Stephanie said, I don't think it's a disagreement over when they should have called the police.

The feeling in my gut grows stronger. James was too quiet, as though he was frightened of saying the wrong thing. It strikes me as odd that he didn't call the police sooner. There's also the reality none of us talked about. With each passing hour, in this brutal cold, it becomes more and more likely something terrible has happened to Hollie.

# 7

## Elise

After a sleepless night, I'm exhausted when my alarm goes off at five thirty. Andrew doesn't stir. As I shower and dress, I wonder how it feels to have no conscience. Then I'm thinking about Hollie; wondering if she's come back. Pulling on a cardigan over my uniform, I tiptoe downstairs, glancing toward Niamh's room, still in darkness.

In the kitchen I make a mug of tea and a bowl of muesli. The certainty that it's too early to be interrupted by Andrew brings a tenuous layer of peace to the room. Unable to stop my mind from wandering, I imagine how different this house would be, how free my life would feel, without him.

Having finished my muesli, I check my schedule on my phone. Today my flight is to Barcelona. At this time of year, I'm expecting an easy day with few passengers. Tomorrow, I go to Malaga; after that, Athens. Beautiful places where the sun shines, where life could be so different. A yearning fills me to be free of this life, of Andrew, followed by a grim determination. I need to get through these intolerable years, let Niamh grow up. *But one day*, I tell myself, *I will be.*

It's still pitch-dark as I go outside and get in my car. Starting the engine, I let it idle while the layer of ice on the windscreen clears, then slowly set off down the drive. When I turn onto the lane, frost sparkles in my headlights, the landscape surreal, a layer of freezing fog coating every branch on each tree either side of the road. As I drive, I can't help looking out for Hollie, even though I know I'm unlikely to see her. Then Andrew comes to my mind, the photo of the naked girl on his phone. He's omnipresent, tainting everything I do.

Reaching the main road, I glance at the road sign. The airport is clearly marked, ten miles away, to the left. I turn on my indicator, then pulling out, I turn right.

# Nicki

The next morning, the search gets under way. It begins close to the Hamptons' home, which in daylight reveals a shabbiness I hadn't seen last night. The paint on the window frames is peeling, the garden overgrown. Beyond the house, there are a number of outbuildings—an unused stable block and a stone building crudely converted into an office that James uses. Hollie could have hidden in any one of these and no one would have seen her.

Searching each area meticulously takes most of the morning. In the stable block are unpacked boxes and old furniture—damp, coated with dust. James's office is no tidier. When he shows us in, he looks mildly embarrassed.

"Hollie rarely comes in here." He pauses, frowning. "Have you spoken to her friend yet? Niamh?"

"Not yet." My eyes scan the books and papers piled messily on the shelves. "I'll go round there after school."

"School's closed." Clearly beside himself with worry, he speaks abruptly. "The heating failed."

"Right." I hadn't known. "I will talk to her, Mr. Hampton." I try to reassure him. "Just as soon as I've finished here."

\*   \*   \*

As I turn into the Buckleys' drive, it's clear they live in one of the grander houses in the village. Gray and imposing, the cold makes it look somehow starker. The windows are dark; there's no sign of life inside, until a sudden movement catches my eye. Then framed by an upstairs window, I see a face.

# Niamh

*It happens on a Friday, two weeks after the day I saw my mother take the call she didn't want me to know about; a week after Hollie and I went into the grounds of Deeprose House, where I thought the light was flickering in one of the rooms; as Arctic air clings on, lowering temperatures, a fine layer of snow carpeting the ground.*

*Freezing fog blankets out the sun, so that for a few days, the world is silent, wrapped in a bone-chilling cold. Hollie remains missing. With the roads too icy to be safe, my school is closed. Pulling on layers of warm clothes, I go for a walk through the village, thinking of a hundred places Hollie could be—like her mother's grave, or Ida Jones's house, or with one of her school friends, somehow knowing she isn't at any of them.*

*I pass no one as I walk; nor do I see any lights in any of the windows. Even Ida Jones's cottage is in darkness. It's as though the village has descended into an eternal night. All the time thinking of Hollie, I take the path to the church, where frozen leaves crunch under my footsteps.*

*Reaching the churchyard, my shiver isn't because of the cold.*

*It's the rows of frozen headstones standing out against the snow; the motionless bell in the tower, its single tone waiting to announce the passing of another soul; the knowledge that I'm surrounded by the dead.*

*I force myself to open the church door; the latch is frozen shut so that at first I think it's been locked. But it opens suddenly. Inside there is no welcoming light, no hope, just the same freezing cold and the sound of mice, as I imagine ghosts closing in around me. Hollie's ghost. Leaving the church, without closing the door, I run.*

*From an upstairs window I watch the car pull up, then go downstairs to open the front door to find a policewoman and a younger policeman looking at me. The woman, with brown hair, shows me her ID. "I'm Detective Sergeant May. We're from Chichester police." She seems to look past me into the house. "Are your parents here?"*

*I shake my head. "They're at work."*

*She nods. "We're making inquiries into the whereabouts of Hollie Hampton. I don't suppose you've seen her, have you?"*

*I frown at her, not sure when she's talking about. Then I hear a car on the drive. "That's my mother."*

*Both police officers turn to look, and DS May nods again. "We'll wait here."*

*Closing the door, I watch from the kitchen window as my mother gets out of her car. Instead of her uniform, she's wearing her big woollen cardigan. As she walks toward the police, it falls open, revealing her navy uniform dress and patterned scarf.*

*After they come inside, I go upstairs. From the top, I listen to them all in the kitchen, hearing the sound of chairs being pulled out, jackets taken off, the kettle being switched on, their voices low. Ten minutes later, I'm in my bedroom when my mother's voice reaches me. "Niamh? Could you come down here?"*

*I'm gripped by nervousness as I go downstairs, wondering*

*what they want to ask me. My mother's face is pale when I go into the kitchen. "This is Detective Sergeant May and Constable Emerson. They're looking for Hollie, Niamh. They just want to ask you one or two questions."*

*I feel their eyes on me as I pull out an empty chair and sit down.*

*"Thank you, Niamh." It's the woman, DS May, who speaks. "I understand you and Hollie used to spend time together."*

*I nod.*

*"When did you last see her?"*

*I think of the last time Hollie was here. "About a week ago?" I glance at my mother.*

*"Did she say anything unusual? About anyone? Or talk about running away, for instance?"*

*I feel myself frown, wondering how to explain that Hollie isn't like most people; that most of what she says is unusual. "Not especially. I mean, she didn't suggest she was about to do anything."*

*My mother looks at me. "The last time I saw her here, she seemed upset about something. Do you know what it was, Niamh?"*

*There's an edge to her voice. Shaking my head, my face is blank. "She didn't tell me."*

*DS May frowns as she looks at me. "What do the two of you like to talk about?"*

*I shrug. "Stuff. School. Music."*

*DS May nods slowly. "Do you know if she has any other friends in the village?"*

*I shake my head at the same time as my mother says quickly, "There aren't any other teenagers in the village—at least, not at my daughter's school. There's the Morby twins, but they're nineteen. They're at university."*

*I watch DS May scrutinize her list, then pause with her finger under a line. "The Morbys live at Apple Tree house?"*

*My mother nods.*

*She turns to my mother. "Your husband, Mrs. Buckley . . . He's a doctor, isn't he?"*

*"He's a GP at the Meadowside practice in Chichester."*

*I watch the policewoman make a note against her list. Why does she need to speak to my father? Why does she need to speak to any of us? Then, as if she can read my mind, her eyes meet mine. "It's just routine, Niamh. We have to talk to everyone. It's surprising how the smallest detail can help us find someone."*

*When the police drive away, my mother looks at me. "You haven't heard from Hollie?" Under her uniform-standard makeup, her skin is pale, her eyes anxious.*

*I shake my head. Doesn't she realize I'd have told her? But as I take in her face, I see that she's clinging to hope, that the police are unnecessary, that Hollie is just going to turn up; that the nightmare will be over. But as my mother knows, some nightmares are never over.*

# 8

# Elise

"The police were here earlier." When Andrew comes in, I watch his face for a reaction to my announcement; see the split-second freeze before he continues as though it meant nothing. "They were asking about Hollie."

This time, his reaction is unmistakeable. "I hope you told them that girl is nothing but trouble." His voice is abrupt, cold. "She's probably run off with a boyfriend. We all know she's more than capable of it."

"James is really worried," I tell him, taken aback by the harshness of his words. "Niamh hasn't heard from her. It isn't at all like Hollie to do this."

"That's nonsense, Elise, as you well know. That girl doesn't care who she upsets."

That he could be so utterly callous in the face of a teenage girl's disappearance appalls me. Then I remember the photo he was looking at on his phone. It was of a girl, not dissimilar to Hollie. Not for the first time, I wonder if my husband is into porn; if maybe that's why he froze when I mentioned the police visit.

"Andrew, that photo—" I start, but he cuts me off.

"That wasn't what you think it was," he snaps. "Do you know how many men with frigid wives look at photos of pretty girls?"

But before I can respond, my phone buzzes. My heart is in my mouth as I see an unknown number flashing up on my screen. Turning away, I answer it.

"Elise Buckley." I listen for a moment, glance at Andrew, then walk a few steps away from him. "I'm sorry . . . I can't talk right now. Can I call you back?" I speak as quietly as I can, but when I end the call and put my phone down, Andrew's staring at me.

"My God." His words are mocking, a look of sheer disbelief on his face. But I see it for what it is. He isn't interested. It's simply a deflection of attention onto me.

"Whatever you're thinking, it isn't that," I say wearily, knowing there's nothing Andrew would like more than to point his finger and find me guilty, as if my having an affair would somehow validate his own extramarital activities.

"Tell me who that was." He barks it out, an order he expects me to obey. As he comes to stand directly in front of me, his presence is suddenly menacing.

"No." Shaking my head, I reach for my phone to keep it away from him.

"Give me your phone." Holding his hand out, he tries to snatch it from me.

Putting my phone in my pocket, I manage to evade him. "It's nothing to do with you, Andrew." Summoning all my dignity, I turn away. "Now if you'll excuse me . . ." As I start to walk away from him, I'm aware that I'm holding my breath, knowing how much he hates being crossed. But I've barely gone two steps before I feel him grab my arm, his fingers closing tightly, roughly pinching my skin. I spin around. "How dare you!" I stare at him, trying not to show my fear. "You're the one who's screwing around. You don't even care who knows it. You're despicable." I hear Niamh move around upstairs and shake my arm free of his grip. "There's only one reason I'm here—and that's Niamh. You do know that, don't you?"

"Lying bitch," he mutters.

Hearing Niamh's footsteps on the stairs, I step back, flashing him a warning look. Then as she comes into the kitchen, I turn toward her. "I was just telling your father about the police being here earlier." My tone deliberately light, I glance at Andrew. "I've told them where the practice is. I'm sure they'll be in touch."

I turn to Niamh again. "I've made chicken curry. Can you set the table?" But under my mask of calm, a torrent of anger rages inside me at Andrew's complete lack of respect for me. I should be upstairs packing, removing myself and Niamh from this toxic house, from Andrew's life, then calling the police, listing the abuse he inflicts on us. Being here isn't good for Niamh. But then a sense of powerlessness overwhelms me. Andrew will never let her go. He's made that clear—nor can I leave her here alone. I'm trapped.

It isn't until the next day, when Andrew's at work and Niamh is still in her room, that I return the call from yesterday, dialing the number with shaking hands, sounding matter-of-fact when an unfamiliar voice answers; waiting as I'm connected.

"Hello. It's Elise Buckley. I'm sorry I didn't get back to you before." As I listen, I feel my world slip sideways. "Oh. Friday? I think that's fine." Swallowing, I rack my brain as I try to remember when I'm working. "Yes. Thank you."

After ending the call, I turn to see Niamh standing there. I wonder how much of the conversation she's overheard, but I can't read her face. "Are you OK, Niamh?"

Going to the fridge, she nods. After getting out a can of Coke, she says calmly, "Are you and Dad getting a divorce?"

My response is too quick, my gasp too loud. "Of course we're not. What makes you think that?"

The way she shrugs, then turns in a single fluid movement, reminds me of Hollie. "That phone call?" When I don't reply, she goes on. "It isn't just that. You argue all the time. Dad's never here. When he is, he eats on his own." I'm astonished when I see tears glitter in her eyes.

Walking toward her, I put my hands firmly on her shoulders. "We are not getting a divorce." I speak with a ferocious determination. "I know things seem a bit difficult just now. But we'll get over it. You mustn't worry." Then I pause. "Have you spoken to your father about this?"

"Yes." Her answer shocks me, that she's talked to Andrew at all, let alone that she's talked to him before me.

I stare at her, incredulous. "What did he say?"

She shrugs again. "Not much." She breaks off, then her clear gray eyes look piercingly into mine. "He laughed. Then he said you'd never leave him."

As she says that, my heart breaks for her. She's a pawn. He's using her, doing what I've always dreaded he'd do, drawing Niamh into his cat-and-mouse games with me. In that moment, I've never hated him more. I imagine him laughing, unkindly, cruelly, knowing he doesn't care what Niamh sees, how she feels. He doesn't protect her, look out for her. The only person who can do that is me. "He's right. I won't." As I gaze steadily at my daughter, the web I'm caught in tightens.

Niamh's nod is barely perceptible. Not knowing how else to reassure her, I play it down, changing the subject. "I had an email from your school. They should have the heating fixed by tomorrow. If the roads are clear, they'll open again the day after. I don't suppose you've heard from Hollie?"

"No." Niamh walks over to the window, gazing ahead. "Where do you suppose she is?"

I go over and stand next to her, making out a flurry of snowflakes in the dim light outside. "I don't know. It's only

been two days. Most likely, she's at someone's house somewhere." I break off, because no one knows, and because the
more time passes, the more worrying her absence becomes. In
temperatures like this, she wouldn't survive living rough.

"I'm scared." Niamh wraps her arms around her narrow
body. "I want to know what's happened."

"I know." I feel exactly the same. "How do you and Hollie
usually keep in touch?"

"Messenger," Niamh says briefly. "Sometimes Instagram.
But, you know. Mostly, she just turns up."

"Try not to worry." I place an arm around her shoulders.
"She'll be OK. We have to believe that she will turn up. I'm
sure the police are doing everything they can."

But I'm not sure. There are no rules when teenagers go missing, just as too many lives are cut short for all the wrong reasons. Right now, Hollie could be anywhere.

# Nicki

Throughout the village, officers knock on doors and search gardens, woods, and fields, but by early afternoon, nothing of any significance has been found.

As I leave the Buckleys' house, I turn to Emerson. "We need to talk to more of the villagers. In places like this, it's impossible to keep secrets. Someone somewhere must know something about Hollie."

"Maybe she left. If she'd decided to run off, she could be miles away by now."

"How? There are no buses through here."

"A friend could have picked her up. Or she could have walked."

I'm silent, then seeing a lay-by, I pull over. "The village church is up there. Let's take a look."

Getting out, Emerson pulls the collar of his coat up as I lock the car and do the same. The path is frozen, the air sharp as we make our way along the path toward the churchyard. As the trees open out, the headstones are gray against the white of the frost. The church is small, dating back about six hundred years, with a small tower in which a single bell hangs. I try the door, surprised when I find it unlocked, but a search of the sparse interior yields nothing. Closing it behind me, as we start walking back toward the road, my phone buzzes.

"May." As I listen to the voice at the other end, I feel the blood drain from my face.

It takes me two minutes to find Furze Lane, then another three to find Deeprose House. Sarah Collins is waiting in front of the heavy, locked gates. "The owners are away. There's a caretaker who has a key, apparently. We're trying to get in touch with him."

"Where is she?"

Sarah's voice is grim. "In the gardens. Milsom and Edwards came in from the fields—there's a fence that's easy to climb through. I assume that's how she got in."

"Can you show me?"

We walk in silence a short way down the lane, where Sarah turns into an opening and climbs over the gate. "Careful. Some friendly farmer has wrapped barbed wire around it."

Heeding her warning, I manage to climb over unscathed, then follow her through thick grass to the other side of the field, where there's a post and rail fence.

"She's just through here," Sarah says quietly.

All the time we were searching, there'd been hope. But as I cross the gardens, then follow Sarah through a hedge into a smaller enclosed part of the garden, hope is gone. In the pool in front of us, we spot her hair first—long, floating around her as she lies facedown in the water.

"She was under the leaves, ma'am." As Milsom speaks, I notice the piles of leaves scraped back around the edges of the pool. "She must have fallen in. She was invisible until we cleared them. The water had frozen over her."

She's wearing the jeans and jacket Stephanie described, but only as Milsom speaks do I notice the ice, encasing her body, her hair, so that only the back of her head protrudes above it.

"We should inform her parents." Sarah's voice is flat.

"Not yet. We need to be absolutely sure." Hearing voices, I turn and find two more officers walking across the garden toward us. That they've come that way must mean they have a key. They're followed by two more carrying a stretcher. There's silence as we stand there, while the ice is broken. Then as Hollie's body is removed from the water and her face is visible, any doubts are gone.

"I'll tell the parents." As I speak, Sarah nods, her eyes grave.

I make my way back to my car, steeling myself. Many things about my job aren't easy, but of all of them, the worst is breaking bad news. When you tell a parent that their child isn't coming back, you know their life as it was has gone forever.

As I pull up outside the Hamptons' house, then walk down the path to the front door, Stephanie opens it before I knock. When she takes in my silence, then my expression, her hand goes to her mouth. Then she turns and runs back in, calling out to her husband.

"*James . . . James?*"

When I go inside, they're standing huddled together in the hallway. "Please," I say quietly. "Can we go through?" I gesture toward the sitting room where only last night, they were telling me about Hollie, all of us hoping to find her alive. Hope that was futile, because she was already dead.

"Where is she?" James's voice is harsh and shaky at the same time.

"We found her in the grounds of Deeprose House." I speak slowly, quietly. "She was in the pool."

Stephanie gasps. "No . . . She's not . . ."

"I'm so sorry." I pause, letting my words sink in. "She'd obviously been there for a while. There was nothing we could do." I watch their faces as they try to twist my words, make them into anything other than the truth, as they struggle to take it in. We've all considered the worst, but when the worst happens, nothing prepares you for the shock.

When James gets up, it's as though he's shrunk. "I want to see her." His face is ashen. "Please take me to her."

"We'll need you to identify her body in due course. Hollie's death will be investigated. It's entirely possible that it was accidental, but at this stage, we can't be sure."

"But why was she there?" Stephanie cries. "She doesn't even know the Penns. She had no reason to be in their garden."

"It's my fault." James's face is gray, his body rigid with shock as he stares at me. "It's all my fault."

"I think we'll probably find it was an accident," I say gently, and Stephanie takes his arm. His words are the natural response of a parent who'd have done anything he could to protect his child.

"But I knew something was going on," he mutters.

Tears roll down Stephanie's face as she tries to reason with him. "Hollie could be impossible," she says desolately. "We both know that. You didn't do anything wrong. You couldn't have known anything like this would happen."

# Niamh

Hollie isn't coming back.

*I saw the single car, its blue light flashing as it passed me on its way to Deeprose House, its siren breaking the silence. There was a fluttering in my veins as I watched, motionless, even before the unmarked ambulance made its way more slowly along the same route, half an hour later, sending a chill through me, because I recognize it.*

*It's the kind of ambulance they send when someone's dead.*

# 9

# Elise

It's Ida Jones who tells me, that night. She doesn't say how she knows, just that Hollie's body has been found.

"Oh no . . ." Remembering the sirens I heard earlier, there's a rushing in my ears as Ida goes on talking. "Wait . . . I can't take this in."

"Terrible, isn't it . . ." Ida's voice trembles. "That poor young girl . . ."

Her call leaves me stunned. In a daze, I go to find Niamh. She's upstairs, lying on her bed with her iPad in front of her, plugged into earphones. When she sees me, she takes them out. "Niamh? Honey?"

She knows from the "honey" something's wrong. As her eyes meets mine, I contemplate the magnitude of what I'm about to tell her. But I have no choice. "Hollie's been found."

She knows from my voice that I'm not delivering good news, but in denial, she gasps in shock. "Is she OK?"

But I'm shaking my head. "Niamh . . . She isn't. I don't know what happened . . ." Going in, I sit on the bed close to her, saying as gently as I can, "Hollie's dead."

"No." Suddenly rigid, Niamh springs up. "She can't be dead." By the window, she stands with her back to me, her body stiff, her denial absolute, but then it's her bed that Hollie was sprawled on, just days ago; her company Hollie sought out when she came here. Even to me, what's happened is incomprehensible. Going over to the window, I put my arms around her, absorbing her dry sobs.

"I need to know what happened," is all she says. "Poor Hollie." She seems to wrestle with her emotions; then her eyes go blank. When I look at her, she seems shut down.

"Ida didn't say. She probably didn't know." I pause for a moment. "Why don't I make us some tea," I say gently, realizing she's in shock. Hollie's death is too close. I can't help thinking, as no doubt every other parent will be doing, *What if it had been my child?* Then I think of James, trying to imagine how he's coping. It's hard enough that he lost his wife a few years ago. And now his daughter is dead, too.

When Andrew comes in, after taking off his coat, instead of his usual glass of wine, he pours himself a large whisky.

"I imagine you've heard about Hollie?"

He takes another mouthful. "Yes. Her body was picked up earlier today."

I'm incredulous. It stands to reason that the medical practice would have heard, but at the very least, I'd have expected him to call me. "And you didn't think to tell me? What if Niamh had heard from someone else?"

"What difference does it make?" Speaking impatiently, he starts toward the door. "I've had a hell of a day. If you don't mind, I'm going to sit down."

"Just a minute, Andrew." My voice is sharp. "Do you know what happened to her?"

I watch as he stiffens, then slowly turns around. "I was there, so yes. She drowned," he says curtly. "There'll be a postmortem. As yet, there's no way of knowing whether it was an accident or not."

An image of Hollie's lifeless body comes to me, her long hair spread out around her under the water, and I feel the blood drain from my face. "Where did it happen?"

"In the grounds of Deeprose House, apparently. God knows what she was doing there."

But as he speaks, my skin prickles. Deeprose House is close to where Ida saw Niamh and Hollie that day, but I don't tell Andrew that. "I've told Niamh that Hollie's been found, but none of the details."

Andrew raises his eyebrows. "You can tell her, if you want. Or I'll do it later."

"I'll talk to her now." Niamh would want to be told, and I don't trust Andrew to break it to her gently. My heart is heavy as I go up to her room. Then as I tell her what I've learned, watching her face, it's as though I'm peeling away a layer of her childhood.

But there are questions that perhaps only Niamh can answer. "Do you have any idea why she might have been there? It's where you and Hollie were walking recently, wasn't it?"

Niamh looks away. "We climbed over a gate into a field," she says defiantly. "She didn't say if it was part of Deeprose House. It doesn't matter, does it? Nothing can bring her back." When she turns to look at me, her face is wet with tears.

Shock ricochets through the village as the news spreads. Everyone here has children in their lives, grandchildren, nieces, nephews, teenagers, none of whom are supposed to be found dead. The next day, knowing I can't go away and leave Niamh, I call work and take a couple of days' leave. She's never been demonstrative, but the extent of her silent calm unnerves me.

While I'm at home with her, I'm aware of the strangest sensation, as though time itself has been paused. It's a morning when I should have been on my way to Zurich, when Niamh should have gone back to school; a morning that in the aftermath of Hollie's death, stretches interminably, as our lives change irrevocably. It takes until the afternoon for the police to arrive. Opening the door, I recognize DS May from last time.

"Mrs. Buckley? May we come in?" There's another woman with her.

Nodding, I stand back to let them in. "Of course. Come through." Closing the door, I lead them into the kitchen.

"This is Sergeant Collins." She gestures toward her colleague. Rather than being in uniform, DS May's wearing a black, well-cut coat and lace-up boots. "I know this probably isn't an easy time, but could we talk to you and your daughter?"

"By all means." I gesture toward the kitchen table. "Do you want to take a seat? I'll go and find Niamh."

"Before you do, Mrs. Buckley . . ." DS May is soft-spoken. "She might find this rather distressing. You see, Hollie drowned."

"We already know." Taking in their surprised glances, I add, "My husband is the GP who came out when you found her. He told me." I start walking toward the stairs. "Niamh? Could you come downstairs?"

As I look up, her pinched face appears in her bedroom doorway. "The police are here."

Niamh comes closer, peering through the balusters. "Have they said any more about what happened to her?"

Shaking my head, I go up the stairs toward her. "Not yet. But they'd like to talk to both of us."

Niamh's intake of breath is sharp and I wonder if it's too much for her.

"If you're up to it?"

Wordlessly she nods, then slowly comes downstairs. In the kitchen, I pull out a chair near mine for her to sit on. "This is Sergeant Collins and Detective Sergeant May—you met last time?" I remind Niamh, nodding toward the policewomen.

"Hello, Niamh." DS May speaks gently. "I'm very sorry about your friend. We'd like to talk to you some more about her. You might be able to help us find out what happened."

"OK." In front of the two policewomen, Niamh seems younger, smaller, as though the news of Hollie's death has reduced her in some way. Then I realize she *has* been reduced; in a village of adults, the two who were allies, are now one.

"How long had you known each other?"

Niamh glances toward me. "Two years?"

I nod. "About that."

DS May's pen hovers above her notebook. "But you didn't go to the same school?"

"No." Niamh stares at her hands clenched on the table in front of her.

"Did you know any of Hollie's other friends?" DS May's eyes scan her notes.

Niamh shakes her head. "She didn't talk about anyone. I don't think she had that many."

"Any boyfriends?"

Niamh glances at me quickly, before shaking her head. "She didn't have one."

"How about old boyfriends? Was there anyone she might have upset, or who wanted her back?"

"I don't think so." An anxious look crosses Niamh's face.

DS May turns to look at me. "Mrs. Buckley, I know we've been over some of this last time, but how well would you say you knew Hollie?"

How do you measure a relationship? "I met her soon after her family moved to the village—about four years ago. She and Niamh became friends more recently. She's spent a fair amount of time at our house. And I used to see her around the village—I go running," I explain. "Sometimes, weeks could go by without a sign of her. But she's a teenager. I never thought of it as strange."

"You know her parents?"

I nod. "Not particularly well, but enough to talk to them in the pub, if our paths happen to cross. We're acquaintances rather than friends. They seem like nice people."

"Hollie got on well with them?"

I frown. If she wants a window into their family life, she's asking the wrong person. "As far as I know, but I'm probably not the best person to ask."

DS May looks at Niamh. "Niamh? Did Hollie say anything to you about her relationships with her father and stepmother?"

Niamh shakes her head.

DS May is silent for a moment. "Hollie's body was found in the grounds of Deeprose House. Do you have any idea what she might have been doing there?"

Niamh's gaze drifts toward the window. Then she looks back at the policewoman. "She used to go into places like that. She'd find her own way in. She never did anything bad. It was more like she was doing it because she wasn't supposed to."

DS May looks interested. "You mean she got a kick out of it?"

"Kind of." Niamh pauses, thinking. "But it wasn't just that. It was more like she didn't like being told what to do. I think she wanted to feel free."

DS May looks at her closely. "Did you ever go with her?"

The hint of pink in her cheeks, Niamh's look of alarm, give her away.

DS May tries to reassure her. "Niamh . . . you're not in any trouble, I promise you. All we're trying to establish is what Hollie was like, what she did, who she saw . . ."

Niamh hesitates, then speaks quickly. "The other day, she climbed a gate up Furze Lane into a field. I was with her. But that's all. I did try to stop her," Niamh adds. "The gate said *private* on it. She said we weren't doing any harm. We weren't."

Glancing at me, she folds her arms.

"Can you tell us when that was?"

Niamh frowns. "About ten days ago? I'm not sure."

DS May turns to me. "Mrs. Buckley, you said earlier, you sometimes saw Hollie when you were out running . . . Where was that, usually?"

"I run five miles, Detective Sergeant." I pause. "Not always along the same route. But quite often, I'd see her in the church-yard."

DS May pushes a strand of her long hair behind her ear. "Didn't that strike you as a macabre place for a teenager to hang out?"

"Yes . . ." I hesitate. "I suppose it was. But Hollie had a vivid imagination. Her mother died just a few years ago and though she's not buried there, I think there was something about the idea of being among ghosts."

It's the same reason any of us go there. To remind ourselves of loved ones who have gone before us. "It isn't as strange as it may sound," I add, then I break off as she looks at me oddly. "I'm not sure what else I can tell you."

It seems as though we've reached an impasse; DS May stands up. "I'll leave you my card. Should you think of anything, however small, I'd be grateful if you called me."

After they go out to their car, Niamh stands at the kitchen window watching them leave, then without speaking, turns and goes upstairs to her room, as I swallow the lump in my throat. It's hard for her, even harder for Hollie's parents. But the reality of Hollie's death affects all of us.

# 10

# Elise

On the Sunday after Hollie's body was found, instead of the handful of regulars, most of the villagers make their way down the frozen footpaths to gather in the church, as well as one or two visitors from outside. I'm relieved when Mia, one of Niamh's school friends, squeezes into the pew next to her. The service is poignant, a reminder of how transient life is, after which the vicar delivers a more personal message.

"We should look out for one another. Small communities like ours are rare places. At times like this, we must stand united. We should all feel able to let our children roam the footpaths. Our children should in turn, feel safe. We have to somehow not let this tragic accident destroy the sense of security that's always existed here."

It's a naïvely optimistic message—and inappropriate, I can't help thinking. We don't know yet if Hollie's death was an accident. Whether or not it was, it will be time, rather than faith, that will lead people to feeling safe around here again.

As we file outside, Sophie catches my arm. "Andrew not here?" As she raises a questioning eyebrow, she seems to lack her usual sparkle.

"Golf." After glancing around to check where Niamh is, I add, "So he says."

She shakes her head. "Bastard. Leave him, Elise. You're better than this."

I'm silent. It's impossible to explain even to Sophie why I can't. Across the churchyard, I see James, his face shadowed with grief. "Poor James. It makes you wonder how much pain one person can bear."

"He isn't the only person who's lost someone." Sophie's silent for a moment. When she speaks, her voice is sober. "How long before the police know more? They're treating this death as suspicious, aren't they?"

"All I know is they're carrying out a postmortem. For now, we have to wait." I glance at my watch. "I have to go. I'm working this afternoon. I'll catch you another time." I start walking, looking for Niamh, and find her head-to-head with Mia. "I have to go home, Niamh. I check in at one. Do you want to walk back with me?"

"Can I go to Mia's?" Niamh looks at me uncertainly.

"Of course—if that's OK with your mother, Mia?" I glance at Mia. She and Niamh aren't particularly close, but right now, Niamh needs company.

Mia nods. "She did say it would be OK on the way here. It'll be fine."

"OK . . ." I glance at Niamh. "I'll call your father—he can text you to arrange a time to pick you up."

Three hours later, I'm sitting on an aircraft bound for Nice. In the south of France, the sky is blue and when we open the aircraft door, the voices are laced with French accents. With my perspective altered by distance, for a few hours, in the calm of the half-empty cabin, Hollie's death seems a lifetime away. But as I drive home, then turn into the village, it comes flooding back; only this time, there are more memories, ones I've tried my hardest to forget.

Andrew's car is in the drive. After I park and go inside, the sound of the television filters through from the sitting room. Slipping off my shoes, I'm on my way upstairs to look for Niamh when I hear Andrew's voice.

"For God's sake, you know I can't." His voice is scathing as he talks on his phone, seemingly unaware I've just come in.

"She won't say anything." There's a silence, before he laughs cynically. "How do I know? For Christ's sake, I'm married to her. Of course I know!"

Unable to stop myself, I walk over to the sitting room and push the door open, pretending I don't know he's on the phone. "Did you collect Niamh, Andrew?" I speak louder than usual, hoping that whomever he's talking to will hear me, too.

Turning around, frowning, he points to his phone. I ignore him. "Niamh?"

"Just a moment," he mutters into his phone, then covers the mouthpiece with his hand. "How dare you?"

"I would have thought our daughter's whereabouts were the highest priority right now." I stare at him coolly, my meaning clear. "Particularly in light of Hollie's death. Did you even read my text?"

I've caught him out. He hasn't bothered. "One of us needs to go and get her," I say pointedly, gazing at the almost empty bottle of wine on the table in front of him. "I imagine that's going to be me."

Tired, I was hoping to have a bath and put on pajamas, but suddenly I've no desire to be in the same house as Andrew. Without waiting for a reply, I walk out to the kitchen, putting on my shoes, just as a car pulls up outside. I hear a door slam, then Niamh appears through the door. "Mia's dad dropped me. He said he didn't mind." Her face is brighter than this morning. It's been good for her to be out. She sounds lighter, less troubled than she has been in days, weeks even.

"Your father got held up." As always, I make an excuse for

Andrew's selfishness. "I've only just got in. I was coming to get you. I'm sorry, Niamh."

"It's OK." As she realizes I'm lying, her eyes lower. My stomach twists uncomfortably. Two minutes in this house, and the lightness is already leaving her.

On Monday morning, life resumes a semblance of normality when Andrew goes to work, Niamh goes to school. There are no arguments. Pulling on a sweatshirt over my running gear, I go for a run, taking a different route that brings me past the Hamptons', where the house looks closed and dark; where the only sign of life is the single police car parked outside.

Farther away from the village, I turn into the pinewoods, taking the wide path through the trees that stretch as far as I can see in neat, regimented rows either side of me. Under my feet, the ground is cushioned by a carpet of pine needles. The air is cold and dry, but still, without wind; just the occasional cry from a passing bird breaking the silence.

After a couple of miles, out of breath, I slow to a walk for a while, pausing to stretch for a couple of minutes, before carrying on through the woods, until a few yards ahead, I see a car.

Something makes me hang back, even though the car is familiar. Then as another car pulls up next to it and both drivers get out, I instantly recognize James. The second man is also familiar, but as I watch them talk, I can't place him. I wonder if this has anything to do with Hollie's death, but I'm too far away to make out what they're saying. Then suddenly, James starts shouting.

Shrinking back into the shadows, staying out of sight, I carry on watching them. From James's air of desperation, it seems the other man has the upper hand. He's taller than James, deliberately aggressive in his manner. Edging closer, I try to make out what they're arguing about. Then James raises his fist and punches the man.

As they look at each other, I wait for it to escalate, but the other man says something, then gets in his car and drives off. I hesitate, not sure what to do. I haven't seen James to talk to since Hollie died. But before I can do anything, he, too, gets in his car and drives away.

I carry on running, in the same direction the two cars took. Then just before the track meets the main road, I see James again. This time, his car is parked to one side. He's on the phone, clearly upset. But then, he's just lost his daughter. As I pass him, it looks as though he's pleading with someone. I raise a hand, but when he sees me, he looks horrified, lifting his hand briefly out of habit rather than anything else before he looks away.

Living in a house where the police are omnipresent, a village where suddenly everyone's watching him, he's clearly come out here to find privacy, not expecting anyone to see him. And it's understandable. There could be any number of explanations for his behavior, none of them my business. The death of a child breaks a parent's belief in the order of things. It isn't supposed to happen that way. Now, he has to find a way to get through this tragedy.

Except not everyone does. James has no anchor in his grief, no other child who needs him. Stephanie can't understand—she has no children of her own. But unless someone has experienced a similar loss, no one can. Despite the flurry of well-wishers and neighborly support around him in these early days, James is alone, as we all are.

It crosses my mind to go to the Hamptons' house to talk to James, but I decide it's too soon, that they need privacy, space to grieve. As yet, the cause of Hollie's death still hasn't been announced.

When news of the postmortem results slip out, Andrew has the grace to call me.

"Hollie had head injuries. They're opening a murder inquiry."

It's almost as much of a shock as when her body was found.

I'd imagined Hollie missing her step, hitting her head on the side of the pool as she fell. "How can they be sure?"

"There's an injury to the side of her head, which would be likely if she'd simply fallen, but they've found a second. They think someone hit her with a sharp object, then she hit her head a second time as she fell into the pool. I have to go, Elise." He speaks coldly. "I have patients."

I'm still struggling to take in this news when I have to tell Niamh. She listens in silence, then gets up and pushes past me on her way to the bathroom, making it just in time before I hear the sound of her throwing up.

As I wait for her to come back, the rain starts.

# Nicki

All weekend, I think of the Hamptons, waiting, as we all are, to find out more about how Hollie died. First thing on Monday morning, the skies are overcast, the first drops of rain falling as I get into my car. By the time I reach the office, it's become a downpour.

I've been there less than five minutes when the DI calls me. As I listen, he explains that the injuries to Hollie's head don't correspond with bruising she would have sustained from a fall. "We're still checking it out, but there's a wound to the front of her head that she couldn't possibly have got from falling against the edge of the pool. It doesn't look like her death was an accident. You'd better get back to the Hampton house. It's likely we're looking for a murderer."

# 11

## Elise

Needing to be home for Niamh, I take a week's unpaid leave. But in the days that follow, as the rain continues to fall, I realize how little I know about the people around me. I talk to Ida Jones now and then, but I only know what she chooses to share with me. When I see our neighbors, conversation is superficial, brief. None of us open our hearts, bare our souls. We all have our own lives and they rarely overlap, just as each of us has secrets. Even Sophie, whom I'm closest to, only sees what she wants to, but then I hide the miserable truth from her, from everyone. She doesn't know what goes on under the surface.

For reasons I can't explain, I don't tell anyone that I saw James in the woods, arguing with another man; that he hit him. But it niggles at me. With the circumstances of Hollie's death now considered suspicious, I know I should share what I saw. I'm expecting another call from the police, just not so soon. This time, DS May turns up alone. Her long hair is rolled into a twist; in a pale blouse and black trousers, she appears coolly confident. Across the table from her, I feel I'm under scrutiny, uncomfortable with her questions.

"Did you have any reason to be concerned about your daughter's friendship with Hollie?"

Did I? Doesn't every parent have concerns about their children's friends? I'd never considered Hollie as anything but harmless, but I know DS May is trying to establish her own picture of a girl she'll never meet. "No more than anyone else." I meet her eyes. "I'm aware of who she spends time with. But she's fourteen. You have to let children grow up, be themselves. I think that's why she and Hollie got on. However unhappy or troubled she was feeling, Hollie was always herself. I think Niamh admired that."

DS May frowns. "You said however unhappy or troubled Hollie was feeling . . . Was she often like that?"

I sigh. Hollie was Hollie. "Not particularly. We're all different, Detective Sergeant. Hollie could be volatile, emotional, high-strung. She was smart, too, but I think it's fair to say she thrived on having a degree of drama in her life." It's how I'd always seen her. She wasn't the kind of person to be content with a quiet life. She should have been an actress.

"What about her father?" This time, DS May looks openly curious. "Can you tell me anything about him? He wrote a best seller, didn't he?"

I nod. "He's written other books since, though I don't think they've done so well. But the family seems to have a nice lifestyle—and Stephanie has her shop."

DS May nods thoughtfully. "Hollie got on well with Stephanie?"

I shrug. "As I told you before, I didn't really spend time with them as a family. I wasn't aware of any animosity between them. I don't think Hollie was always easy, but Stephanie meant well, and when she married James, she took on a grieving stepdaughter. It can't have been easy for any of them."

"You sound as though you knew Hollie quite well." DS May watches me carefully.

"It's a village." I sit back, looking at her. "There aren't many of us here. Because Hollie spent so much time with Niamh, there was a certain familiarity between us. Do you think that's strange?"

She shakes her head. "Of course not. To be honest, I'm struggling to find anyone other than her father who knows Hollie more than just in passing."

I shake my head. "There was something. The last time I saw her in the churchyard, she was definitely upset. She'd taken the day off school. In fact, I asked her what she was hiding . . ." I look at DS May, remembering Hollie's agitation. "She said there was nothing. But she was lying. I'm sure of it."

DS May nods. "I'm seeing her class teacher tomorrow. She may be able to throw some light on whatever was going on. Unless you think Niamh could help us? If Hollie was hiding something, she may have confided in her."

Knowing Niamh doesn't find it easy talking to the police, I'm torn between protecting her and wanting to help. I nod. "I'll ask her. Niamh tends to keep things inside. She finds it difficult to express her emotions. It's just the way she is."

"It might be really helpful. Perhaps I could come back later on? When she's back from school?"

"She's usually home around four."

After DS May leaves, I stand at the kitchen window, watching her hurry across the drive and get in her car. As she drives away, I wonder who else in the village she's talking to about Hollie. I shiver, glancing at the sky, which is heavy with rain that shows no signs of easing.

In the quiet of the house, unwanted thoughts fill my head, until I have to get out. It's too wet outside to go for a run, so I pull on my coat, dash to my car, and set off for Sophie's. The road has flooded in places, the streams on either side already overflowing. Outside the Calders' house, a torrent of water pours down their drive. Managing to sidestep it, I get to the door, but it's Julian who opens it.

"Elise! How are you?" He speaks with his usual air of bonhomie, but he looks surprised to see me. "You must come in. Dreadful, isn't it?"

Unsure whether he's talking about Hollie or the weather, I hover on the doorstep. "I was hoping to catch Sophie—is she around?"

"Hasn't double booked again, has she?" Julian looks at me curiously. "She went to Chichester. Something to do with a fundraising lunch..." Breaking off, he frowns. "At least, I think that's what she said."

But I'm not in the mood for Julian's small talk. "Don't worry. She wasn't expecting me. I was just passing. I'll catch her another time." I start backing away toward my car. "Tell her I called by?"

Back in my car, I start the engine, watching as he closes the front door. Pulling away, avoiding the worst of the puddles, even with my windscreen wipers on full, I'm forced to drive slowly, barely able to see the road ahead until I reach the dual carriageway. Accelerating, for a while I drive aimlessly, playing loud music. Hollie's death has gotten under my skin. Feeling emotions I don't want to face, I try to bury them.

I end up at Stephanie's florist shop, driven there by a need to talk to her that's subconscious rather than intentional. When I go inside, her eyes are red, her shoulders slumped. Her efforts to rally herself to greet a customer evaporate when she sees it's me.

"Elise." Even heavier than usual makeup doesn't hide the paleness of her skin.

"How are you holding up?" I pause. "I'm sorry, that's a stupid thing to ask. It's such a horrible day. I was driving past. I thought I'd just pop in."

She nods. "It's nice of you. Everyone else is staying away. I haven't had a customer for days. I'll put the kettle on—if you have time?"

It's what people do. Stay away, because they don't know what to say, when what's most needed is basic human contact. But condolence calls are too much of a reminder that death can happen, at any time, to any one of us. Suddenly uncomfortable, I'm struck by that same urge to make an excuse and leave, but stop myself and nod. "Thanks."

She looks mildly surprised. "The kettle's through here."

I follow her through a doorway behind her desk into a smaller room. There are photos on the walls of beautiful flower arrangements, presumably some of Stephanie's work. Down one side, there's a long table and in one corner, a compact kitchenette. I recognize the scent of narcissi and hyacinths in the air—then notice the rest of the space is filled with spring flowers.

Stephanie sees me looking at them. "They're for the funeral."

"They're beautiful." The flowers are fresh shades of lemon, white, pale blue, and pink. At the mention of a funeral, my heart jumps. Hollie's disappearance, the discovery of her body, then the police involvement, and now her funeral—everything's moving so fast. "Have you a date?"

"Next Thursday. It's early to get the flowers in, but I want to make sure they're fully open . . ." Her voice wavers. "Oh God . . . Hollie's dead and I'm talking about flowers." Her voice is tearful. As she looks at me, her face is etched with grief.

"It's what you do," I tell her quietly, going over to the worktop to finish making the tea. "I'll do this. Why don't you sit down?" Perching on one of the chairs, she doesn't argue. A minute later, I hand her one of her mugs.

"Thank you." Getting out a tissue, she wipes her face. "The day after her body was found, I had to come in early to work on some wedding flowers. Beautiful, they were . . . It was the kind of fairy-tale wedding that every girl dreams of at some point. Putting together all those bouquets and boutonnieres, all

I could think was, 'Hollie will never get married, never have children . . .' " As her voice breaks, more tears stream down her cheeks.

Hollie may not have been her blood daughter, but Stephanie's clearly heartbroken. A feeling of powerlessness overwhelms me, but at times like this, there are no words, nor is there anything I or anyone else can do to help her. I let her drink her tea, then quietly ask, "How is James bearing up?"

"Honestly?" She raises her tearstained face to look at me. "He's a mess. I'm trying to be there for him, but he's all over the place. Losing his first wife, now Hollie . . . it's too much for anyone."

"He has you," I say gently. But she's right. It is too much; the worst, most unnatural loss.

"I don't know how he'll get over this." More tears roll down her face.

I don't say anything. I don't believe people do get over a loss like this. What happens, over a long period of time, is that it somehow becomes assimilated into their lives. But nothing can ever be the same as it was before.

Then Stephanie shocks me. "The thing is . . ." She hesitates. "I'm sure there's something else going on." She's tense as she looks at me. "Please don't tell anyone this, will you? But I think he's hiding something from me."

I stare at her, trying to work out whether she's hinting at something. "To do with Hollie, you mean?"

Her eyes widen, and then she tries to backtrack. "Nothing like that. I shouldn't have said anything. I'm sure it's nothing."

My ears prick up as I remember the man James met in the woods that day I saw them. I watch her. She suspects something. I know from experience that there are gut instincts you can't ignore. "What makes you say that?"

"Oh, I don't know." She looks evasive. "Why does anyone think someone's keeping something from them? Private phone calls, hiding what he's looking at on his laptop . . . he's drinking far more than he used to, too. But this all started a long time before Hollie disappeared."

A chill comes over me. "Have you asked him about it?"

"I've tried . . ." Her voice wavers. "He pushes me away. Tells me lies." She shakes her head sadly. "James and I used to be so close. But that's gone. And now poor Hollie . . . Nothing stays the same, does it? You can't ever trust that life will be OK, because nothing lasts."

I'm silent, trying to remember when my life last seemed OK. When Niamh was born? Days after, I'd discovered Andrew was having an affair—his second, as far as I know. I cast my mind back further, then I stop, because my life is far from OK. It's been that way as long as I can remember, but I can't dwell on it. I turn to Stephanie. "With Hollie's funeral coming up, maybe now isn't the time to confront him about it, but if you and James are good like you say, you'll get through this. For now, you need to take each day at a time. You have enough to think about." I pause for a moment. "If I can do anything . . . you know where I am. Call me, Stephanie—or come round. Anytime."

As I walk away, already I'm regretting saying that to her. Not just because my instincts are to protect my privacy, but because Andrew hates people turning up uninvited. The more people who know his whereabouts, the harder it becomes to hide his indiscretions. We're the epitome of the perfect family, if only in his eyes. He has no intention of letting that image slip.

# Niamh

*In death as in life, in my mind, Hollie takes center stage. On the bus, everyone's talking about her. At school, it's the same. Bad news travels faster than good.*

*Through the bus window, I stare at the rain painting everything gray, while all I can think of is Hollie, in the churchyard amongst the headstones, staring at the ghosts; running across a field, her long hair flying out behind her; her body floating, lifeless, cold.*

*In the time it takes to run from the bus stop to my house, my clothes are soaked through. In the kitchen my mother's talking on her phone, while I go upstairs and change my clothes. When I come down, she's waiting for me.*

*"How was your day?" She looks anxious.*

*"OK." I shrug, then go to the fridge for a drink.*

*My mother's voice comes from behind me. "Niamh, the police want to talk to you again. They think Hollie may have told you something that might help them get to the bottom of what's happened to her."*

*Opening the can, I take a mouthful, as my mother goes on.*

*"DS May was here earlier. She wondered if Hollie might have confided in you."*

Through the window, raindrops scatter the beams from a car's headlights into a thousand tiny shards, as my mother says, *"That's probably her."*

DS May and Sergeant Collins look as though they've been standing in the rain for hours. I feel my insides twisting as they take off their coats, accept my mother's offer of tea. At the kitchen table, DS May gets out her notebook.

*"Thank you for talking to us again, Niamh. It's just that you're one of a very small number of friends Hollie had. We need to make sure we haven't missed something."*

Coming over, my mother places mugs on the table, pulls out another chair next to mine.

DS May goes on. *"I know we've asked you before, but can you tell us what you and Hollie used to get up to again? Where you went . . . who you saw . . . ? Try to remember. Was there anyone you may have met along the way?"*

Gazing at her, I bite my lip. She doesn't understand. There's so much I don't know. The only person who knows what happened is Hollie.

*"I can't tell you anything,"* I say at last, looking at both of them.

*"Niamh."* There's a warning tone in my mother's voice.

*"It's true."* I turn to her. *"We watched movies. Sometimes Hollie told me that stuff was wrong at home, but she never actually said what it was."*

DS May's frowning at me. *"Was this recent, Niamh? Hollie telling you something was wrong?"*

I nod.

*"And you've no idea what?"*

*"She said she couldn't trust the one person she should have been able to depend on. I asked her to explain, but she wouldn't. I don't know anything else."* I stare at her, wondering if she be-

*lieves me. Then it's too much. Pushing back my chair, I stand up and walk upstairs.*

*In my room, I lie on my bed, the way Hollie used to—on my back, hands clasped behind my head, staring at the ceiling, before rolling over, pushing myself up with my elbows so that I can see the window. I'm still lying like that, watching the trees blowing in the wind, when my mother comes in.*

*"Niamh, you really shouldn't have walked off like that. The police need your help. You have to answer their questions."*

*I shake my head. She still doesn't understand. "I can't."*

*My mother comes over and sits on my bed next to me. "Look, I know this is upsetting. But surely you want to help the police find whoever did this to Hollie?"*

*Sliding off the bed, I get up and walk over to the window. It's almost dark, the rain still beating on the glass. I turn to face my mother. "She made me promise."*

*There's a moment of silence before my mother reacts. This time, she doesn't hide her irritation with me. "She's dead, Niamh. Don't you think this is more important?"*

*I stare at her. I'm not the only one who's holding something back. Then I say it. "Have you told them everything?"*

*As my mother's face pales, I know she hasn't. But I'd known that before I asked the question. When she goes downstairs, I know it's the last time she'll try to push me. She knows what will happen if she does.*

*From the top of the stairs, I listen as she talks to the policewomen, fobbing them off. "I'm sorry. Niamh isn't feeling well. She's finding this incredibly traumatic—we all are. Maybe it would be better to come back another day. In the meantime, I'll talk to her."*

*"Of course. It's a difficult time. I understand that." DS May's voice carries up the stairs. "You have my number. If Niamh thinks of anything, or wants to talk to us, give me a call."*

*"Of course."*

*Even from my room, I can hear the obvious relief in my mother's voice. There's a murmur of voices, before the back door opens and closes, followed by the sound of my mother's footsteps as she comes back upstairs.*

*She pauses in the doorway. "I haven't told them you were seen in the grounds of Deeprose House."*

*I stare at her. "You don't believe me, do you? You believe whoever said that, even though I've told you we were in the field." I'm lying, but that isn't the point. It's the fact that my own mother takes a stranger's word over mine.*

*My mother raises her voice. "When the police are talking to everyone in the village, don't you think they're going to find out?" Then she takes a breath. "We both know this is about Hollie, and that's all. You need to help the police. It's important." Across the top of the stairs, a pair of headlights swing into the drive.*

*"Your father." My mother stares at me. "I'll leave it to you to tell him about the police questioning you—if he asks."*

*I nod. We both know he won't ask. He never asks me anything, but I don't mind that. It means I don't have to cobble together satisfying answers to pointless questions. Silence makes everything so much easier.*

# 12

# Elise

"Don't bother cooking. I have to go out at seven." When he comes into the kitchen, Andrew drops his bag by the table and puts the kettle on. "I won't have time to eat."

Usually I don't ask him what he's doing, but I've had enough of walking on eggshells around him. I'm his wife. "Where to?" There's sarcasm in my question.

"What's this?" he mocks, getting a mug out of the cupboard. He doesn't ask me if I'd like one. "Have you suddenly decided you care?"

"Let me see." I stare him in the eyes, deliberately taunting him. "Is it the golf club, Andrew? Or the pub? Oh, silly Elise. It's Friday, isn't it. Everyone knows where Andrew goes on Fridays—everyone except his stupid wife. But do you know what, Andrew? She isn't as stupid as you—"

While I'm talking he comes over, stopping inches in front of me, before interrupting. "Bitch," he mutters through gritted teeth. Then he raises his arm and slaps me. Above the sound of his hand on my cheek, I hear a gasp of breath. At the top of the stairs, out of the corner of my eye, I see Niamh.

My face throbs. "You need to watch it, Andrew," I mutter under my breath and walk away from him. Near the door, I stop. "Emotional distance and infidelity are one thing." I keep my voice low, not wanting Niamh to hear. "But I'm not sure how physical abuse would sit with your practice manager."

"Prove it." His eyes are like lasers, boring into me, while he seems to forget we have a witness. "But I'm warning you. One mention, Elise, and I'll dredge up those notes from four years ago. I bet the airline would love to read them. The police, too."

His words hit me harder than any blow delivered by his hand. He's talking about a breakdown I had, which, in my desperate state, triggered me to take an overdose. For months after, he held it over me, reminding me constantly that if I'd been thinking of Niamh, I would have asked for help.

Desperately unhappy at the time, I told him I wanted us to separate. I can still remember his look of contempt, his cruel smile as he told me that I could leave, but no one in their right mind would give me custody of a child—he'd make sure of that. I'd realized at that point, he didn't care even slightly about me or Niamh. All he was interested in was controlling me.

I'd told myself I'd stay, just until I could find a way past him. Meanwhile, Andrew removed my breakdown from my medical records—but that had been for his sake rather than mine. He hadn't wanted anyone to know he had a suicidal wife.

"Fuck you." I turn away so that he can't see my face. However it looks to anyone else, I'm trapped, married to a monster. But as he walks away, his phone in his hand, something clicks into place inside my head.

Andrew knows what I saw on his phone the other night. He may believe he holds the winning hand. And for now he does. But when the time is right, I'll tell the police his nasty little secret. At any time, I can potentially bring him down. He holds a position of trust and responsibility. What I've seen could have serious consequences for him.

That I know how to ruin Andrew gives me iron strength, armor through which his unkindness can no longer pierce. For years I've felt imprisoned by him, powerless to change my life. But not now. Hollie's death is a reminder that life is short. I've let too much time pass already. And Andrew deserves what's coming to him.

Two days later, on a morning when I'm alone, Stephanie turns up unexpectedly. As she stands on the doorstep, she's clearly distraught, her tears blending with the rain on her face.

Her eyes are desperate as she looks at me. "I'm so sorry, Elise . . . I didn't know who else to turn to."

"Come in. You're soaked." Only when I close the door and she starts to sob does the extent of her distress become clear. "What's happened? Let me hang up your coat."

Wiping her face, she awkwardly shrugs off her coat and passes it to me. Underneath, her sweater is soaked, too. "Come and stand by the radiator. I'll go and get you something to change into."

Upstairs, I find a lambswool sweater in a dull shade of blue and take it down to her. "The cloakroom's through there." I indicate a door just beyond the kitchen. While she goes to change, I put the kettle on.

When she comes back, she's slightly more composed, but as her eyes flit around, it's clear she needs to talk about something. For a fleeting moment I wonder if it's Andrew, then dismiss the thought. If she was having an affair with my husband, I'd be the last person she'd come to with her problems.

Finally, she sits down, and I get out two mugs. "I've made a pot of coffee. But if you'd prefer tea, it's no trouble."

She shakes her head. "Coffee would be good." She hesitates. "Thank you, Elise. I'm so sorry to turn up here like this."

"It really isn't a problem. Let me finish making this; then we'll talk."

She sits down, and I take the coffeepot and milk over to the small table by the sofa under the window. There's a wood-burning stove, which I hadn't bothered to light earlier, but even without it, the sofa is soft and it's the coziest corner of this house. Pouring the coffee, I pass her a mug. "Now, tell me what's happened."

As she starts to talk, her composure evaporates. "James will kill me if he knows I've talked to you." Her voice cracks.

"James won't find out," I tell her firmly.

Mopping her face, she sighs shakily. "We're in trouble, Elise. I mean James is, but it affects us both. He's massively in debt. The mortgage is in arrears—I only found out yesterday. Unless a miracle happens, I think we're going to lose the house."

It seems desperately unfair that after losing Hollie, they're faced with this. "Have you spoken to the bank? They might give you some time. They can't just repossess it overnight."

She shakes her head, blinking away her tears. "It's hardly overnight. This has been going on for a year. Believe it or not, James has hidden it from me. I'm never there when the post arrives and emails always go straight to him . . . It was irresponsible of me, but I've never thought anything of it. I can see now how stupid I was to have trusted him, but I've never had any reason not to. Anyway, it's too late." She sounds desperate. "We're going to lose everything. I have no idea what we're going to do."

I'm frowning. "But you have your shop. And what about the books he's written? Surely they must make some money?"

"They do. It used to be enough." She hesitates. "But not now."

Something in her voice makes me frown. "What's changed?" As I watch her closely, it's clear she isn't telling me everything.

"James invested in a business and he owes them money." She says it quickly.

"So can't he sell?"

"It seems not." She doesn't look at me. "James is up to his neck in something. For ages he didn't tell me. In fact, I've only just found out. He was conned . . ." But instead of sympathetic, she sounds bitter. "He didn't know what he was letting himself in for. There was supposed to be a contract. He was led to believe he'd make a lot of money . . ."

I stare at her. "There has to be something he can do. Have you gotten legal advice?"

Stephanie's eyes drop. "It's not that simple. James was desperate, Elise. His last book was rejected by his publisher." She pauses, as though she's trying to work out what to tell me, then raises her eyes to meet mine again. "He met someone who told him about a surefire way to make a lot of money. What the man didn't tell him was how, exactly . . ." Her voice shakes, then she sighs. "I may as well tell you. It's a porn site, Elise. The people running it con people into looking at it by telling them they're looking for investors for an app they're developing. Once someone looks at it, they're on a list. Everyone who buys in, like James, gets added."

"James actually bought into a porn site?" I'm not easily shocked, but the thought of someone I thought I knew getting into something like this is utterly abhorrent.

"I know." Stephanie covers her face with her hands. "It's completely vile, Elise. He can't sell, and now he's being forced to pay huge amounts—more than we can afford—just to remain anonymous. It's a nightmare."

As she speaks, I'm thinking of the image Andrew was looking at on his phone; then the man I saw James talking to, the argument they had. "The man who's conning him, do you know who he is?"

"He's local—that's all I know. James got swept into his circle out of pride—and vanity. James likes to impress people. I think he thought this man was a doorway into a circle of wealthy, powerful men, which it was, of course . . . But for the worst possible reasons."

I stare at her in disbelief. "He should go to the police."

She looks up sharply. "You won't tell them, will you?"

"No, but you or James should." I pause, frowning again. "Why on earth hasn't he?"

"Because he'll be arrested," Stephanie whispers. "Some of the photos . . . they're of children, Elise."

"God." Suddenly I feel sick. How could he get involved in child porn? "That's even more reason to get the police involved. You can't protect him, Stephanie. There's no excuse for something like this."

"I know." As she looks up at me, she looks old, aged by worry and shame. "He swears he didn't know. But it will be the end of his writing career."

It will be far more than that, but it doesn't mean she should protect him. "That's his problem. He should have thought of that before he got involved. He hasn't had anything published in a few years, has he?"

She shakes her head sadly. "The irony is, he's just finished a new book. He was about to send it to his agent, but then Hollie went missing."

Suddenly I shiver. I'm thinking of how Hollie was in the days before she disappeared. She'd seemed more erratic, more distracted than usual, even for her. "What if Hollie had found out?" There's a look of horror in Stephanie's eyes as she looks at me. I go on. "She definitely seemed upset about something. What if her death is connected in some way? I don't see how you can rule it out."

"You're right." Her voice is low but she doesn't meet my eyes. Then as I watch her, I shiver again, realizing she's thought of this already and she still hasn't told the police. Her voice shakes. "I need to ask you one favor."

I sympathize with Stephanie and James over Hollie's loss, but I can't feel anything other than disgusted about what she's told me. "What is it?"

She hesitates. "I know it's a lot to ask, but if you're talking to the police at all, about Hollie, you might find it hard not to let on about what I've told you." Her eyes fill with tears. "But can you wait a few days? If we could just have Hollie's funeral . . . I don't want her memory tainted by whatever her stupid father has done. For that one day, I want everyone to be thinking about her." Even in her distressed state, she's fiercely determined to keep Hollie's name out of whatever James is involved in. "After that, the police can arrest James, for all I care. I won't be around to see it."

Her words surprise me. "Where are you going? What about the shop?"

"I've given notice on the lease." Her voice is emotionless. "There are a few weddings and parties booked in, but I've found another florist to honor my commitments. Where will I go? I don't know yet. But anywhere that's far away from here."

"I can't promise." If the police question me directly about what I know, I'm not prepared to lie. But then I put myself in her shoes. I can understand why she's asked me. "I won't tell them unless they ask. But after the funeral . . . If you don't tell them, I'll have to, Stephanie. For Hollie's sake."

If she was hoping for more from me, she doesn't say anything. She stays long enough to finish her coffee, putting her mug down now and then, as if she wants to say more before thinking better of it. As she leaves, cowed by grief and shame, she seems smaller somehow, and I think about how desperation drives people to extremes. First James and his investment, and now Stephanie, prepared to lie to the police; each with motives they've justified to themselves, when their only priority should be finding out what happened to Hollie.

Then the headline comes back to me, the one I saw on the flight before all of this started. Maybe only ten percent of people are good, but given extreme circumstances, who knows what any of us are capable of?

# 13

# Elise

In the light of what Stephanie's told me, I wonder how many other people are embroiled the way James is—in an immoral, illegal business that they're too frightened to blow the whistle on. At the same time, another question enters my mind. *Could Andrew be?*

In my heart, I know my husband is capable of anything. He isn't a doctor out of compassion. It's for the aura of authority and integrity that accompanies his title; his cloak of infallibility; the fact that his words carry more weight than other people's. It astonishes me how even now, so many people don't question their doctors, even though doctors are human, as capable as anyone else of making mistakes.

In my mind, I conjure the face of the man I saw James arguing with in the woods, sure that I know him somehow, yet still unable to remember where from. Two days before the funeral, I go back to work, reporting one early morning for a flight to Barcelona. The flight is busy, so that after we've taken off, I don't get time to look outside until we're flying over the south of France. The cloud carpeting the landscape as we left the UK is far behind us and from the small window in the forward door, I can see snow-capped mountains, just before the land flattens out to meet the sea.

As we start our descent into the city, I'm distracted for a couple of moments while I make a final check of the cabin. By the time I return to my view, we're low enough to make out buildings and the network of streets bathed in winter sun. Then the aircraft turns to head out over the sea briefly. The port comes into view, then open water, before we turn and make our final approach.

After we land, I study the rows of faces in front of me, imagining lives that are so different from mine. Then as the last of the passengers disembarks, I'm gripped by an urge to make an excuse to go to the terminal building, to merge into the thousands of people there before disappearing from everything I know. I come close, for a moment believing I could, until I think of Niamh.

It's a reality check that causes my mood to slump. Like many of us, I live a life bound by responsibility—as cabin crew required to get this flight home; as Niamh's mother; and now, in the light of what's happened to Hollie and what Stephanie has told me, there's an additional burden on me, an obligation to help expose the truth.

I push it to the back of my mind as we fly back, but two hours later, as we make our approach into Gatwick, I think of the hold Andrew has over me. Am I really so different from Stephanie? Weak, playing along with Andrew's game for my own reasons, instead of letting the truth come out and dealing with the fallout? As the aircraft wheels touch down, I realize I'm not like Stephanie. She isn't weak at all. After the funeral, she's going to cut herself loose from James. It's exactly what I need to find a way to do.

After we park on our stand and the return passengers start to disembark, my eyes fix on a man speaking angrily to his wife.

But instead of looking upset or anxious, she humors him, touching his arm with affection. I watch his anger evaporate; then he laughs quietly, kissing her on the cheek. It's a brief moment that reminds me of everything that's wrong in my marriage; a reminder that only I can change it.

While I drive home, I feel uncertainty escalating around me, as if unstoppable change is in the air. It's a feeling that's heightened that afternoon, when I drive into Chichester for an appointment. Later, when I get home, I switch on the radio and turn the music up. Then, out of character for me, I open a bottle of Prosecco and pour myself a large glass. I don't care what anyone else thinks. There's no reason for me to, when the world's increasingly unpredictable and the only person I can rely on is myself.

Finishing the glass, I pour another, as an upbeat track comes on the radio. Caught in a moment of recklessness, I start to dance—wildly, uninhibitedly, because no one's watching and because I feel like it. It isn't until the music subsides that I hear the knock at the door.

Catching my breath, I smooth my hair behind my ears and open it to find Sergeant Collins and DS May standing there.

"Mrs. Buckley? I hope we're not disturbing you. Would you mind if we came in for a moment?" Their faces are impassive. If they saw me through the window, it doesn't show.

Standing back, I open the door wider. "Of course not." The cloud of uncertainty I felt earlier is back, hanging over me. "Come through."

They follow me inside, hovering for a moment, until I gesture toward the table. "Would you like to sit down?"

DS May shakes her head. "Thank you—but this won't take long."

I watch her eyes glance around the kitchen, taking in my half-drunk glass, then glancing at the clock, before she carries on. "Can you remember where you were the day Hollie died?"

I gasp. Am I a suspect? "I was at work—on a flight. I'll have to check where to."

"If you wouldn't mind?"

My feeling of uncertainty grows stronger as I get my phone, logging into the crew portal before bringing up my flight schedule. "I went to Barcelona."

Making a note, she nods, before going on. "I wondered if you knew Niamh was with Hollie the day before she disappeared."

Shaking my head, I frown at her. "You must be mistaken. It isn't possible. She would have been at school." But I was flying that day, too. I've always trusted that she goes to school. I've no reason not to, but in reality, I can't be sure where she was.

The expression on DS May's face is grave. "We have reason to believe that Niamh took the day off. According to the school, you emailed them to tell them she had a dental appointment."

I stare at her, feeling my grip on reality loosen further.

"Did you, Mrs. Buckley?"

I try to take in what she's said. Niamh must have been at school. In that moment, I'm paralyzed, torn between needing to protect Niamh from whatever Hollie was caught up in and telling the truth. Except that the truth is I don't know where Niamh was that day. My voice is hoarse. "I can't be sure. I'd have to check the calendar . . . Maybe the school made a mistake. Did they say if she'd missed any other days?"

To my relief, she says, "To the best of our knowledge, this was the only one, which makes it all the more important. Did Hollie have some kind of grip over your daughter? Enough to make her take a day off school, for whatever reason?"

"Not that I'm aware. It's best if I talk to Niamh." But as I watch them, DS May and Sergeant Collins glance at each other.

"She's usually home around four, isn't she? Would you mind if we wait?"

# Niamh

When I see the police car parked on the drive outside my house, I think about turning around and going somewhere else—anywhere else. Then I see my mother standing at the kitchen window. When she sees me, she raises a hand.

As I go inside, I see the two policewomen sitting at our kitchen table. I know they're waiting for me—otherwise why else would they be here?

"They want to talk to you, Niamh." My mother sounds jittery. "They say you were with Hollie on one of the days she was missing from school."

"Yes." I'm not going to lie. "But there's a reason I didn't tell you." I glance at her. "Before, I mean."

Shaking her head, she looks furious for a moment. Then she looks worried. In a flash, I get why. She thinks I know more than I'm saying about what happened to Hollie.

"I made Hollie a promise," I tell DS May and Sergeant Collins. "Just because she's dead, doesn't mean a promise should be broken."

DS May nods slightly. "So Hollie was upset that day. Upset

*enough that she persuaded you to take the day off school. Wasn't there anyone else she went to when she needed to talk to someone?"*

I shake my head. *"She didn't have anyone else. I was going to get on the bus, as usual, but she was desperate."*

*"So what happened after you didn't get on the bus?"*

*"We came back here. I got changed, and we went out again."*

*"But first, you emailed your school, telling them you had a dental appointment."*

I nod.

*"Niamh." My mother sounds shocked.*

*"Of course, some of your teachers picked up that you weren't in lessons." DS May pauses. "So what did you and Hollie do after that?"*

There are things you don't tell your parents, that they don't need to know or wouldn't understand. I recall that day when Hollie was at the bus stop waiting for me.

*"Can you not go to school today?"* Her eyes were huge with dark circles under them, as though she hadn't slept in days. *"I'm going mad, Niamh. I need you."* The words broke out of her in a sob.

I thought about the classes I'd miss, the trouble I'd get into when my mother found out. *"If I don't go to registration, they'll call my mother."*

Her eyes didn't leave mine. *"Can't you tell them you have a dentist's appointment? I'll never ask you to do anything like this again."*

I paused, thinking of the online portal between the school and parents. I'd memorized the log-in details they sent my mother. *"I suppose." I paused. "What are we going to do?"*

*"I don't know. I don't care."* Hollie always spoke theatrically. *"Your bus is coming, Niamh. You have to decide. Please . . ."*

As I heard the bus coming closer, the desperation in her voice *swayed me. A day off school wouldn't make any difference to anyone.* "OK."

"*Is your mum at work?*" *As we walked away down the road, Hollie spoke hurriedly. When I nodded, she said,* "*Can we go back to yours? Shouldn't you change?*" *She looked at my uniform anxiously. As the bus came into sight, Hollie grabbed my arm.* "*Quick. Before the driver sees us.*"

*By the time it reached the bus stop, we were out of sight. From the garden, I heard the bus slow down for a moment, then when the driver saw I wasn't there, gradually accelerate and pull away. Running ahead of me across the garden toward the house, Hollie seemed more anxious than usual.* "*Hurry up, Niamh. You need to email the school, remember? Before they try to call your parents.*"

*Unlocking the back door, I closed it behind both of us, then got my laptop, logging in and sending the email to the school, before shutting it down again. I turned to Hollie.* "*What now?*"

*There was a strange look on her face. Then she said,* "*My dad's done something.*"

"*What?*" *Before she could speak, I added,* "*I need to change, Hollie. Come upstairs.*"

*As I went upstairs, I tried to imagine what her dad might have done. But after all that, she didn't tell me. While I changed, she was restless, flitting around my room. Then as I pulled on a sweater, she said,* "*I have to show you something.*"

"*What?*"

*But she was already going downstairs again. In the kitchen, she picked up my jacket and handed it to me.*

"*Where are we going?*"

*Shaking her head, she opened the back door, standing outside impatiently.* "*Come on, Niamh. It has to be now, or someone will see us.*"

*As the same urgency that gripped her filtered into me, I closed the door and hurried to catch up, jogging to keep pace with her quick steps. As we reached the lane, she glanced around, as if to make sure we weren't being watched. When she broke into an easy run, I did the same, following her along the pavement, watching her unzipped jacket flapping behind her. "Hollie." When she didn't slow down, I shouted after her. "Hollie . . . Stop!"*

*There was a mystified look on her face as she turned round. For some reason, I was annoyed. "What are we doing out here? Someone will see me. I'm supposed to be at school, remember?"*

*Jogging back to me, she grabbed my hand, then stroked a strand of hair off my face. "It'll be OK, Niamh. But I have to show you something. It's important."*

*I was relieved when no cars passed us. We carried on, more slowly. As we passed Ida Jones's cottage, I glanced up at her windows, grateful when I saw they were dark. Then we passed Furze Lane and crossed the road, taking an unmarked path through the woods.*

*Clouds were rolling across the sky, lowering, threatening rain. Under the canopy of branches, the woods were dark. It took fifteen minutes for us to reach the house. Telling me to stay hidden, Hollie hurried around the front to check the drive.*

*"No one's home."*

*I followed her to a window she made me peer through, into a small room that looked like someone's office, with photos on the desk. Photos of young girls. Then she told me what she'd been keeping from me; made me swear not to tell anyone else.*

*"Everyone has secrets, Niamh. But now my secret is your secret, too."*

*Even now, I have to keep her secret. "She told me her dad had done something. It must have been quite bad. Then she made me go a long way to this house that belonged to someone she didn't know. But that was it." It seems an age ago it happened, but that's how it feels when someone dies. It's the difference between life with and without; before and after.*

"*Where was the house?*" *DS May's pen is poised, ready to write it down.*

*I look at her blankly.* "*Through the woods somewhere.*"

"*Not Deeprose House?*" *When I shake my head, she adds,* "*Would you be able to take us there?*"

*Can I remember the twisting path Hollie took?* "*I'm not sure I could.*"

"*It's really important, Niamh. If I go with you, could we try to find it?*"

*I shrug.* "*Maybe.*"

*DS May is quiet for a moment. When she speaks, she sounds irritated.* "*She didn't tell you any more than that, Niamh, about her father?*"

*I shake my head.* "*That was the trouble with Hollie. She'd tell you she'd discovered something, and how terrible it was, but then she wouldn't actually tell you what it was.*"

# 14

# Elise

Niamh looks at me. "I don't know anything else. I should have gone to school." Sounding mildly resentful, she shrugs.

"Hollie could be very persuasive," I tell DS May and Sergeant Collins.

"So I see." But DS May's voice is gentler as she addresses Niamh. "It's interesting that she always came here, rather than you going to her house."

"Hollie's father works from home. I think she felt freer here," I try to explain. "Both Andrew and I are out most days."

Her attention turns to me. "How often are you away, Mrs. Buckley?"

Suddenly I'm uncomfortable. "It varies. Mostly, my flights are short haul. Sometimes I'm away overnight, but it's rare."

"I see." Nodding, she goes on. "And you were working the day before Hollie disappeared?"

I watch as Niamh starts. "Yes. I'm sure I was. I'll check my flight schedule." Getting up, I go to get my phone, clicking on the page I've downloaded. "I had an eight thirty check-in for a flight to Malaga. I would have left the house by six thirty and got home around five that evening."

"Could you send us a copy for our records? That way, we can rule out the need to question you further."

My heart beats erratically at the realization that I'm a suspect. "Yes. Of course." Then I frown, because it can't just be me. Surely we're all suspects. "You're questioning everyone?"

DS May leans forward. "Mrs. Buckley, we have to. Until Hollie's murderer is found, we will continue talking to everyone in her life. Somebody, somewhere, must know something."

Her words make me uncomfortable. Both Stephanie and I are keeping information from the police, but not for much longer. Hollie's funeral is two days away. After that, I'll tell them everything they want to know.

On the day of Hollie's funeral, for a short while the rain lets up, leaving watery skies from which comes weak sunlight as we assemble outside the village church and Hollie's coffin is carried in. At the rear of the church, I study the backs of everyone who's come here today. In our small corner of England, we've paused our lives to spend this hour paying our respects. The church is filled with simple spring flowers, which I imagine to have been arranged by Stephanie. Each step of the way, she holds her husband's hand, her show of solidarity with James unfaltering. They appear united in their grief; no one would guess what's really going on between them.

When it's time for the eulogy, it's James who stands up. As he walks to the front of the church, you could hear a pin drop. He talks about the pain of losing the daughter he'll always miss, then asks for everyone to be patient and give them time to grieve. His eyes flicker over the congregation, pausing slightly on me. In that second, I know Stephanie's told him.

Whatever the circumstances, whatever wrong James may have done, I can't help but put myself in his shoes. As I look around, I see that the service leaves no one unmoved. To my right, Andrew is tall and somber in his black suit and tie, his expression emotionless. As I glance at Niamh's fair head on my other side, there's a lump in my throat. It's why I tolerate Andrew. I couldn't bear to lose her. To lose a child . . . it doesn't bear thinking about. But what for most of us is our worst nightmare, for James and Stephanie is reality.

After the funeral, as everyone filters outside, I see DS May and Sergeant Collins standing together on the fringes of the small crowd. On the other side of the churchyard are two more uniformed officers. Whether they're expecting trouble and playing it safe, or merely observing us, their presence is nonetheless unnerving.

While Andrew plays the concerned doctor, I pause, watching DS May's eyes fix on James, his head bowed and shoulders slumped, then move to Stephanie, her hair newly colored, wearing an understated navy dress. She barely leaves his side. Both of them are clearly devastated. Despite her outburst to me, it doesn't look at all as though she's about to leave him.

Sophie walks toward me. "God-awful day, isn't it, Elise?" Leaning forward, she kisses me on both cheeks. "Sorry I missed you the other day. Julian was a bit worried, actually. He thought you were rather upset."

"It was one of those days," I say evasively. "I can't even remember what was going through my mind. You're right, though. It's a terrible day. It doesn't get much worse."

Sophie gives me an odd look. "Are you going to the pub? James and Stephanie have invited everyone. We're going."

Wondering how they're going to pay for it, I shake my head. Then across the churchyard, I catch sight of the man James was arguing with in the woods. Glancing across at James, I watch him, wondering if he knows the man is here. Just then, he looks up, sees the man, then takes Stephanie's arm and steers her away.

"Sophie? Do you know who that is? Over there—on his own, by the hedge?"

Cringing, I look away as Sophie stares at him. "That's Phil Mason. You met him, Elise. A year ago—at our summer party. You asked me who he was then, too. Andrew was talking to him for ages. Why do you want to know?"

As she says that, pieces start falling into place. I remember him and Andrew deep in conversation, drifting away from everyone else, and fear strikes me.

"I knew I recognized him. I couldn't remember where from." I keep my voice casual. "What does he do?"

Sophie frowns. "He works for some software company. Don't ask me for details—you know what I'm like with anything technical. But he's done well. It's made him quite a wealthy man."

As I study him, I'm silent, wondering if he's the one who's blackmailing James. But if it is, surely he wouldn't be here? Then behind me, I hear Stephanie's voice. "Are you joining us at the pub, Elise?"

For a moment, I see the truth of what she's going though. It's there in the desperation flickering in her eyes. "I'm sorry," I hedge, floundering around for a believable excuse. "I won't be able to. To be honest, I don't want to leave Niamh alone."

"You can always bring her." It's a mixed message. She wants me close—but not too close.

"Thank you. I think I'll take her home. It's such a sad day—" Seeing Stephanie's eyes fill with tears, I break off, then add, "I'll come by the shop in the next few days. If you're going to be there?" I watch her start. She knows I'm referring to what she told me in confidence, about giving up her lease and going away for good.

"Of course I will. I'm hardly going to be anywhere else." Her voice is overly bright.

I frown at her, knowing the lie is for Sophie's benefit, as well as for anyone else who might be eavesdropping. Holding her gaze, I speak quietly. "Take care, Stephanie." But she's already turning to walk away.

There's a strange atmosphere as all of us stand there, but I'm not prepared for what happens next. Over everyone's heads, I glimpse Andrew in conversation with Phil Mason. As they shake hands, it seems amicable enough. Then I watch James, in mid-conversation with Ida Jones, suddenly break off and stare in their direction. When Andrew turns and walks toward him, the look in James's eyes shocks me. It's a look of pure hatred.

While Niamh and I walk home together, the rain returns, the force steadily intensifying so that we only just make it back before it becomes a downpour. While Niamh goes upstairs to change, I put the kettle on and make a pot of coffee, my head buzzing with thoughts about Hollie's funeral.

The more I replay what I saw, the more convinced I am of the existence of some kind of triangle between Andrew, James, and Phil Mason. I wouldn't put it past Andrew to be involved in anything nefarious and I already know from Stephanie what James is embroiled in. Then there's the argument I stumbled upon, between James and Phil; there's Phil's wealth. Quite what they are to each other, I don't know, but instinct tells me it isn't good.

Thinking back to what Stephanie told me about James's so-called investment and how it's bankrupted them, my blood runs cold. It's easy to point the finger at her, to blame her for not being more aware of their joint finances, but if Andrew had got involved in something similar, would I know?

The truth is, I don't know half of what he does. I didn't even know he and Phil Mason were friendly. Light-headed, I go into his study, closing the door behind me, before sitting at his desk. Quietly, I open the drawers, glancing at the few letters inside, which seem innocuous enough. But if Andrew was involved in anything, I know he'd be careful to completely cover his tracks. If there's anything here, it's because he wants me to find it. I wonder if he knows what a mess James has got himself into.

Judging from the look James gave him, there's clearly ill-feeling between them. Before going to change, I think about asking Stephanie if she knows why.

But my suspicions don't leave; instead, I feel them take root. It's late when Andrew comes back from the pub, stinking of whisky and cigarette smoke, slurring his words. "What's for dinner, Elise?"

Dinner's long gone. Niamh and I ate two hours ago. "I assumed you were eating at the pub. I didn't realize you knew Phil Mason," I say calmly. "Are he and James friends? I suppose they must be, otherwise why else would he have been at the funeral?" I watch the telltale freeze in his expression, before he comes over and stands in front of me.

"It's a small village, Elise. Of course I know him. What exactly are you trying to say?" There's a warning note in his voice. Before I can speak, he goes on. "But a word to the wise. Phil's a powerful man. He's not the kind of person you go around asking questions about. Do I make myself clear?"

I stare at him, wondering if he's threatening me. But I cut him short. He's too drunk to attempt a rational conversation. "It was an innocent question, Andrew. There's cold chicken in the fridge. I'm going to bed." I walk out, leaving him fumbling in the cupboard for the whisky bottle. With any luck, he'll drink himself to sleep on the sofa long before he makes it upstairs.

# Nicki

The longer Hollie Hampton's murder remains unsolved, the more convinced I become that the villagers are closing ranks. Usually the whole world has an opinion on what's going on with a murder investigation, but not in Abingworth. They're too reticent, too reluctant to talk about almost anything.

"It's as though there's some unspoken agreement, sir. Either that, or a secret they all know about."

The DI looks nonplussed. "Still no more on the porn ring?"

I shake my head. "Not yet. But that can't be it. They wouldn't all be in on it."

"No." He's thoughtful. "It's too much of a coincidence that Hollie's body was found in the same area we believe the porn ring to be based."

"It could just be coincidence, sir," I remind the DI.

"Yes." But he doesn't sound convinced. "Niamh Buckley . . . Do you think she knows anything about Hollie's death?"

I shrug. "I wouldn't like to say. Her loyalty to Hollie is commendable, if a little misguided, given the circumstances. But she's fourteen years old and her friend has just died."

"Maybe talk to her again. Win her trust, May. What about the mother?"

"The last time I saw Elise Buckley, she had half a bottle of Prosecco inside her. She's protective of her daughter. But on the whole, she seems fairly black-and-white."

"And her husband?"

"Andrew Buckley's the GP who signed the death certificate when the body was found. I've spoken to him on the phone since. He's businesslike, professional—and busy."

He scratches his head. "We've at least got a name. Philip Mason, May. We need to establish his whereabouts and bring him in for questioning in relation to the porn ring. But no one seems to know where he is. I've got a photo, somewhere." The DI rummages through the array of papers on his desk, then produces it with a flourish. "That's him."

As I study it, I recognize him. "He was at Hollie's funeral. Where does he live?"

"A mile or so out of Abingworth. Someone's been over there. Apparently, his house is locked up, the curtains and blinds drawn. It looks as though he's gone away.

"We need to find him." The DI speaks through gritted teeth. "Do you think during one of her free-spirited jaunts, Hollie might have stumbled across something and he had no choice but to get rid of her?"

I shrug. "Maybe. I don't know, sir. It's impossible to say."

"Tell me about the funeral."

I nod. "I'd say most of the village was there. The church was packed. It was really sad, as you'd expect. There was nothing out of place."

"And after?"

"Most of them went to the pub," I tell the DI, frowning, re-membering that Andrew Buckley was there, while Elise and Niamh hadn't made it, which I thought strange initially. But given Niamh's age and the circumstances, it was understand-able.

He sighs. "All we can do is keep talking to them. Keep asking questions. There's always someone who knows something. We just have to find them."

He's right. People don't always act as you think they might. There's often someone who may not realize they're sitting on a vital piece of information, just as there's always someone in a village who sees most of what goes on, yet stays in the background.

When I reach Ida Jones's cottage, I wonder if she could be that person. Her lips are pursed as she lets me in. Her unruly gray curls are scraped back into a bun. She comes up to my shoulder but despite her age, looks strong. As she shows me into her sitting room, she gestures to the sofa.

"Do you want to sit down?"

"Thank you." The heavy dark furniture and dated three-piece suite remind me of my grandmother's house. "I'm sorry to turn up like this, Mrs. Jones. I'd like to talk to you about Hollie Hampton."

She nods; then her eyes are suddenly far away. "I thought you might. But I'm not sure there's much I can tell you."

"Well . . . You could start by telling me about her. How well you knew her. Where you saw her, what you knew about her, her relationships . . ."

"She was quite a sweet young thing. But flighty, I called her. She was friends with young Niamh, but I expect you know that. It's hard on young ones to lose a friend." Her eyes mist over.

"Mrs. Jones . . . How well do you know the Hamptons?"

"Them?" She looks faintly surprised. "You'll know that James is a writer and Stephanie's a florist?"

As I nod, she goes on. "I might be wrong, but after his first book, I don't think he's had much luck. It's her shop that keeps them going."

"Is that so?" My ears prick up. It's the first suggestion I've heard of any financial difficulties. "Do you know the Buckleys?"

"Oh yes . . ." Ida Jones is more forthcoming. "I see Elise from time to time. The doctor though . . ." Her face clouds over.

My instincts are on full alert. "What about him?"

"Between you and me, he's not a nice man. I won't say any more than that." Her face is mutinous.

"Mrs. Jones . . . If you know something about Dr. Buckley that could help us, we need to know."

She's shaking her head. "It won't help you find who killed poor young Hollie." She hesitates. "But there are rumors. Villages are full of rumors." Her eyes give nothing away. "He likes women. That's all I'm saying."

I'm not altogether surprised. If her husband's fooling around, it might explain the slight hostility I sense in Elise Buckley. I push Ida Jones for more information, but she won't be drawn. Then she frowns.

"I almost forgot. I saw Elise with Hollie not that long back. They were by the church. I think they were arguing about something. I'd just started talking to them when my phone rang. It was my daughter—by the time we'd finished our chat, they'd sorted it out." Then she says, "Hollie and Niamh were all over the place together. They didn't take too much notice of boundaries, those two. But they were harmless."

"Where did they used to go, Mrs. Jones? Do you know?"

"How would I know?" She glares at me for a moment. "Ask young Niamh. She's the only one who could tell you."

Without knowing how, I've struck a chord. Either that, or she's slightly mad. I try to defuse her. "How long have you lived in the village, Mrs. Jones?"

"It's gone thirty years, twenty of them without my Derek. I've seen a few folks come and go, you know. Met most of them, too."

"Have you seen any strangers hanging around, or noticed

anything unusual?" I watch her face for any clues, but she shakes her head.

"It's different these days. Folk don't have time the way they used to. There's the pub, but it's full of outsiders. Even the church . . . folk go there on high days and holidays. We used to go every week. Shame." She shakes her head.

High days, holidays, and funerals, I can't help thinking. But I take her point that in a short time, close to a thriving town, village life has changed almost beyond recognition. I'm curious. "Do you feel like you belong to a community?"

She seems to think for a moment. "Oh yes," she says softly. "When something terrible happens, people rally round. We've always done that."

"Like now, you mean?" I feel myself frown.

She looks up sharply. "Exactly."

As I drive away, replaying her last comment, I'm sure I missed something. *When something terrible happens, people rally round. We've always done that . . .* I'm almost certain it wasn't Hollie she was talking about. But if not Hollie, who was it?

After what Ida Jones has implied about the Hamptons' financial situation, I pay a visit to Stephanie Hampton's shop, hoping to talk to her away from her husband. But when I get there, it's in darkness. Checking the clock in my car, I realize I've timed my visit badly, guessing she's closed for lunch.

Her shop is one of a few arranged in a courtyard of converted farm buildings. Now that I'm here, I'm curious. Getting out, I take the half dozen steps to the door, peering in through the glass. From what I can see of the dim interior, it looks as though Stephanie is waiting for a delivery to arrive. There are few flowers and it looks empty, but after Hollie's death, it stands to reason that Stephanie's mind would be on other things.

Or would it? If Ida Jones is right and this shop is keeping the Hamptons afloat, in its current state, it's less than inspiring. Going back down the steps, I walk along to the next building, glancing at the window display filled with wedding paraphernalia. Above the door, gold letters spell out TIGER LILY.

I open the door and go inside, taking in the rails of wedding dresses as I'm greeted by a young woman wearing a tape measure slung around her neck. "Can I help you?"

"I was hoping to catch Stephanie next door."

Clearly hoping for business, the woman's face falls.

"I'm DS May. I'm investigating the death of Mrs. Hampton's stepdaughter. I don't suppose you know where she is?"

She shakes her head. "I'm sorry. I don't . . . Her hours have been a bit erratic lately. Hardly surprising . . . Can I help in any way?"

I pause for a moment. "How well do you know Mrs. Hampton? I mean, you have complementary businesses. Do you refer brides to each other?"

"I did." A shadow crosses the woman's face. "I don't like saying this, but I'm being a bit careful now. The other day, one of her suppliers came in. He was chasing her for an unpaid bill. I don't want to refer my brides to her for their flowers if her business is shaky."

I nod. It sounds as though Stephanie's on a downward spiral. When a business isn't doing well, word gets around, customers stay away, making it worse. And of course the situation won't have been helped by Hollie's death. "Can I leave you my card? If you do think of anything, will you call me?"

Back at the office, I go over everything we know for the umpteenth time, then check in with Sarah Collins, to see if they've got any further with Operation Rainbow, the name the porn ring's been given.

It isn't until later that afternoon that my phone buzzes and an unknown number flashes up on the screen. I'm even more curious when I find out who it is.

# 15

# Elise

I leave it a couple of days after the funeral before I go to see Stephanie. It's early afternoon when I get to her shop. When I walk in, the shelves are empty, the display of flowers half what it used to be. She's at a table, poking white roses into a display of winter foliage.

"Have you told James?" I ask her.

"That I'm going? I suppose it's obvious." Her voice tight, she glances around the shop. "I haven't told him in as many words."

"I wanted to ask you something." I hesitate. "Do you know if James and Andrew have fallen out?"

"I wasn't aware that they were ever friends." There's an odd look on Stephanie's face. "Why do you ask?"

"I don't think they were friends. Not as such . . . But they always seemed to get on reasonably well socially." To my knowledge, they probably only met up two or three times a year. "It was just that at Hollie's funeral, I caught James looking at Andrew. Let's just say it wasn't friendly."

I watch as Stephanie stiffens. "I've no idea why." Both of us are silent; then she adds, "I don't know what you want me to say."

"Nothing. I just thought I'd ask you, that's all." I change the subject. "Are you planning to talk to the police before you leave here?"

She hedges. "I don't want to, but I'm going to have to, aren't I? It's the last thing I feel like doing, to be honest. They'll probably want to know where I'm going."

"Don't tell them you're going anywhere." If I were she, that's what I'd do—have everything packed and ready to go first, so that once I'd told the police, I could drive away. "Tell them what you need to about his 'investment,' then just leave."

"You think?"

I shrug. "Look, it isn't for me to say." It depends what her conscience will let her live with. "But it's his problem, Stephanie, not yours. I guess you have to do the right thing, but after that . . ."

She shakes her head. "I've done what I can for James, but he's a fool. I would never have imagined he'd be stupid enough to do what he's done. What kind of a man does that?" Her voice is shaking, but her eyes are blazing as she looks at me. I understand how she feels. He's betrayed her. She goes on. "I keep asking myself—why? Why me? Why us? It seems too unfair, too unbelievable, that so much could go wrong all at once."

I nod silently. My circumstances are different, but lately, I've thought the same—there's Andrew's infidelity, his abusive ways, Niamh's silence. But then she says pointedly, "There's no use my trying to explain to you. You have no idea, Elise, how it feels. But how could you?"

Her words take me aback, because I know exactly how she feels. I stare at her. "The truth is that none of us knows what each other's lives are like. Not really. How can we?" I'm challenging her, wanting her to see how wrong she's got it. That appearances are meaningless, that her assumptions about me are way off, because she has no idea what my life is really like. No one does.

But she doesn't get it. "Yes, but look at you, in that big house, married to the doctor, your daughter safely at home every night . . . You don't need to work but you do it anyway. For fun, I suppose, in that uniform, giving you the perfect excuse not to be here." Her words are loaded with bitterness.

"What are you insinuating?" Quietly seething, I stare at her. "What makes you think you know what my life is like?"

Her mood suddenly changes. "Oh God." Stephanie looks mortified. "I'm so sorry. I should never have said that."

"No, you shouldn't," I snap, but I'm already turning around. Marching out before she can say anything, I close the door hard behind me, almost walking into Ida Jones.

"Elise, my dear. How are you? How's little Niamh?"

Hastily composing myself, I stop for a moment, but Stephanie's words are still ringing in my ears. "We're fine." When she frowns at me, I try to soften my voice. "We're fine, thank you . . . I just called in to see Stephanie. It's a difficult time for her."

Ida's eyes linger on me. "You look a little upset. Are you sure you're alright? It can't have been easy for you, either, what with—"

But I interrupt. "I'm fine. Really. Thank you." I glance up at the shop window. "I'm sure Stephanie will be pleased to see you."

"Yes." It's as though Ida's speaking to herself. "Come for coffee, dear. So much has happened. I haven't seen you in such a long time."

I've a sudden need to get away, to be alone. I nod. "I'll be in touch when my next flight schedule comes out."

As I drive away, I'm still angry with Stephanie. I know her life is collapsing around her, but she has no right to make assumptions about other people. By the time I reach home, my anger hasn't dissipated. In the house, I throw my bag on the table, then grab my phone, and without hesitating, call the number DS May gave me.

She answers straightaway. "DS May."

"Hello. It's Elise Buckley." I'm floundering, suddenly less sure of what I want to say, terrified I'm opening a Pandora's box. But I can't go back. "There's something you need to know."

In the thirty minutes before DS May's car pulls up in the drive, I swing between fobbing her off with something incidental rather than telling her the truth about James, but in the end, I decide I have a duty to tell her. James is involved in a business that harms children. There's no question in my mind that I should have gone to the police the moment I found out. But there's Stephanie, too. I saw a different side to her earlier. Whatever she said she'd do, I don't trust her.

"Come in." I hold the door open, and DS May walks inside. In a printed cord skirt and suede boots, she looks like someone's mum, rather than a policewoman.

"What was it you wanted to tell me?"

I take a deep breath. "I don't know the actual details, but James Hampton is caught up in something. Stephanie, his wife, told me about it."

DS May frowns at me. "What exactly is he involved with? I take it he still is?"

I nod. "As far as I know. Someone offered him the chance to invest in an app. All I know is it's to do with porn." I hesitate. "I've been told there are images of children."

She leans forward. "How sure are you?"

"Fairly sure. Stephanie was very upset."

"How long has she known?"

I try to remember if Stephanie told me. "I'm not sure, but not long. She was horrified when she found out," I emphasize, not wanting DS May to imagine Stephanie was involved in any way.

DS May's eyes are fixed on mine. "Can you tell me exactly what she said to you?"

"She told me they were in financial difficulties. James hasn't had a book published for a while. He was offered an investment opportunity. He was led to believe that he'd make a lot of money. It was only later that whoever took his money told him he was on a list. If he didn't want his involvement made public, he had to pay huge sums of money, to the point that they are now bankrupt."

DS May shakes her head slowly. "What else do you know?"

"Nothing really." I hesitate. "I regularly go running. One morning, I took a different route, that comes out in the woods up the lane."

"On the way in from the main road?" When I nod, DS May writes it down.

"As I came out of the trees, I saw James's car. I was about to go and speak to him, when another car turned up. It parked next to him and this man got out. They had an argument."

"Did either of them see you?"

I'd deliberately stayed in the shadow of the trees. "I don't think so."

"Did you hear what was said?"

I shake my head. "I was too far away. But they were definitely arguing. The other man's manner was quite aggressive. James was clearly upset. In the end, he punched the man."

"Mr. Hampton punched him?" DS May speaks sharply.

I nod. "Afterward, the other man drove away. James followed."

"This other man . . ." DS May fiddles with her pen. "Do you know who he was?"

"I recognized him." I pause for a moment. "I couldn't place him until I saw him again at Hollie's funeral. Sophie knew who he was. His name is Phil Mason."

She interrupts me. "You're sure?"

I nod. "Sophie was, at least. She said we'd met at one of their parties. I didn't remember, but . . ." About to tell her that Andrew clearly knew him, I break off.

"But what?" She's frowning at me.

"My husband was talking to him at the funeral. They've probably met in the pub. All I can say is that James didn't look too pleased to see him there. That's about all I know."

DS May makes a note, then looks up at me. "When did Stephanie tell you all this?"

"Just before the funeral. She asked me to wait a few days—to let them have the funeral without the entire village knowing what James had got involved with."

Her face is unreadable. "And at the time, you didn't think you should have told us?"

"Of course I thought I should." My face feels flushed, and I glance away, trying to remember exactly what I'd been thinking. "But they'd just lost a child. To me, respecting their grief took precedence over everything. I could understand her wanting to have the funeral without everyone talking about what James had got caught up in. Anyway, Stephanie was going to call you herself—as far as I know, she still is."

"Mrs. Buckley . . ." DS May pauses. "Next time anything like this happens, please don't keep it to yourself. You could be charged with perverting the course of justice." She sounds less than impressed.

Heat rises in my cheeks. "I did what I thought was right."

"I understand that. But it wasn't your decision to make. We would have spoken to Mr. Hampton and established the facts for ourselves. It wouldn't necessarily have interfered with the funeral." She pauses. "When did you last see Mrs. Hampton?"

"Today." I look at her. "I went to her shop."

"Is she still there now?"

I glance at the clock on the wall. "If it's quiet, she closes early. You may have missed her."

As DS May starts getting up, I add, "What happens now?"

"Obviously we have to talk to both her and Mr. Hampton. Have you told anyone else what you've told me?"

"No."

"Be careful, Mrs. Buckley." Her face is grave. "Desperate people are capable of extreme things. If you're concerned at any time, call the police."

"What's going on?" As I register what she's saying, I feel the blood drain from my face.

"We're not sure of anything right now, but besides James Hampton, there may be other people in the village who are involved in the same . . ." She hesitates, before adding, ". . . business. I would be very careful who you mention this to."

As I see her out, I know she's warning me. But it's only after she's driven away that I realize what I forgot to tell her—that I'm sure Stephanie's told James that I know.

# Niamh

When I think back to Hollie's funeral, all I remember is it being wrong. The sadness, the hymns, and DS May across the churchyard watching everyone. As I watch him talking to people afterwards, I wonder if James Hampton has any idea what Hollie knew about him. Not that it matters. When you're dead, nothing matters.

I can't talk about what's happening, just feel it, under my skin, in my bones, imagining Hollie's body without life. I think of her wide, brown eyes, her hair flowing behind her, her constant agitation with the world around her. Hollie's world was never going to be right. There were too many problems out of her control, that she couldn't resolve.

Hollie felt more than most people. She lived harder, experienced more intensely, hurt more deeply. I noticed it with Dylan, how a light burned between them, dazzling everyone. When he went, Hollie's world darkened forever.

At the funeral, I wanted to shout at all the villagers, that Hollie should still be here; that her death is another that shouldn't have happened. But behind the tears that vanished as soon as they walked out of the church, none of them cares.

*The night after the funeral, I overheard my mother ask my father about Phil Mason; heard his answer, warning her not to interfere.*

*"A word to the wise." His answer was another of his lies. It was Hollie who told me. Phil Mason knows my father very well. Her death isn't the end of this. Nothing will ever be the end of this.*

# 16

# Elise

The grayness of the evening is broken by a single blue light, followed by a siren. My first thought is that it's connected to James Hampton, and I wonder whether the police have arrested him. I don't hear any more until later, when Andrew comes home. Without speaking, he pours himself a drink, downing it in one gulp before pouring another.

"I suppose you should know," he says at last, dispassionately, unemotionally. "Stephanie Hampton tried to kill herself."

I'm suddenly light-headed, overcome by dizziness. Feeling my way to the table, I pull out a chair and sit down. "What happened? Is that where you've come from? The Hamptons'?"

He doesn't say. "She took an overdose. I was in the pub. I was supposed to meet James, but he didn't turn up. Then I got a call from him. When I got there, the police had already arrived." He frowns. "I'm not sure what they were doing there. Anyway, they called an ambulance and she's been taken to Chichester hospital."

"God." Then I think back to how Stephanie had been earlier today, when I saw her. She'd been battening down the hatches in the shop. Maybe it was she who'd called the police, to pass on to them what she felt morally bound to tell them. When she'd said she was leaving, I'd believed her, but I'd never imagined this.

I frown, trying to work it out, realizing that after Stephanie had spoken on the phone to the police, they must have driven over to question James. In the meantime, unable to watch James arrested, in another part of the house, she must have taken an overdose. Her solidarity at the funeral hadn't been an act. She had genuinely loved James, but already devastated by Hollie's death, couldn't bring herself to live with the knowledge of what he'd done. With Hollie gone, there was no one else to keep her here. "Poor Stephanie. What are the chances that she'll recover?"

"God." Andrew looks at me. "You are so cold, Elise. The woman's just lost her stepdaughter, she takes an overdose, and all you can do is sit there, cool as a cucumber, asking *what are the chances she'll recover,* as if you're asking what we're having for dinner. Jesus."

The strength of his response astonishes me. Slamming his glass down, he tops it up, then goes on. "I've no idea. Her pulse was weak, her heart all over the place. God knows what she's taken."

He's a doctor. He should realize it isn't coldness, that I'm in shock, racked with guilt, because I feel instrumental in what she's done. For once, I let his caustic remarks wash over me. I think of Stephanie's remark, about going somewhere far away. Maybe all along, this was what she'd intended. She would have known time was running out. After her outburst this morning, she knew I had no reason not to go to the police. But she'd been jittery when I went to the shop. Maybe she'd already decided she couldn't go on.

"Stephanie was worried about James." I watch Andrew's face, and as he turns around, DS May's warning comes back to me, about being careful.

"Did she say why?" His eyes bore into me.

I shake my head. I can't tell Andrew what I know. I don't trust him. "It was a passing comment. I assumed it was because Hollie had died—isn't that enough to rock anyone? Stephanie didn't confide in me, Andrew. I don't know her that well." Pausing, I deflect him, because I want to know. "Why were you meeting James tonight?"

"No reason." He looks away. "I thought that after the funeral, he might appreciate the company."

"How caring of you, Andrew." I can't keep the sarcasm out of my voice, knowing he isn't capable of unselfish acts, that there always has to be something in it for Andrew. "Especially when you're not even friends. In fact, the last time I caught him looking at you, I'd say he seemed positively hostile."

"Really? You have no idea what you're talking about," Andrew says smoothly. "People can change. At least"—he pauses, a disparaging look on his face as his eyes rest on me briefly—"some of us can."

I know he's trying to stir me up, to distract me, but my instincts tell me it's a smokescreen; that I've touched on something he doesn't want me to know.

"Do you know which ward Stephanie's in?"

His voice is matter-of-fact. "She was taken to Accident and Emergency, then admitted to Russet ward."

Getting up, I go to find my phone.

"What are you doing?" Andrew sounds annoyed.

"Calling the hospital. I want to know how she is."

"Don't be ridiculous." Andrew's tone is scathing. "You've just told me you're not even friends."

"Like you and James, Andrew, I'm sympathetic. They've just lost Hollie." Unlike him, I'm being honest. But he snatches my phone away.

"Call them in the morning, Elise, if you must. Right now, you'll take up valuable time when they should be saving lives. It's not as though they'll be able to tell you anything. It's too soon."

"What about James?"

For a moment, Andrew loses his bluster. "When I left, the police were with him. I expect he's gone to the hospital by now."

I stare at him, trying to work out whether he's bluffing or not, but it's impossible to tell. If the police were with James, after what I told them earlier, and if Stephanie had spoken to them as well, the chances are they'll have arrested him. "I'll call him—just to check."

This time, Andrew doesn't try to stop me, just stands there watching me as I find James's number, but my call is unanswered. Eventually I leave a message. "James, it's Elise. I heard about Stephanie. I hope you're both alright. I'll try to call you tomorrow."

The next day, I get up early for a flight to Rome. Apart from a couple of men who'd drunk far too much in the departure lounge, the outbound sector is quiet. As we touch down, then taxi toward the terminal building, I'm suddenly thinking of Stephanie, wishing that instead of taking an overdose, she could have got on a flight and disappeared, somewhere like here, in a city rich in history and culture, another world where she could start again. But instead, she's unconscious in a hospital bed.

After the aircraft parks, and all the passengers have disembarked, I quickly check my phone and find a voicemail from Andrew. It's clipped and to the point, no emotion in his voice as he tells me, *I thought you'd want to know Stephanie died.* As the return passengers board, I'm on automatic. All I can think is what a waste of a life. The flight back to Gatwick is surreal, life suddenly tenuous, no less because I'm at thirty-five thousand feet, aware that there's only a few millimeters of metal between life and certain death.

After landing, I try to call James, but again it goes to voicemail. When Andrew gets home that evening, other than citing organ failure as the most probable cause of Stephanie's death, he has nothing to add about either of them.

In the days that follow, when I run past the Hamptons' house, the windows are closed and curtains drawn. Even at night it's in darkness. I wonder how long before the bank fore-closes, before what's left of James's life is gone. Oddly, my husband is suddenly home earlier, around more often. It takes a while for my brain to work it out, but all of a sudden, I see what's been right under my nose.

While he's out, I pour away every last drop of Andrew's beloved Scotch, then take the red wine outside and hurl each bottle into the dustbin, listening to the glass shatter. Then I'm forced to wait, mentally preparing what I want to say to him. When he comes in from work and goes to the cupboard where the whisky usually is, he glares at me.

"Elise. My Scotch isn't here." He speaks impatiently, accus-ingly.

The words I've spent most of the afternoon rehearsing evap-orate as I turn to face him. "You're a fucking liar, Andrew. It wasn't James you were meeting in the pub the other night. It was your lover. Don't try to lie your way out of this. I've worked it out. While James's life has been going down the drain, you've been fucking his wife."

# 17

# Elise

"Me and Stephanie? You really are insane." Andrew looks at me, aghast. Then when he speaks, his voice is patronizing. "You need to go back to the specialist, Elise. Maybe there's something he can give you."

It takes all my strength to hold his gaze. I won't let him get to me. It's bad enough to put a face to the woman Andrew's been screwing. To know that I tried to befriend her, to know that she's now dead after taking an overdose. But with each passing second, much more is becoming clear in my brain. "But it got complicated, didn't it, because Hollie found out."

Instead of frowning, blustering his way out of it, he shakes his head. "This is ridiculous, Elise. Yes, I've been seeing someone. But we both know that. It isn't a secret. Hardly surprising when you're so cold toward me."

Andrew's done this before, twisting the truth, making his behavior my responsibility. His audacity is breathtaking.

"I'm not in the habit of sleeping with men who shag around," I say curtly, trying to keep him focused, adding, "We're talking about Stephanie, Andrew, not me. She's the reason Hollie got in contact with you. She found out you were having an affair with Stephanie. She even told Niamh she'd found out something about her father." I've had enough of his way of twisting the truth. "It's true, isn't it?"

Shaking his head, Andrew's silent for a moment. "I don't know how she found out. But there was more to it. I don't know how she got my number. I suppose Niamh must have given it to her. She came to the surgery." When he sighs heavily, I frown. It's a change from his usual heavy-handed, domineering way. "If you really want to know, I'll tell you. Now and then, a teenage girl gets a crush. Don't make one of your facile comments," he says sharply, so I force myself to stay silent. "It's a quirk of human nature. Usually girls seeking a father figure. Anyway, Hollie made an appointment to see me. She said she had a lump in one of her breasts. I told her I'd ask a chaperone to come in, but she said she didn't want anyone else in with us. Said she was shy . . ." A cynical laugh comes from him. "Let me tell you, there was nothing shy about what she did. After telling me to stay away from her stepmother, she made a hell of a fuss—accused me of touching her inappropriately. She even wrote a letter to the practice manager. Of course, they knew nothing had happened. But even so, it was hugely embarrassing."

Damaging to his professional image, too. The phrase *no smoke without fire* comes to mind, because something doesn't ring true. "So, why do you think she did it? Why did she want to set you up?"

"I didn't reciprocate her crush," he says crisply. "You and I both know, Hollie was a mess. She was all over the place. It was probably she who slashed my tires . . ." He shakes his head. "I have to say I'm quite glad that Niamh is free of her." He sounds critical, dismissive of Hollie's suffering, as he glances at the cupboard. "Bloody stupid, throwing away that Scotch."

For a moment I'm staggered that he can switch from talking about Hollie to his Scotch, without drawing breath. "You're missing the point, Andrew," I say acidly. "Maybe she knew about you and Stephanie and she was looking for a way to get back at you." I shake my head. If I knew Hollie at all, she would have wanted to protect her father. "Frankly, you deserve far worse." I pause, before breaking our unspoken agreement. "How long had you been seeing each other?"

Picking up his jacket, he walks out. Seconds later, when I hear his car start, I know we've crossed a line. But as I sit in the silence of the kitchen, I know life is too short to spend in an atmosphere of intimidation and fear; I've wasted enough years without love. Even though Andrew will do his damnedest to force me to stay here, the time has come to do something, not just for Niamh's sake, but for mine, too.

The day after Stephanie's death, I receive another visit from the police. It's a sunny morning when DS May and Sergeant Collins arrive. I'm taking advantage of the fine weather, pruning back last year's growth on the roses that ramble along the wall, enjoying a peace that's long been absent from my life. As DS May walks across the garden toward me, I pull off my gardening gloves.

"I'm sorry for turning up like this." DS May looks apologetic. "Do you have a moment? I wanted to talk to you about Stephanie Hampton."

"Will it take long?" I glance at my watch. "It's just that I have an appointment in an hour's time."

"If we can run through a couple of things, it would be helpful." When DS May doesn't offer to come back another time, my heart sinks.

I nod. "You'd better come in."

At the back door, I pull off my boots and leave them outside. The kitchen isn't as tidy as it usually is—un-ironed clothes piled on the table, this morning's breakfast dishes yet to be cleared. "I'm a bit behind. But do sit down." I move the pile of washing onto the sofa, stacking the remaining plates and carrying them over to the sink, before joining the two policewomen at the kitchen table.

DS May's notebook is already open. "Mrs. Hampton did call us. She confirmed what you'd already told us. It must have been shortly before she took an overdose, because by the time we got there, she was unconscious. But as you were one of the last people to see her, I wanted to ask how she seemed to you."

"Stephanie?" I blink at her. It seems weeks, not days ago, that I saw her. "She was grieving for Hollie and worried about James."

"Was there anything she said that suggested she was thinking of killing herself?"

I sigh. "She told me that after she'd spoken to you, she was going away. Somewhere far away from here—I think that's what she said."

DS May frowns at me. "She didn't imply anything more sinister?"

"No. At the time, she really didn't. Of course, now . . ." I look up at DS May. "It's easy to interpret her words completely differently. I was on a flight to Rome the day she died. When I got there, I was thinking of her—how she could have got on a flight to anywhere—started a new life, rather than taking an overdose. Then I checked my phone and found a message from Andrew, telling me she'd died."

"Your husband was her doctor."

I nod. "Yes. To be honest, he's doctor to half the village." Then I look at her more closely, suddenly suspicious. "Why do you ask?"

As DS May's eyes meet Sergeant Collins's, I'm uncomfortable. Somehow, they know about Andrew and Stephanie. Folding my arms, I sit back, watching them. "Go on."

"This is awkward." DS May looks uncomfortable. "We have information suggesting that your husband and Mrs. Hampton were intimate."

I feel another layer of dignity stripped away. I shrug, wondering how she knows. "So it would seem."

"You knew?" She looks surprised.

"I only found out yesterday. After Stephanie had died." When they look surprised, I add, "Oh, I knew he was having an affair—just not who with. Andrew's had several affairs. I tolerate them."

DS May's face is blank. "Plenty of women turn a blind eye to their husband's infidelity. But considering Mrs. Hampton had confided in you, you must have been shocked."

I think back to how she came here, then what Stephanie said, the last time I saw her, just before I walked out of her shop. In the light of what I know now, it makes more sense. "She told me I didn't know how lucky I was." I shake my head. "I think she loved James, but he'd screwed things up between them. Maybe she needed someone more solid—like her good old, reliable doctor." Even I can't believe I'm defending the woman who was sleeping with my husband.

DS May looks at me oddly. "You were OK with that?"

"Absolutely not. Don't try to understand my marriage, Detective Sergeant. It really doesn't bear scrutiny. I'm here for one reason only. My daughter."

"Why don't you leave him?" She makes no attempt to hide the genuine curiosity in her eyes. "You're an independent woman. If you separated, half the proceeds from selling this house would buy you a lovely cottage, even around here. Children are often better off with divorced parents than stuck in the middle of a war zone."

"This house is not a war zone." My response is too sharp. "Anyway, Andrew would destroy me." Watching their faces, I try to explain. "He likes the image. This house." I gesture around the large proportions of the kitchen. "His daughter, the private school she goes to . . . The fact that we're together, when so many marriages flounder. Status is important to Andrew. He's a doctor. It's important that his patients believe in him." It's about control, too, but I don't tell them that. I have to bide my time before I reveal the truth about Andrew. From their expressions, I know I've painted enough of a picture for them to understand how he is. Then I add carefully, "None of us know how it is to be someone else. I don't think any of us should judge." I'm thinking of Stephanie, obviously, but myself, too. Still watching them, I lean back in my chair again. Then I catch sight of the clock. In a hurry, I get to my feet. "I'm sorry, but if there isn't anything else, I have an appointment I need to get to."

I wait for them to ask me where I'm going, but they don't. As they drive away and I tidy the kitchen, then get ready to go out, it seems no coincidence that the blue skies of earlier are clouding over, the sunlight gone. A minute later, rain starts to fall.

# Nicki

In the aftermath of Stephanie Hampton's suicide, we question her husband. His wife and daughter dead, James is broken. Even so, on the subject of Phil Mason, he remains frustratingly silent, even though I tell him what we've learned not just from Stephanie, but from Elise Buckley, too.

When we take a break, in the DI's office, I try to explain where we're at. "It's as if he has some kind of loyalty," I tell him.

"Then we need to get to the bottom of it, don't we?" he says impatiently. "What's the time?"

"Twelve, sir."

"Right. We'll question him together this afternoon. You and me, May," he clarifies unnecessarily.

When we go into the interview room, James Hampton barely looks up from where he's slumped over the table. Beside him, his lawyer's face is blank. "This is DI Saunders, Mr. Hampton. We have a few more questions for you."

The DI clears his throat. "I understand you bought into a business through Philip Mason. Is that correct?"

The lawyer looks mildly irritated. "My client has already confirmed this to your colleague, just as he's confirmed he had no idea what he was getting into."

"I see." The DI leans back in his chair. "Didn't know it was porn, is that what you're saying, Mr. Hampton?"

When James shakes his head, the DI says, "Answer yes or no for the tape, Mr. Hampton."

At James's muttered *no*, I glance at his lawyer in surprise.

"I'd like to remind you that you're duty bound to tell the truth, Mr. Hampton." Speaking sharply, the DI pauses. "You see, what you're telling us is that you invested a substantial amount of money without checking out what you were buying. Is that correct?"

It's clear James is caught somewhere impossible. But the DI's right. No one invests without knowing where their money's going—or had he been stupid enough, desperate enough, to do just that?

"A minute, sir." I mutter something to the DI, then turn back to look at James Hampton. "Mr. Hampton, would it be fair to say that Phil Mason impressed you?"

For the first time, he looks up, meeting my gaze fleetingly. "I suppose you could say that. He was a successful businessman. He'd made a lot of money . . . He offered me a chance to do the same."

I frown, half wanting to believe him. But I'm not convinced.

Nor is the DI. "So, even though you had money problems yourself, you handed over all the cash you could get your hands on to a man who'd impressed you with his wealth, taking him at his word. There was no contract of any kind, was there?"

James nods miserably. "He said that if we had a gentleman's agreement, it would save a fortune in tax."

The DI glances at me, then back to James. "Porn and tax evasion, eh? I'd really like to have a chat with your friend. Do you have any idea where he might be?"

He shakes his head. "I haven't seen him since the funeral."

He sounds convincing. Phil Mason is clearly a cool customer if he's bold enough to persuade people in that way. "Have you heard from him at all?"

"No."

"When did you first realize where your money was being invested?"

James looks haunted. "I transferred the money into his account. Then a few days later, he called me. Said he'd like to come over and catch up with where things were. He came into my office ... He said there were half a dozen websites that would be making me money, then he suggested we take a look at one of them. He'd left his laptop in his car, so of course, I suggested we use mine ..." He pauses, his face ashen as he remembers. "What came up were images. He tried to tell me that if he wasn't supplying them, thousands of other people would be. He even told me there were safeguards in place and that the images were of teenagers over the age of consent ..." He rests his head in his hands for a moment. "He told me the girls needed to make money. He said tens of thousands of people make money from the porn industry in various ways." He shrugs. "I believed him. I needed money, badly. I knew this kind of thing went on."

"Go on, please." The DI's voice is curt.

"I received the first return on my investment. I didn't think too much about where it had come from. I was just relieved to have some money coming in. Then one evening, I'd had a couple of drinks. I took another look at the website. This time, I looked at more pictures than Mason had shown me on my laptop. That was when I discovered images of children."

I turn to the DI. "We have the details, sir."

The DI's face is implacable, his eyes riveted to James Hampton's. "What did you do then?"

"I called Mason and told him I wanted my investment back.

I offered to repay the money I'd received, but after that, I wanted out."

"What did he say?"

James Hampton's voice is heavy. "At first, he tried to charm me around to his way of thinking. When I wouldn't go along with it, he turned nasty. He said that purely by virtue of the fact that I'd looked at the site, he could expose me to the police in connection with pornographic images of children and that the only way to prevent him from doing so was to pay him off."

"And you believed him."

James nods. "At that point, I was wishing I'd kept my mouth shut. If I had . . ." He shakes his head. "I wouldn't have lost anything, would I? I might even have ended up richer."

For a moment there, I'd almost felt sorry for him. But that last remark reveals the depth of his self-interestedness, that he could make a case for his involvement being morally OK when it's obvious it wasn't. Beside me, the DI stiffens. "Perhaps. And you'd have found yourself in far deeper trouble further down the line." He pauses. "When did your wife find out?"

At the mention of Stephanie, a look of regret crosses his face; at last he shows some remorse. "Recently. I hid it from her." He says it as though his secrecy makes what he's done less abhorrent. "But she found a letter from the bank a few days before she died."

He pauses and the DI says, "So as well as bankrupting you, your deal with Mason has effectively led to the death of your wife."

James says nothing, but the DI is relentless. "Let me get this right." The DI studies the page he's holding. "On the afternoon your wife took an overdose, she went home to an empty house. She called DS May, then told her everything she knew about your involvement with Mason. Then she took an overdose, not expecting to be found in time. You were out at the time, but DS May called you on your mobile. She told you she'd been talking to your wife and she wanted to see you both at home. Even then, you didn't realize your secret was out?"

He shook his head. "I thought it was to do with Hollie. I drove straight home. I was surprised. Stephanie had told me she had a late meeting that day—she quite often stays late to talk to prospective brides about their flowers."

"Mr. Hampton . . ." I pause. Just as it was with Elise Buckley, there's no easy way to ask this. But we need to know. "Did you know your wife was having an affair with Andrew Buckley?"

In his chair, he seems to rock slightly. "It wouldn't surprise me," he says at last through gritted teeth.

I give him a moment, before asking again. "Are you saying you knew about them?"

This time, unable to control himself, he snaps at me. "No. I didn't."

"Had you been to your wife's shop recently?" I watch him closely.

"Not for a while."

I nod. "I guessed as much. If you had, you'd have noticed business was far from booming. I'd say she was running the shop down, with every intention of closing it."

James looks horrified. "But she told me the shop was doing fine. Bookings were up. She said we'd get through this." As he falls silent, I know what he's doing. He's replaying every excuse she made to stay late at work, to be out at weekends, wondering if any of it was true. It's what happens when someone cheats. You question everything.

"I suppose you believed what you wanted to believe." I pause. "An examination of her books will give us a better picture." I look at him. "Your lives were falling apart, weren't they, Mr. Hampton? Your career, your finances, your marriage, Hollie's death, then your wife's . . ."

Fists tightly clenched, he holds it together. "It's this fucking village." His voice is full of hostility, the strain clearly visible on his face. "We never should have moved here. It's been bad from the start, right when Hollie met Dylan."

"Dylan?" I'm puzzled. I've never heard his name mentioned before.

He utters a brief, cynical laugh. "Right there, that one word, tells you how little you know about what's gone on around here. Ask Elise Buckley. No, on second thought, ask her bastard of a husband. They know far more than I can tell you."

"Who is Dylan?"

"The boy Hollie loved, with all her heart. But he screwed her up—destroyed her. If you're looking for her murderer, it started with him."

# 18

# Elise

I have to swap a flight to go to my husband's lover's funeral, keeping up the appearance of the doctor's loyal wife, smartly dressed, the cracks in our marriage hidden by layers of makeup. I wonder how many people are laughing at me as I take my place at his side. Either two funerals in the village within two months are too much for most people, or the fact that Stephanie took her own life brands her as undeserving in some way. The church is only half-full, the flowers pitifully lacking.

James sits at the front, with two men I've never seen before on either side of him. He speaks to no one. There is nothing uplifting about the service. It's only after it's over that I realize the two men are plainclothes police. Their presence confirms my suspicions that the police are holding him in connection with what Stephanie told them. After waiting around only until her coffin is carried out through the door, they escort him away.

The villagers may have let her down, but as I walk outside to the churchyard, it's as though nature has done its best for Stephanie. The funeral may have been sparse in every sense, but out here, primroses crouch in the shadier corners alongside brave stems of the first bluebells; under our feet, the grass is sprinkled with violets and the palest lilac of wildflowers, the paltry efforts of the congregation during the few hymns out- shone by the chorus of birdsong.

As a rule, Andrew avoids touching me. But today, in a ges- ture that's proprietary rather than affectionate, I feel his hand lightly against my lower back as he nods toward the path. An- drew clearly doesn't want to hang around. "Shall we go, Elise?" It isn't a question, but I've no more desire than he has to stay here any longer than necessary.

As we walk home, I casually tell him what the police told me. "They know about you and Stephanie." Beside me, I feel him tense.

When he speaks, his voice is measured. "I'm assuming it wasn't you who told them."

"Do you think I enjoy being made to look stupid?" I spit the words out in disgust.

He ignores me. "It rather makes one wonder who did." I know it's for my benefit that instead of annoyance, there's amusement in his voice.

As I keep walking, pulling my coat around me, nausea rises in my throat. I'm sick of him, of everything he does. "Have you a new one lined up? Lover, I mean?" My tone is intentionally, inappropriately light, spelling it out that he can do what he likes, but I won't let him get to me.

"Don't be ridiculous," he snarls.

"Me? Ridiculous?" But my emotions are too stretched. In spite of my best intentions, I lose it. "You're the one who's fucking ridiculous, Andrew. Look at you. Your entire life is a façade. Us, your affairs, your holier-than-thou act with the vil- lagers. But do you know what? No one's fooled. And even if they were, they soon see through you. It'll catch up with you, Andrew. Don't think it won't."

I feel his fingers around my arm, knowing that if my coat wasn't thick, there'd be red bruising where he's pinching me. Recklessness seizes me. "What are you going to do?" I'm deliberately goading him, unable to stop myself. "The mighty doctor with the wife that's so important to him? Everyone knows you're a fake."

In the split second before he reacts, I know I've pushed him too far. His hands close around my neck as he slams me against a tree. "Bitch," he hisses, closer to losing control than I've ever seen him. "You think you're so clever, don't you? You'll never win, Elise. I know too much about you." He pauses. "Do you know how easy it would be for me to kill you?" As his eyes bore into mine, panic rises in me. In that moment, I know he's capable of anything—even murder. A sob escapes me as I imagine Niamh left motherless, but far worse than that, being left with *him*. Then, relaxing his grasp, he arranges his face in a rictus of a smile. "But that would be too easy." Pretending to dust off my coat, he tucks my hand under his arm. When he speaks, it's as though he's enjoying himself. "It's so much more fun watching you suffer."

At home, I lock myself in my bathroom, carefully taking off my clothes, examining the red marks on my neck before applying concealer over them and pulling on a high-necked sweater, aware that as time passes, Andrew's behavior grows more extreme. What will he do next time?

That question is followed by another thought. *Could Andrew have killed Hollie?* Had she goaded him, forced him into a corner, pushed him too far? All those evenings, weekends, when Andrew's been out, I've had no idea where he's been. I've assumed he's been meeting his lover. How convenient it is, that the one person who could have verified his whereabouts is now dead.

Or did Hollie find something out? Something that Andrew was also involved with? There's the image I saw on his phone that I've yet to tell the police about. Out of everyone in this village, there are two people I can imagine being capable of murder. Having seen him talking to James Hampton, the first is Phil Mason. The second is my husband.

Whenever I've seen him, Phil Mason's presence has disturbed me. There's a cold watchfulness about him. He's a hunter in a world where the rest of us are fair game. After seeing him with James, then Andrew, watching his iron self-control at Hollie's funeral, I know he's a man I want to stay away from.

When I think back to how upset Hollie was the day I met her in the churchyard, I can't help but wonder if she'd discovered the porn business James had invested in. It would explain why she was so agitated. Maybe she discovered that Mason was blackmailing her father, then confronted him, before he killed her? I stop myself. It's wild speculation; I have no proof. Hollie's body was found in the grounds of Deeprose House. I've since learned that Mason lives a couple of miles from there.

On impulse, I get up and pull on a jacket. The air is cold, but walking briskly, I'm warm by the time I reach Ida Jones's cottage. As I knock on her door, I'm wishing I'd called her first, to check that she was home, but then I hear the latch lift, the door opens, and Ida's face appears.

"Elise! What a lovely surprise." She falters, studying me for a moment. "Would you like to come in?"

"Thank you. I'm not working today," I say, by way of explanation. "I hope I haven't interrupted you?"

"Oh no, dear. Not at all. I was going through some old photos." When I follow her through to her sitting room, her small dining table is covered in them. "Young folk these days don't appreciate them, do they? Everything's on their phones. All very well till they lose them . . ." She sounds wistful. Then she brightens. "Now, come into the kitchen and I'll put the kettle on. Would you like a cup of tea?"

"Thank you." I'm ridiculously grateful for the warmth, not just of her cottage, but her presence, as I'm suddenly made all the more aware of its absence in my life. Her kitchen is dated, the pine units in need of a coat of paint, but her curtains are fresh and there are pots of herbs on her windowsill; it's homely.

Hugging my arms around me, I watch her warm the teapot.

I can't remember the last time I saw anyone do that. Then she gets two mugs.

"How's young Niamh? It's never easy for the young ones— not at her age, not losing her friend like that."

"No. She's quiet. It's rocked her. It's impossible for her to understand why anyone would have wanted to kill Hollie."

"It's difficult for any of us to understand." Offering me a mug, Ida picks up the other and starts toward the sitting room. "Let's sit down."

As I sink into the sofa, I feel the tension leave my body, then exhaustion overtake me, so that it's a minute or so before I'm aware of Ida watching me. "I'm sorry." I'm embarrassed. "I don't know what came over me."

"These are sad times," Ida says quietly. "Those two poor people, and so close together. From the same family, too . . . I don't know how that man is coping." As she mentions James, I wonder if she knows what he was involved in. She goes on. "Have you seen him at all?"

I shake my head. "Only at the funeral. But not to talk to. He left immediately after."

"I was sorry not to make it." Ida looks sorry. "I had a hospital appointment this morning. I do hope enough people were there."

"Not really." My voice is hard, but it's true.

Ida hesitates before speaking. "There's no accounting for what some folk will and won't do." For a moment, I wonder if she knows about Andrew and Stephanie. But she changes the subject. "So, what about you, dear? How are you?"

Her question takes me by surprise. As tears fill my eyes, I try to wipe them away without her noticing. Her frown deepens. "Elise, dear. What's wrong? Whatever it is, you do know you can talk to me."

I look at her, touched by her kindness, but where do I start? Knowing that even if I tell her everything, nothing will change.

# Niamh

*I try to remember Hollie alive, free, happy, the way she was when she was with Dylan. If he hadn't gone, none of this would have happened. But everything has consequences. Dylan abandoning her changed Hollie's life. But there were implications for all of us.*

*For a while I avoid the churchyard, but in the end, it pulls me back. Hollie's grave doesn't yet have a headstone, but Hollie wouldn't care about that. Her voice is in the air, the wind blowing her name into my mind: "Remember me as I was, Niamh . . . Don't let anyone forget . . ."*

*As I stand beside her grave, the sun warming my back, I try to imagine the night she died. Hollie's last minutes, her body in shock as cold, dark water engulfed her, her fear as it closed over her, the fight to reach the surface when there was nothing she could do; when she realized she was dying. I wonder how long it took, before she stopped thinking, before oxygen stopped reaching her brain; before her body went limp; how much later rigor mortis set in.*

*Did her ghost swim to the surface, then stand on the side looking down at her? I wonder where it went after that, or if she's with other ghosts. Then I wonder if she'll ever come back.*

# Nicki

Despite the absence of anything other than the most tentative connection between Mason and Hollie, the search for him is stepped up, but apart from his passport being traced to a flight he boarded to Paris a week ago, he's untraceable. But people like Mason often have multiple false passports and places to hide. He could be anywhere.

Andrew Buckley continues to prey on my mind. I know the power that people like him have—to maintain control, force silence, hide the truth about themselves. I arrange to visit him at his home. I haven't spoken to him since he signed Hollie's death certificate. But in light of what James Hampton said and what I know about Buckley's personal life, I'm curious to hear what he has to say.

As I drive toward the village, the countryside bears long-awaited signs of spring. Grass verges show new signs of growth and the branches bear the faintest tinge of green. After one of the wettest winters I can remember, they're signs of hope.

In the shelter afforded by the tall stone walls that surround it, spring has already arrived in the Buckleys' garden. Trees bear pale pink blossoms and in the borders, clumps of primroses and bluebells are interspersed with verdant shoots of what's to follow. I linger, taking it in, unaware that Andrew Buckley's watching me from the window. When I knock at the door, he opens it immediately.

"Come in, Detective Sergeant. I'm afraid my wife's at work. I hope that isn't going to inconvenience you?" His manner is smooth, authoritative.

I can't help but wonder if it's by accident or design that he's arranged to meet me when she isn't here. "Not at all. I have a few questions to ask you. It shouldn't take long."

His face is impassive. "Absolutely. Would you like to come through?"

Instead of the kitchen, where I've spoken to Elise and Niamh, he shows me through to a large sitting room, extravagantly furnished, with tall sash windows that look out onto the garden.

"Do have a seat."

Getting an impression of how it is to be one of his patients, I sit on one of the armchairs, while he sits down opposite me, on the sofa.

"So how can I help?"

His deliberate affability isn't lost on me. Getting out my notebook, I take a deep breath. "You're aware we're holding James Hampton?"

He nods, his face sober. "I had heard." He frowns. "May I ask why?"

"Do you know a Philip Mason, Dr. Buckley?" I study his face for a telltale giveaway sign, but there's nothing.

"I have a drink with him now and then. He only lives a couple of miles away, but I understand he's away a lot on business."

"Your wife said you were talking to him at Hollie's funeral."

"Was I?" As he frowns, apparently trying to remember, I can't work out whether his look of blankness is contrived.

"Yes. He was there. I did talk to him. We were saying how terrible it was that Hollie had died."

Even though he's saying all the right things, instinct tells me not to trust him. "I understand you and Stephanie Hampton had an involvement."

His eyes narrow. "Who told you that?"

"We've heard it from a number of sources." I speak slowly, noticing the telltale tightening of his jaw. "I take it they're correct?"

Slowly arranging his hands in his lap, he considers his response. "Stephanie and I were intimate." He looks at me. "Plenty of people have affairs, Detective Sergeant." There's the faintest hint of warning in his voice as he goes on. "Can I ask you what relevance this has to the police investigation of Hollie's murder?"

I hold his gaze. "Dr. Buckley, I'm sure you're able to understand that after a murder and a suicide, we need to know as much as possible about the deceased." When he doesn't say anything, I continue. "Mr. Hampton suggested that I ask you about Dylan. He said that Hollie was in love with him, but he left her. He said it destroyed Hollie. Initially, he told me to talk to your wife. But then he backtracked. He said you were the person to talk to."

There's a look of disdain on his face. "He's got his facts wrong, I'm afraid. It wasn't Dylan who left Hollie, Detective Sergeant." I watch Andrew Buckley shake his head, taking his time. When he speaks, his tone is measured. "There are issues of doctor-patient confidentiality, but I know . . ." As I go to interrupt him, he raises a hand. "Hollie Hampton had problems. They were worse than most people realized. I was going to refer her to a psychiatrist—I hadn't told anyone, but I was increasingly convinced she was suffering from a personality disorder."

I've heard various accounts of Hollie's free-spirited nature and her bunking off school, but nothing like this. "What makes you say that?"

"It's difficult." He pauses. "There wasn't just one thing. Since she and Niamh were friends, she spent quite a bit of time here with us. As a doctor, obviously you see traits that other people don't notice. She was unpredictable, exceptionally flighty, highly emotional . . ."

"I imagine her medical notes reflect this?"

He shakes his head. "It was a tricky situation. There was an incident at the surgery."

At the mention of an incident, I frown. "What happened?"

"She made an appointment to see me. It had to be me, apparently—the receptionist told me she was insistent. She told me she had a lump in one of her breasts. Of course, I told her I'd ask a chaperone to join us before examining her—it's standard practice. But she got extremely upset. She said she trusted me because I was Niamh's father . . . I fell for it. It was a complete setup. As soon as she'd taken off her top, she screamed at the top of her voice. When someone came to investigate, she told them I'd assaulted her."

"And you hadn't?"

"God, no." Andrew Buckley looks horrified. "Hollie wrote a letter of complaint and the practice manager got involved. Of course, everyone realized what had happened. That kind of thing is rare, but not unheard of. It's usually girls or young women seeking the attention of a father figure."

I'm puzzled. "But that would hardly apply to Hollie. It seems as though she and James had a good relationship. Why would she do that to you?"

"She'd found out about me and Stephanie." He pauses briefly, adjusting the lime-colored cushions behind him on the sofa. "I'm not proud, Detective Sergeant. My marriage isn't what it should be, in spite of my best efforts. None of us are saints."

I wonder what Stephanie got out of their affair. From what

I've seen, I'd challenge any woman to have a loving relationship with Andrew Buckley. My impressions are of a man who's cold, domineering, unsympathetic, but there are two sides to every story and it isn't my place to judge him.

But unless I've imagined it, he's deliberately maneuvered the conversation away from my initial question. "Tell me, Dr. Buckley . . . Dylan . . . Where does he come into this?"

Andrew Buckley looks at me sharply. "As I've explained, Hollie had a number of problems. I'm not sure he does come into it."

Something flashes in his eyes. Too used to calling the shots, he doesn't like it when it's the other way around. "That's not what James Hampton said." Determined to keep him focused, I watch him closely. When he doesn't respond, I add, "Don't worry. If there's nothing you can tell me, maybe I should talk to your wife."

"There's no need." His voice is calm, his words measured— and loaded with contempt. Knowing he's cornered, Andrew Buckley makes no attempt to hide his discomfort. "To be honest, I'm surprised you haven't found out before." Despite his attempt to somehow turn this around and make it look as though it's the police who have done something wrong, I don't react. It's obvious I've hit on something. "Dylan and Hollie were in love—as much as two teenagers can ever really be in love." He speaks disparagingly. "They went off the rails, as anyone will tell you. They weren't good for each other. Hollie was difficult. When he met her, Dylan lost interest in everything else."

I still don't understand the secrecy around Dylan. "So what happened? I know he left . . . Do you know where he is?"

"Dylan died," he says shortly. "After he and Hollie split up, he took an overdose. It was a ludicrous waste of a life. He was sixteen years old. There's a lot about that girl people don't know. She really messed Dylan up when she left him. I probably shouldn't say this, but to be honest, I'm quite glad she's out of Niamh's life."

He speaks cynically, bitterly, as though on some level, he blames Hollie for Dylan's death. I'm astonished that in a small village, no one else has thought to mention this. That sense I had before comes back to me, of the villagers closing ranks. "You knew his family?"

"If you'd bothered to check your records, you'd find everything there." His words are loaded with sarcasm. Then a shadow crosses his face as he speaks through gritted teeth. "He was my son."

# Nicki

When Andrew Buckley tells me Dylan was his son, I'm shocked. "I had no idea."

"Why would you?" His voice is accusing. "It was two years ago, Detective Sergeant. Since then, it's been a difficult time for all of us. My daughter has lost her brother and my wife is emotionally fragile. She had a breakdown after he died. She still isn't back to how she used to be." His description of Elise bears no resemblance to the woman I've talked to. There's a vulnerability about her, but there's also grit. The loss of her brother, however, may explain why Niamh finds it so hard to talk about Hollie's death. He goes on. "We're trying to get on with our lives. Dredging up the past is incredibly painful."

I nod. "I can imagine."

"It probably explains why no one's mentioned him to you." His voice is calm again. "James is desperate to pin Hollie's death on someone. I do understand that. I believe he held Dylan responsible for Hollie's state of mind. When people are at the end of their tether, they do the most unlikely things."

\* \* \*

As I drive away, I replay what Andrew Buckley told me, thinking about the comment he made. *To be honest, I'm quite glad she's out of Niamh's life.* I'm wondering just how much he wanted Hollie out of the way. Enough to kill her? Or maybe Dylan's the secret I've sensed people in the village holding back from me. But his death was two years ago. It's highly unlikely that it has anything to do with Hollie's death.

Andrew Buckley appears to be a respected doctor. His marriage isn't happy, but that's not unusual. His daughter is self-contained, but given the obvious problems between her parents and the fact that she's lost her brother as well as her friend, it isn't surprising. During my conversation with Andrew Buckley, I saw different sides of him, ranging from professional, astute, opinionated, to cutting and manipulative, interspersed with measured shots of compassion and understanding, designed to leave me believing that whatever he says, he cares. Yet I'm left with the overriding impression that he doesn't. The only person Andrew Buckley cares about is himself.

At home back in Chichester, I let myself in, closing the door and standing there briefly, letting the day's tension ebb away, before going into the kitchen and putting the kettle on. The house is still too quiet, even though three months have passed, during which my wounds have started to heal. But thinking about Joe leaving is still like pouring acid on them.

Making a cup of tea, I force myself to get my laptop, then once it's up and running, type *Dylan Buckley 2016* into the search bar. A few rows down, there's a link to a press release. It's only three lines, stating that his death was due to an overdose of a prescription drug.

Searching further, I find the date of his funeral, which was at the same church where Hollie's was held, in the village. It occurs to me his grave must be there, too—I make a mental note to search for it. Then I find an obituary page that's been closed.

Realizing it's a long shot, I try Facebook, trawling through lists of people by the name of Dylan Buckley, then have a far better idea. There can't be many Niamh Buckleys in the world. Typing in her name, I find I'm right. Out of only two, I recognize her face instantly.

When I bring up her page, it's clear that Niamh keeps most of her posts private, but fortunately for me, not her friends list. I scroll down them, and Hollie's avatar comes up, then near the bottom, Dylan's. I click on it. As I start reading, I take a deep breath. If Andrew Buckley knew what was here, I wouldn't mind betting he'd be furious.

"Sir, I had an interesting conversation with Andrew Buckley yesterday. It turns out that Hollie Hampton had a relationship with his son, Dylan."

Even the DI looks taken aback. "I didn't know there was a son. When was this?"

"Two years ago. Apparently he killed himself when Hollie ended things between them."

The DI looks up. "How come we didn't know about this?"

"We do, sir. I've looked up our records. Dylan Buckley took an overdose. He was found dead at home. But it isn't the Buckleys we're investigating right now. According to Dr. Buckley, Hollie messed Dylan up. He told me he was glad Hollie was out of Niamh's life."

The DI speaks sharply. "He actually said that? Do you think he meant it?"

"I don't know." I'm frowning. "It was a throwaway comment that most people wouldn't think twice about, but Andrew Buckley isn't prone to throwaway comments. Pretty much every word that comes out of his mouth is measured. He also made it clear that he doesn't want me talking to his wife about Dylan. Something about her being fragile, and how they were trying to get on with their lives."

"It sounds reasonable enough to me."

I shake my head. "If it was anyone else, you'd think he was protecting his wife. But not him. Both of them have alluded to the fact that their marriage isn't what it should be. The other thing is, Elise Buckley isn't fragile. She's calculating, but not in a self-interested way. I'd say she's protecting herself and her daughter—from him."

"Where's this coming from?" He looks at me curiously.

I take a deep breath. "Let's just say, when you've been there, you know the signs." I pause. "About Dylan, sir . . . I've asked for his medical records and anything else we can find on him. I found his Facebook page last night. There's a whole load of stuff on there I'm sure Andrew Buckley doesn't know about."

"Such as?"

"A whole series of unflattering comments. There are messages from Hollie, too, telling him how much she loved him." Heartbreaking messages, that completely disprove what Andrew Buckley said about it being Hollie who left Dylan. "Buckley's obviously lied about what happened between them, but I don't know why."

The DI gets up. "By all means look into it, May, but I think we need to stay focused on Hollie. Any luck locating Mason?"

"None. He's probably lying low until Hollie's killer is found. He has a big empty house a couple of miles from the village. Surely he has to come back?"

When I return to my office, there's an email about Dylan's death certificate and the coroner's report. The cause of death is cited as an overdose of antidepressants; the death certificate is signed by Andrew Buckley. No inquest was held. I imagine Andrew Buckley doing whatever it took to minimize the attention his son's death must have drawn to him. While I'm reading, my phone buzzes. It's Sergeant Collins.

"Sarah?"

"It's James Hampton, Nicki. Apparently, he wants to talk."

# Niamh

*Before we were friends, I learned about Hollie slowly, from her hand entwined with Dylan's, her long hair tangled with his. Eyes that glanced wildly around, her melodic voice. A world of sunshine and laughter that for a year belonged to them. The way people were drawn to them, wanted to be like them. But it was impossible to replicate what existed between them. It was about much more than falling in love. They were predestined, Hollie told me, much later, after he'd gone.*

*They were like two blazing stars that collided, dazzling everyone they met. Dylan was a talented artist and Hollie wanted a stage career. They had the future mapped out. When my parents were out, I used to listen to their conversations.*

*"I can't stay here. It isn't a life." Hollie's eyes were bright with an unquenchable thirst for adventure.*

*I stared at her, wondering what she meant.*

*"One day, Niamh . . . you'll want to get away from here as much as we do."*

*Both of us glanced at Dylan at the same time, as he sat at the piano and started to play, a faint smile on his lips.*

*Getting up, I drifted away as Hollie's laughter reached me. I didn't have dreams of the magical life they sought. But I wanted to. I wanted to be like them, but I wasn't sure I ever would.*

# 19

# Elise

On my first overnight stop since before Hollie went missing, in Marrakech, I walk for hours through the streets, losing myself in new sights and sounds, imagining how it would be to live here. In the market, I traipse through colorful stalls, stopping at one on impulse to pick out a beaded bracelet for Niamh, ridiculously touched when the old woman I buy it from presses a small stone into my hand.

Her face is lined from the hot sun and a life that's hard, but there's peacefulness, a kindness in her eyes, as I look at her. "No." Assuming I'm being conned, I try to give it back, but she shakes her head as she closes her hands over mine, nodding just once. *It's a gift . . .*

I wonder if she saw the part of me that's shut off. But for the rest of the day, as I take in the Moroccan heat, a culture that's vibrant with history, color, beauty, I feel my world expand around me. When we land back at Gatwick, it contracts.

It isn't just the gift, but the contrast that throws perspective on my life, leaving me more determined than ever to break away from Andrew. That I was suspicious of a stranger's unexpected gift is suddenly representative of everything that's wrong in my life, where kindness is rare, where people don't look out for each other. Holding up my stone, the sunlight catches a scattering of crystals embedded in it.

Once I'm home, the familiar large rooms and big windows feel suddenly like prison walls I need to escape. Going upstairs, I pull on running clothes and in minutes, I'm back outside. The clouds that blocked the sun when my flight landed this morning have burned off, leaving a clear sky. In front of the kitchen window, the garden is bursting into life, the wisteria on the house a haze of lilac against the gray of the stonework. It's beautiful, but it doesn't touch me the way it used to, I try to tell myself. Then I remember the truth. From the start, it's never really touched me.

As I reach the main road, I break into a run, waving as I pass Ida Jones's house, seeing her across the garden, her small frame bent over; it looks like she's weeding. I keep going, spurred on by a drive to move, to set change in motion. In my head I start to work out a plan, knowing the first thing I need to do is find a house.

The status of owning a large country house is what brought us to Abingworth. But suddenly I don't care whether I buy one or not. What matters is that Niamh and I have our own space, where we're free of Andrew. I imagine a small cottage, a little untidy, with secondhand furniture and maybe a cat; the opposite of our impressive, stark, toxic family home. As I take the path toward the church, I think of Hollie, struck by a pang of heartbreak that it's too late for her. Her life is over, but Niamh and I are still here. I owe it to my daughter, to live the kind of life I really want for her. In a way, it would be a betrayal not to.

I still have to deal with Andrew, the impenetrable barrier between me and freedom, but I can't let him stop me. Not any longer. Too much time has already been wasted. I won't be blackmailed into staying with him. Once I've found a cottage and moved out, he can carry out his threats. I'll talk to the police if I have to, tell my side of what happened. If there's a risk involved that I'll lose everything, it's a risk I have to take. Or nothing will change.

As I turn into the path beneath the trees, the ground is soft with layers of leaf mold cushioning my feet. Then I emerge from under the trees and see DS May across the churchyard amongst the headstones.

When I notice where she's standing, my stomach turns over. Glancing over my shoulder, I think about turning around. I don't particularly want to talk to her, but then she looks straight at me. Raising a hand, I walk toward her. In a denim jacket, her long hair loose and slightly windswept, she looks younger, softer than she usually does. "Detective Sergeant." I can't keep my eyes from wandering to the grave she's standing beside.

"Mrs. Buckley?" She looks awkward all of a sudden. "I spoke to your husband a couple of days ago."

Suddenly I'm numb. From where she's standing, from the look on her face, I try to imagine what Andrew's told her. As I stare at my son's grave, I've no idea what to say to her. "He told you about Dylan," I say at last.

She hesitates. "He did. But it was James Hampton who told me first—about Dylan and Hollie." She looks at me. "I'm so sorry. I suppose it explains why Hollie was in the graveyard so much. Look, I'm sure you've come here for some quiet. I'll leave you alone."

As she walks away without saying anything else, a sense of powerlessness rises in me, followed by despair. Whatever Andrew's said to her, it'll be what he wants her to think about how Dylan died, rather than the truth.

For a moment, I'm gripped by an impulse to run after her and tell her the whole desperate story. But there's nothing to be gained. Dylan's death can't be related to Hollie's. It was too long ago. Far more likely it's related to the porn ring James got tied up with, or something else no one knows about.

As I stand there, the sun's rays catching Dylan's grave, there's a lump in my throat. The initial agony of loss has dulled into a raw ache that's become a part of me. I will never get over losing him. His death was a consequence of events that should never have happened, which I should have been able to stop. But for him, just like for Hollie, it's too late.

When Niamh comes in, I give her the bracelet I got her in Marrakech, watching her take it out of the small brown paper bag, then turn it in her hands. I realize it's of inordinate importance to me that she likes it. "Do you like it?"

She nods. "It's really pretty." She sounds guarded, probably wondering why I've bought her a present when it isn't something I'd usually do.

"It came from a market. The woman who sold it to me gave me this." I show her the piece of rock embedded with crystals.

Reaching out a hand, she touches it. "It's cool." There's interest in her eyes. "Why did she give it to you?"

I look at her for a moment. "That's exactly what I wondered." I pause. "She was insistent I take it. I think that it was simply an act of kindness."

If it resonates in any way, Niamh doesn't say, just shrugs, then after a while, goes upstairs to her bedroom. Placing the crystal on the table, I turn on my laptop, then start to look at a local property rental website, grateful that I have a job and a reasonable income. I look at the details of a couple of small houses. They're closer to Chichester than Abingworth, but if I'm going to move, I need distance from everyone here.

One in particular catches my eye, not just because it's pretty, but because I could afford it easily on my airline salary. It's a terraced townhouse on a quiet road on the outskirts of Chichester. From the street, a flight of steps lead up to a freshly painted front door. The photos show a house that's light and spacious, with a garden at the back. I glance toward the stairs, then hearing the faint sound of Niamh's television coming from her room, I pick up my phone.

# 20

# Elise

"Next time you talk to the police about Dylan, perhaps you could let me know." Acid words trip off my tongue as Andrew walks into the kitchen.

"Why?" he demands, standing there. "Are you worried, Elise? Frightened you'll say the wrong thing?"

"He was our son, Andrew." My eyes fill with tears. "How dare you use his death to manipulate me."

His eyes narrow. "There's no manipulation going on. The trouble with the truth, Elise, is that sadly, for you, it hurts."

I can't remember the last time we had a conversation that didn't degenerate into a fight. He's goading me again, but I stand my ground. "It's your version of the truth against mine." I throw my hands up. "I don't know. Maybe we should talk to the police about what happened that day. Give them the facts. Let them decide." I stare at him. I've no idea why I haven't thought of this before, but it's the obvious solution to lay our cards on the table and let someone else form a judgment.

"You're mad. You do know that, don't you?" His voice is scornful. "Any psychiatrist worth his salt would have a field day with you." But again I don't respond. It's what he always says when he senses he's losing ground.

"We both know I'm not." As our eyes meet, something shifts between us. No longer can he cow me into acquiescence, just as he no longer has the moral high ground. I can tell from his hesitation, Andrew's not as sure as he usually is. "If you pull that one, I'll get an independent assessment from someone out of the area. Don't fuck with me, Andrew. I've had enough."

Without bothering to look at him to see the impact my words have had, I fetch my jacket and go outside, needing to remove myself from his toxic presence, to stand in fresh air and cleanse my lungs. Walking across the grass to a more hidden corner of the garden, I realize how desperate I am for a sense of calm in my world. A white clematis, just coming into flower, catches my eye. Its delicate stems trail over the wall, its daisy-like flowers softening the stone. Farther on, I see the first of the pale roses are blooming. For a transient moment, their fragrance reaches me, bringing with it a nostalgic desire for the past and a time when life was simple. It's a scent that takes me back to my own childhood, one that was surrounded by family.

Suddenly, I miss my sister desperately. I'd been close to her until Andrew destroyed our relationship, just as one by one, he's destroyed all my friendships in his escalating need for control. Without any allies to turn to, there's nowhere else for me to go, and he can behave exactly as he likes toward me.

It's the sad truth of what my life has become, but it's taken until now for me to see it. Instead, I've hidden from everyone, cutting myself off because it's easier than justifying his behavior, explaining why I stay with him. But I can't go on like this. Nostalgia hits me again. If only there was someone I could talk to, who'd understand what's going on. But Andrew holds the trump card. Because of him, I have no one.

\* \* \*

That evening, I cook a bowl of pasta, serving up a plate each for myself and Niamh, which we eat together at the kitchen table. Andrew has half a bottle of Scotch inside him when he comes into the kitchen.

"Fucking pathetic, Elise," he snarls, with no thought for the fact that Niamh is sitting there, listening to his every word. "Thinking you can exclude me."

I glance at her, shaking my head slightly. "I didn't want to interrupt you, Andrew. There's plenty in the pan." In my head I'm thinking that very soon he'll be cooking his own dinner.

Instead of going back to the sitting room, he comes and joins us at the table, even though Niamh and I have finished eating. Niamh's eyes scan mine, her face anxious. "Would you like more?" I ask her, but she shakes her head.

As we sit in silence for a few minutes, Andrew's foul mood is like a stench pervading the room. In the end, it's too much for Niamh. Getting up, she rushes out. Then I hear her feet on the stairs. Glaring at Andrew, I get up to follow her.

"Stay here, Elise," he growls. "I want to talk to you."

"There is nothing you can say that I want to listen to," I say, then go upstairs, knocking gently on Niamh's door.

She's distraught. "Why is he like this?" she sobs. "He's so horrible to us. He's horrible to you. Why can't he be nice?"

Putting my arms around her, I hold her tightly. "Listen," I whisper fiercely. "Your father can't go on doing this—to either of us. I won't let him. Hold on, just a little bit longer. But it isn't going to be forever, Niamh. I'm going to do something."

I sleep fitfully that night, preoccupied by the reality of what's ahead. The next morning, I get dressed in my uniform and leave the house early, knowing exactly what I have to do. If the day goes the way I'm hoping it will, by the time Andrew gets home tonight, a very different future will have been set in motion. One over which he has absolutely no control.

# Nicki

Due to events that are out of my hands, two days pass before I'm able to talk to James Hampton. When I reach the interview room, he and his lawyer are already in there.

"Mr. Hampton." I sit down. "This shouldn't take long. I'm just waiting for DI Saunders to join us."

As I finish speaking, the door opens and he comes in. "A moment, May?" He nods toward the door. Getting up, I glance at James Hampton briefly.

Outside the room, out of earshot of anyone else, the DI's jumpy. "Mason's passport's been picked up. Seems he got on a ferry to Portsmouth. Local police are down there as we speak. We've traced him back to Santander, in northern Spain, where he was picked up on CCTV driving a black Audi. Fingers crossed, we've got him."

I frown at him. I can't believe that after avoiding us for so long, Mason will make it that easy for us. "Why's he back?"

The DI shrugs. "Maybe he's hoping to flog his investment opportunity to a few more losers. Maybe he needs the money."

"We should get someone over to his house. Straightaway."

The DI nods. "I want you to go. Take Emerson—or Collins, if she's not busy. He's only just landed at Portsmouth. At this time of day, it'll take him at least an hour to get there, probably considerably longer."

Glancing at my watch, I nod, even though the DI's assessment of the time scale seems overly optimistic. "Shall we go in, sir? Hampton's already been in there a while."

"Don't go all sympathetic on him, May. He's a bloody criminal." The DI is brisk.

I know he's right, but Hampton's like any number of people who are desperate—and weak enough to allow themselves to be drawn into criminal activity. Desperation and hopelessness lie at the root of so many crimes.

"Do we know why he wants to see us?"

The DI shakes his head. "Haven't a bloody clue."

James Hampton's lawyer looks impatient as we go back in. Once we're sitting down, he starts talking. "My client would like to tell you who else he thinks is involved in Operation Rainbow."

Sitting back, the DI folds his arms. "I thought your client had already told us everything he knows. Don't you realize you have a duty?" He addresses James Hampton. "Withholding information from us isn't going to go down well in court."

At the mention of court, James Hampton looks startled. As he glances at his lawyer, I get what he's up to. So does the DI. He thinks he can buy his way out of this. "If I were you, I'd advise my client to tell us exactly what he knows, or on top of everything else, we'll add perverting the course of justice to the list of charges against him." After addressing his lawyer, he turns to James Hampton. "What is it that you'd like to say?"

"I don't have proof." His face is ashen. "But I think you should talk to Andrew Buckley."

It wouldn't surprise me if Andrew Buckley was involved. Finding proof, however, is another matter. The DI strides down the corridor. "Get Buckley in for questioning. Find out if he knows what Mason's involved in." He doesn't let me get a word in. "And get over to Mason's. Is Collins going with you?" I check to see if she's answered the text I sent earlier. "Looks like she's nearly there. Sir, don't you think this sudden accusation of Andrew Buckley is simply Hampton grinding his axe? Buckley was having an affair with his wife, and Buckley's son was instrumental in Hollie going off the rails—at least, that's what Hampton would like us to believe. I think he was attempting to buy his way out. Did you see his face when you mentioned court? I'm not sure I'd take him entirely seriously." I check my watch. "I really need to get over to Mason's."

As I drive, I search for a credible reason why James Hampton would wait until now to tell us he had information that would incriminate Andrew Buckley. But I can't think of one. Trying to work out how long it would take Mason to drive from Portsmouth to his house in Abingworth, I put my foot down. If he's in some top-of-the-range Audi, he could have got here in no time at all.

As I approach Abingworth, the stone walls of the village houses suddenly seem sinister. It's like no other village I've ever been to, not just because there's so little interaction among the villagers. Everything about this place is hidden—not just people, but their homes, their lives, their secrets. As I drive, the distant drone of a low-flying helicopter reaches my ears. Pulling over, I watch its outline rising higher behind the trees.

It looks as though it's just taken off. Suddenly, I know where it's come from. Putting my foot down hard, I drive as fast as I dare to Mason's house, only slowing when I notice Sarah's car in front of the locked gates.

Getting out, I look at her. "That was him, wasn't it?"

She nods. "I think so. The helicopter must have landed behind the house. I couldn't see it until it took off. I'd been here about ten minutes before it started up."

Shaking my head, I imagine Mason in his house, laughing as he looked out of the window and saw her car, knowing how easily he could get away from us. Getting my phone, I call the DI. "Sir? Mason just left his house—by helicopter. He was airborne about two minutes ago." I listen for a moment, then hang up and look at Sarah.

"He's going to try to track the helicopter. Chances are, it won't fly high enough to be picked up by radar." I knew he wouldn't make it easy for us. Mason's too sharp to let himself get caught. I'm wondering where he's headed, just as a car pulls up and a young man in a suit gets out.

Imagining another of Mason's potential investors, I show him my badge. "DS May. I'm with Chichester police. Have you come to visit Philip Mason?"

The man looks uncertain. "I have an appointment with him." He looks at his watch. "In ten minutes."

It looks like we interrupted Mason's plans to stay around. "May I ask if you've come here to discuss a business investment?"

He frowns at me, then glances at Sarah. "I wouldn't call it that." He pauses. "I'm an estate agent. I've come here to value his house."

By having a helicopter hidden out of sight, Mason's covered all eventualities. As Sarah's eyes meet mine, I ask quickly, "You have a key?"

"As it happens, I do." He looks at us suspiciously. "Mr. Mason did say that in the event he couldn't manage to be here, I could let myself in."

"Can you give me a minute?" I nod toward Sarah, picking up my phone to call the DI. My call goes straight through. "Sir, Mason's arranged for an estate agent to let himself in to value the house. He has a key."

"Then what are you doing out here talking to me? Get in there. Find something."

"Yes, sir." Ending the call, I nod toward Sarah, then the estate agent. "What's your name?"

"Adam Matterson."

"Thank you, Adam. That was my boss I was speaking to. He'd like us to go in with you."

Adam looks taken aback. "I'm afraid I can't let anyone else in with me. Mr. Mason was most explicit when I spoke to him."

"Mr. Mason is wanted in connection with a serious criminal offense." I pause, not taking my eyes off him. "I'm afraid you don't have a choice."

Reluctantly, he presses a combination of numbers into the keypad next to the gate. Immediately it starts to open, then after we've driven in, closes behind us. The drive sweeps around in front of the house to what looks like a parking area, where I pull up beside Adam's car and get out.

"What's it worth?" I stare up at the impressive elevations. The house is old and gracious, too much so for someone like Mason. Its exterior has also been immaculately restored.

"It's hard to say until I've been inside." Clearly not pleased that he's had to let us in, Matterson is brusque. "I'd imagine anywhere between five and six million. Now, if you'll excuse me, I have to get on."

Inside, the house is no less vast, its grandeur understated, its history evident in mullioned windows, arched doorways, the stone floors worn smooth from age. While Adam walks from room to room recording measurements, Sarah and I start our own search.

As we walk into yet another beautiful room, she shakes her head. "Some house, isn't it?"

I nod, not wanting to dwell on where Mason's money came from. I start carefully looking through a chest of drawers, finding nothing personal. We search more drawers and cupboards in each room. But everywhere we look, it's the same. Everything is neat and orderly and sparse, as though Phil Mason always expected the police to come here and search his house.

When Sarah finds his office, my hopes rise that at last we'll discover something. "It's some office."

She's right. A large desk is positioned by the window, with breathtaking views across the landscaped gardens toward the coast. There's a state-of-the-art screen and keyboard, a pair of speakers positioned discreetly, and heavy curtains hanging in the windows, but that's all.

When a search of the desk reveals nothing, Sarah looks at me. "Frustrating, isn't it? You'd have thought there'd be something."

I shake my head. "There wouldn't be, would there? Not if he was prepared to let an unescorted estate agent wander around. I wouldn't mind betting the whole house is completely clean. But we still need to look. Keep your eyes out for letters and photos. Anything that might tell us where he is."

I'm hoping that we'll stumble upon wherever Mason's hidden his personal effects. When our search turns up nothing of interest, we wait in the kitchen while Adam finishes up measuring the outbuildings. When he comes back in, he looks perplexed.

"Is something wrong?"

He shakes his head. "It's probably nothing. It's just that some of the measurements don't add up. I was redoing them to check I hadn't made a mistake."

Suddenly I'm interested. "What did you find?"

He's visibly less hostile than when we arrived. "If you follow me, I'll show you."

As we follow him across the garden to an L-shape of converted farm buildings, my eyes are drawn to the swaths of spring flowers breaking up the grass; the landscaped pond, which like everything about this house, is impressive. Everywhere I look, it's as though no expense has been spared, but my enjoyment of the surroundings is tarnished by the knowledge of where Mason's money has come from.

Beyond the garden is another large, open stretch of mown grass where I imagine the helicopter landed. The farm buildings themselves have been stylishly converted, the courtyard in front of them heavily graveled. Unlocking a door, Adam leads us into a room toward the corner of the L. "If you look here . . ." Showing us a floor plan, he indicates the space he's measured. "You agree that fits with the plan?"

As far as I can see, it looks in order, but then he takes us outside, through the next door along, into a similar-sized room. Showing us his floor plan again, he points to the wall. "Even if you look outside, you can see there's quite a lot of space behind here that isn't accounted for."

His words are confirmed by the measurements on the floor plan, but even without them, it's obvious. There's even a fireplace built into the wall he's talking about, which has been made to look as though it's been there forever. "So how do we get in?"

Hurrying outside, I walk around the back of the building, following the narrow path that vanishes into the rhododendron bushes growing behind. Pushing my way through, I find a door into what could quite possibly be the area of space that's been bricked off. My heart starts thumping. There's no question we've found something.

"That door isn't marked on the floor plan." Adam's voice comes from behind me.

Mason surely couldn't have imagined an estate agent would miss this. But then I remember. We interrupted him. Who knows what he was going to say to Adam? Standing back, I stare at what Adam's holding out to me: his bunch of keys.

I try each one in turn, but none of them fit. Then I shove my shoulder against it, but it doesn't give even slightly. Handing the keys back to Adam, I get out my phone.

The DI answers immediately.

"Sir? There's a computer in Mason's office. Forensics should take a look at it. But that's not all. We've found a locked room amongst some converted outbuildings at Mason's place. The estate agent doesn't have a key, nor does the space appear on his floor plan."

"We need to see what's inside, May. Can you force it?"

"We've tried. It's pretty solid, sir."

"Right. I'll get someone over to help. Stand by."

I turn to Sarah. "The DI wants us to check it out." I glance at Adam. "Could you give us the code for the gate? If you've finished what you're doing, you don't have to hang around. But if you could leave the keys with us, it might be useful. We'll make sure everything's locked and if you give me the address of your office, I'll drop them back to you later on. Meanwhile, if you hear from Mr. Mason, I'd be grateful if you didn't tell him we've been here."

It's clear from Adam's face that he's out of his depth. When he hands me a business card, I add, "You might want to be careful. Mason's slippery. If he leaves you any contact details, call me." I hand him a card.

After leaving us the code, he starts to walk back toward the house. I look at Sarah. "The DI's sending someone over. It might be a good idea for you to wait on the drive."

As she walks away, I cross the gravel onto the grass, gazing at the open space that stretches into the distance, wondering if Mason owns the woods beyond, too. My blood chills at the thought that people can justify exploiting the vulnerable for their own gains, even as I recognize it's something that happens all too often. There are too many powerful people driven by pure greed and self-interest. James Hampton doesn't fit that category—he's just weak, and Mason caught him when he was desperate. I have no shadow of a doubt that Andrew Buckley does. But in spite of what James Hampton told us, there's still no proof that he's involved.

It isn't long before my thoughts are interrupted by the sound of voices coming closer. Turning around, I see Sarah with a couple of uniformed police making their way across the grass. They didn't waste any time. Then, to my surprise, I see the DI coming behind them. By the time he reaches us, he's out of breath.

"Too much time behind a bloody desk," he wheezes. "Right, May. Let's not hang around. Where's this door?"

"This way, sir." I lead them around to the back of the L of buildings, then along the overgrown path. "This is it."

Standing back, I watch him try the door, then shove his not inconsiderable bulk against it, but just as earlier when I tried, it doesn't budge. Nodding at the uniformed police constables, he stands to one side.

When two of them together fail to force it open, one of them opens the bag they've brought with them, then starts to work on the lock. It takes a few minutes, but finally the door opens silently, and one of them reaches for a torch. But when they shine the beam around the room, it's completely empty.

# Nicki

I follow the DI inside, disappointment washing over me as the beam of his torch illuminates empty space and dusty floorboards. But as my eyes scan the room, they settle on the floor. "Sir? That far corner . . ." The DI's beam flashes back to the spot I'm talking about. "The floorboards are different." As I look more closely, I see it isn't just the corner. There's a four-foot strip of floorboards along the length of that wall that are considerably narrower than all the others.

"Emerson? Pry those up, will you?"

In silence, we watch as the floorboards come up easily—too easily, revealing a narrow staircase. Stepping forward, the DI nods at Sarah. "Collins? Stay here. Keep an eye out, will you? The rest of you—" He glances at me and the two policemen. "With me, please. Let's check this out."

At the bottom of the stairs, the DI shines the beam of his torch around, settling it on a switch. Then as the lights come on, I gasp at the row of screens. There must be half a dozen, each with a chair in front of it. Along one of the walls, there are shelves on which discs and folders are stacked. The DI goes farther in and calls me. "May?"

As I reach him, he's holding back a curtain, revealing an area holding a large bed. It's covered in black sheets, and above it a number of cameras are mounted on the wall. I feel sick, imagining what goes on here.

"Looks like we've discovered the HQ of Mr. Mason's little empire." His voice is grim. "Ask Collins to secure the scene. Then call forensics. I want them over here, right now."

"Sir." I head upstairs, then outside to where Sarah's standing. "We were right," I tell her. "It looks like it's all there." Moving my phone around, at last I manage to get a signal. "He wants you to secure the scene. I'm calling forensics. This could be the break we've been looking for."

When I go back down to Mason's cellar, the DI is still carefully looking around. "They're on their way, sir."

"Thank you. See if you can find anything, May. Photos, names . . . anything . . ."

In the dim light of Mason's cellar, even the air seems laden with darkness.

"He could have flown the girls in. No one would have known what was going on here. Look at these." The DI passes me a handful of photos of naked and semi-naked girls.

It's a measure of how depraved so many people are that what might have shocked even a few years ago, has become normalized, acceptable; that porn is mainstream; that there is a growing market for acts of escalating obscenity. But it's how the human brain works. And as long as there's a demand, there will always be another Mason.

But to use children and young girls is to cross an unacceptable line. As I look at the photos of girls of a variety of ages and nationalities, I find their exposed bodies distressing enough, but far worse are the expressions in their eyes. Some are obviously drugged, oblivious, while others are simply terrified. Unable to take any more, I go outside.

Leaning against the wall, I glance at Sarah. "Hampton deserves everything he's going to get," I tell her briefly. "As for Mason . . ." I shake my head, failing to find the right words.

"Even in our job," she says slowly, "you think you've seen it all, but there's always a lowlife that manages to surprise you. Doesn't say much for the human race, does it?"

I shake my head. There are many good people in the world, but at times like this, it's easy to believe that they are out-weighed a thousandfold by the bad. "We just have to make sure we get him." Mason—and everyone else involved. To let them carry on with what they're doing is inconceivable.

# 21

# Elise

By the end of the day, I'm at last clear about what I'm going to do. Having viewed a small cottage on the outskirts of Tangmere, I've managed to fast-track the usual rental process by paying a deposit and putting down three months' rent in advance. It feels momentous, even though it's the easiest part of my plan. What's to follow is going to be much harder.

By the time I get home, I've decided not to wait to tell Niamh. I need to remove her from Andrew's toxic influence right away. It will take us less than a day to pack the clothes and personal things that used to be so important to me. But I'm aware of a shift in my mindset. Only one thing matters, and that's freedom.

Already I've mentally listed what I want to take—surplus china and cutlery in the kitchen that we've never used, spare bed linens, but most important are my photographs, books, the old case I have that's filled with mementos of Niamh and Dylan growing up. As unwanted emotion wells up in me, I smother it before it can take hold. There will be a time to face the pain, but for now, I have to be strong.

When Niamh comes home, I wait for her to get herself a drink and go upstairs to change. When she comes back down, I seize the moment.

"Niamh? I need to talk to you about something." When she looks up, her eyes are troubled; then I watch the familiar guarded look mask them. "Come and sit down." I walk over to the sofa, sitting down, waiting for her to do the same. She seems reluctant as she perches next to me. I study her face. "You know how the other day, I told you I was going to do something to change things? Well, I've found a house, Niamh. For you and me." I watch her blink several times. "We don't have to stay with your father anymore, or put up with the way he treats us. It isn't how families are supposed to be. You do realize that, don't you?" To my horror, she starts to cry. I try to reassure her. "It will be OK. I'll make it OK, I promise you . . ."

Just then, I hear Andrew's car, back two hours earlier than I expected him. Before I can say anything else, Niamh gets up, then runs from the room, just as he throws the back door open. Even before I see his face, I can sense his mood. Not trusting myself to speak, I go upstairs to find Niamh, suddenly terrified she'll tell Andrew what I've done.

At the top of the stairs, I knock softly on her door, then push it open. Sprawled on her bed, Niamh is sobbing her heart out.

"Niamh," I whisper. "Honey . . ." The endearment is unfamiliar to both of us. "What is it?"

My blood chills as I make out her words through her muffled sobs. "I don't want to go."

"*Niamh . . .*" Beside her, I'm frozen. I'd been so convinced I was doing what we both wanted. Now, I don't know what to say. "We'll have a lovely home. It will be happy . . ." I'm desperate for her to believe me.

She sobs harder. "No . . ."

"I don't understand." I'm utterly bewildered. "He's hateful to you, Niamh. To both of us." But it's what she's used to; what we're both used to. She doesn't know any other way to be. The thought horrifies me, as I understand how blind I've been; how damaged she is. I sit on the edge of my daughter's bed, and the reality hits me. I think of what she's seen and heard; how she's lost her brother, and then Hollie; in that moment, I recognize that she's more frightened of Andrew than I'd known.

# Niamh

*Sometimes it isn't possible not to hurt people. But life is full of impossible choices—between right and wrong, what to tell and what must forever remain a secret.*

*Hollie knew that. There was a weight resting on her. It came from knowing what other people had done. Even when she wanted to put things right, she couldn't. Too much had happened. The damage ran too deep. It was too late for anything to change.*

*My dilemma is my parents. The light shining in my mother's eyes when she told me she'd found a cottage for us to move to. The happy life she imagines for the two of us, in which everything will change. Light that's shattered by my father's cruelty, his darkness. My father will find a way to stop her. He won't let us leave. He'll do anything, including hurt her, if that's what it takes to make us stay.*

*There is no escape from my father—not for me. I have an impossible choice. Do I go with my mother, knowing my father will destroy her, or do I let him destroy me if I stay?*

*All I can do is somehow stop her. I have no choice, because otherwise he will destroy her, just as he killed Dylan, with the blunt words, rejection, hatred, cruelty, that leave no trace. Pushing him too far. Blaming the pills my mother left out the morning Dylan took an overdose. But she wasn't the one who left them out. It was my father. He doesn't care who he hurts to get what he wants. My father is capable of anything.*

# 22

# Elise

Hearing Andrew downstairs, I go to my bedroom, close the door, then go over to the window. I feel the walls close in, knowing that if Niamh refuses to leave, I'm trapped. I'd thought she'd embrace the chance to get away from here. I never imagined she'd want to stay.

As I think of a future with Andrew, the sense of freedom I felt earlier evaporates. Instead, my life feels like a jail sentence, the house a prison, to which Niamh holds a key she can't give me.

Knowing my only hope is to talk to her again, I get up. But as I reach her bedroom, I hear voices coming from downstairs. Tiptoeing to the top, I crouch down, trying to make out what Andrew's saying. I hear Niamh's voice, and suddenly I know what she's doing.

My heart thumping, I tear down the stairs. I almost trip, but when I reach the bottom, Niamh rushes out of the kitchen and past me, her face ashen.

"Niamh..." But my cry is lost as she runs upstairs and slams her bedroom door. Swallowing, I walk into the kitchen, trying to hide my sense of dread.

Leaning against the worktop, Andrew is cool as a cucumber. For a moment, relief floods over me. Niamh hasn't told him, after all. But it was obvious something had upset her.

"What did you say to Niamh?" I stare at him, guarded.

Shaking his head, he smirks. "I simply told her that you and I were going to have a little chat."

There's a feeling of dread in the pit of my stomach; while my eyes are riveted to his. "What about, Andrew?"

His voice is deadly quiet. "Your naïve little plan, Elise. What else?"

I stare at him. "You can't force me to do anything. Not anymore."

"Can't I?" His upper lip curls into a snarl. "I can do whatever I like."

I try to suppress the fear that's rising. I swallow again. "What do you want?"

"I want my wife to stop dreaming up ludicrous ideas and feeding them to our daughter," he says lightly. "I'm not letting you leave, Elise. I'll do whatever it takes to stop you."

As he steps toward me, his threat isn't even thinly veiled. Fear swirls around me. In that moment, I know I'm in danger. But I also know I have to stop giving in to him—otherwise nothing will change. "We have to talk, Andrew." My voice is desperate. "This is no way to go on. You'll have another affair—we both know that. It's over between us. It's been over for years. We don't love each other."

But as I look at him, I know our relationship was never about love. It's about control—it always has been. As if reading my mind, he nods slowly, then his hand reaches out and he clasps my arm.

I try to shake it free, but his grip is too tight, pinching my skin. "Let go." I say it as forcefully as I can. Then I feel the first of his blows across my face. It's swiftly followed by another, then another, as the full force of his anger is unleashed.

# Nicki

At home that evening, I frown at the missed call on my mobile, then try to call back but it goes to voicemail. "This is Elise Buckley. Please leave a message."

A few minutes later, when there's another missed call, I guess that her phone is unlocked and in her pocket; I don't give it any more thought. The next morning, however, when I arrive at work, I get a shock.

It's Sarah Collins who tells me. "Elise Buckley was admitted to hospital last night. Apparently, she had a fall—coming downstairs."

My face wrinkles into a frown as I think of the missed calls. "How did you find out?"

"The DI wanted us to ask Andrew Buckley to come in—he wants to talk to him about Mason. He sounded flustered, then he said he couldn't, because his wife was in hospital and he needs to look after their daughter."

But I'm already shaking my head, alarm bells ringing. "He may have said that, but believe me, Andrew Buckley wouldn't be taking time off to look after Niamh. Her mother is cabin crew—he doesn't bother when Elise is away. Niamh's used to looking after herself." There's more to this, I'm sure of it. "I'm going to the hospital. She's in Chichester hospital?"

When Sarah nods, I grab my keys.

As I drive, I'm wondering if Elise really has fallen or whether she's covering up an attack by her husband. Too much about Andrew Buckley reminds me of my ex-husband, just as Elise reminds me of how I used to be. I know what it's like to be caught in a psychopath's web, how it feels when they block your escape route. How, little by little, they chip away at your self-esteem, until you feel worthless. I've seen it in Elise's eyes. She doesn't believe she deserves better.

I'm going on gut instinct, but if Andrew Buckley has beaten up his wife, it brings into question everything he's told us. More immediately, my concern is for Elise. Mercifully, the hospital car park is quiet, but it's too early for visiting hours. I stop in reception to find out which ward Elise is in; as I start walking, my phone buzzes. It's the DI. I know I should answer it, but instead, I let it go to voicemail.

Elise is in a small ward with two other women. Her back is to me as I walk toward her bed. A few steps away, I pause. "Elise?"

I watch her shoulders stiffen, then as she turns over I see the full extent of her injuries. Her face is red, bruised, bloody, one of her eyes swollen, half-closed.

"Oh, God . . ." I'm horrified. Going closer, I pull a chair up. "What happened?"

"I fell." She mutters the word, but her eyes turn away from me.

It's impossible to believe that her injuries came from a fall. It looks as though she's been punched in the face, more than once. Wondering where else she's been hit, I don't say anything for a moment. "Elise?" Leaning toward her, I speak gently. "Did Andrew do this to you?"

I watch shock wash across her face as she looks at me, her eyes filled with fear. "No. You mustn't say that. He'll kill me."

Listening to her, I'm aware of memories dredged up from the

past. There was a time when I lived in fear, when I wanted to die rather than face another day with the man who abused me. "I know," I tell her softly. "I know what it's like to be where you are. You have to leave him."

Her eyes meet mine and I see her pain. Then, as her head rolls sideways, she utters one word, "Niamh," and instantly I see what she's doing. She's protecting her daughter.

"You're frightened about what will happen if you leave." When she nods, I go on. "We can find you somewhere safe. Andrew won't be able to get to either of you. Think about it . . ." But as I speak, her eyes stare past me.

"Go," she whispers. "Please . . ." There's desperation in her gaze.

Turing around, I see why.

"Good morning, Detective Sergeant. How unexpected." Andrew Buckley speaks with cold calm.

"I had to call in to see someone," I lie. "I was very sorry to hear that Elise had such a bad fall." I glance at her. "You clearly need to do something about your stairs, Dr. Buckley." His face is unreadable. "I understand DI Saunders has been in touch?" I add, my eyes not leaving his. "If you could come in at your earliest convenience, I know he's keen to talk to you."

I don't want to leave her alone with him, but I have no choice. Surely in hospital, he can't hurt her. On the way out, I pause at the nurses' station, just in case. "I think Mrs. Buckley needs pain relief." As I glance over my shoulder, Andrew Buckley is standing, his arms folded, at the foot of his wife's bed.

On my way out to my car, I check my phone to find three missed calls from DI Saunders. When I call him back, he's less than pleased.

"I've been calling you, May. Where the hell have you been?"

"To see Elise Buckley, sir. She's in hospital. Her husband's been using her as a punching bag."

"Dear God. Did she say as much?"

"Almost. But she didn't have to. There's no point in bringing him in. She won't testify against him. She's terrified." But I don't have to explain that to him. We see it far too often in too many abuse cases. "You called, sir?"

"Hampton's given us the name of someone else he says is involved in Mason's business dealings. His name is Julian Calder. I'd like you to talk to him. Don't give anything away. Just ask a few questions about Hollie, gauge his response, and go from there. I'll get someone to text you his address."

By the time I've reached my car, my phone has already pinged with a text giving me the address. As I set off, I can't stop thinking about Elise Buckley; knowing I can't give up on trying to help her in some way. I plan to go and talk to her when her husband isn't around; persuade her that she needs to find a way to get away from him.

The Calders live in a large thatched cottage on the far side of Abingworth village, on a bank above the lane. I park at the roadside, where a flight of stone steps lead to the front door. When I ring the bell, a woman answers.

"DS May, Chichester police." I look at her. "I'd like to talk to Julian Calder. Is he here?"

An uncertain look crosses her face. "What's it about? Julian's my husband."

"We're still investigating Hollie Hampton's murder." When she doesn't move, I add, "Is he in?"

She nods. "Come in. He's in his study. It's this way." After she closes the door, I follow her along a paneled hallway, each of us silent until she says, "We've both told the police everything we know." She stops outside a half-closed door, then knocks quietly. "Julian? The police are here."

She pushes the door open, and Julian Calder gets up from the chair at his desk. He's of medium height, overweight, and balding under light brown hair.

"DS May, Chichester police. I'd like to talk to you about Hollie Hampton, Mr. Calder. May I come in?"

"By all means." His manner is expansive, his charm a little

too much, given the reason I'm here. He gestures toward an armchair opposite his desk. "Do have a seat, Detective Sergeant. How can I help?"

"Thank you." Sitting down, I take my notebook out of my pocket. "Mr. Calder, how well did you know Hollie?"

Sitting down again, he frowns. "Not that well. We don't have children. I know her father, but that's the only reason I ever had contact with her."

Nodding, I go on. "You haven't seen anyone suspicious hanging around? Or had her father mentioned any concerns to you?"

Raising his eyebrows, he looks at me pointedly. "I've answered these and more questions already, Detective Sergeant."

He has an arrogance that reminds me of Andrew Buckley. "I'm sure you have." I pause. "But a teenage girl is dead, Mr. Calder— probably murdered. I'm sure you can appreciate we're only being thorough. I won't keep you long."

I watch his eyes shift, but this time, he doesn't say anything. "How well do you know James Hampton?" I ask.

"Quite well." He glances away. "We used to drink at the same pub."

"In the village?" When he nods, I ask him, "Did he ever confide in you—or discuss business concerns?"

Calder frowns. "I'm not sure what you're getting at, Detective Sergeant. We talked about various things—I couldn't possibly list all of them."

Knowing they drink in the same pub, I keep my face blank as I ask the next question. "Did you—or he, ever mention Philip Mason?"

The pause before he speaks gives him away. "No." He shakes his head. "I don't think so. I've met Phil once or twice, of course—in the pub, but that's all."

"His manner totally changed, sir," I tell the DI. "He made it clear he didn't want to talk to me. One minute he was being belligerent, but the instant I asked about Mason, he changed. He didn't want to give me anything to pick up on."

The DI frowns. "Did he tell you anything about Hollie?"

"Completely drew a blank." I shake my head. "I can't believe someone hasn't come up with even the smallest clue about what happened."

He's silent for a moment. "Maybe they have and we've missed it. Go over everything again, May. We need to find the needle in Abingworth's haystack."

I nod. But at the prospect of days at my desk, reading through everyone's notes, my heart sinks. We're no closer to knowing if there's any connection between Hollie's death and Mason or anyone connected to him. But there's still one person who might know something. "Before I do, there's one more person I want to talk to, sir."

Outside Niamh's school, I wait near the bus stop, searching the dozens of faces of students pouring out through the school gates. When I see her, she's alone, her face shut off, unreadable. As I walk toward her, she looks up.

"Hello, Niamh. Do you mind if we have a chat quickly?"

She shakes her head. "I'll miss my bus."

I hesitate. "If you like, I could give you a lift?"

As she stands there, I wonder what's going through her head. I'm fully expecting that she'll insist on catching her bus, but then she nods. "OK."

As we walk toward my car, I tell her I saw Elise. "I saw your mum this morning." I watch a startled look cross Niamh's face. "I had to go to the hospital anyway," I add.

Niamh looks anxious. "Was she OK?"

I sigh. "Not really. But she will be. Here. This is my car." As I walk around to the driver's seat, Niamh gets in. After starting the engine and driving away, I go on. "Is everything OK at home, Niamh?"

"Yes." Her voice is small.

"What about your dad?"

Niamh doesn't speak. Beside me she just shrugs.

I sigh. There's no easy way to do this. "Last night . . . did you see what happened to your mum?"

"No." Her answer is too quick, too tight. "I was in my room. She said it was an accident."

"How well do you get on with your dad?" I know I haven't imagined her sharp intake of breath. But again, all she says is, "OK."

In the end, I have to ask. "Was it you who called me last night? After your mum fell? From her phone?" My voice is gentle, wanting her to trust me.

But if it was, she isn't going to tell me. She shakes her head. "No."

In the end, I give up. It's obvious Niamh doesn't trust me enough to tell me what really happened. As we reach Abingworth, she becomes increasingly agitated. "Can I get out at the bus stop?"

"Of course." Realizing she's worried about her father seeing her in my car, I slow down, then pull over at the bus stop. As she opens the car door, I pass her my card. "Niamh, if you're ever worried, or you want to talk about anything, you can always call me."

Nodding briefly, she takes the card, then gets out and slams the door. The last I see of her is as she crosses the road and disappears into the Buckleys' drive.

# 23

# Elise

The day my husband hits me puts my plans back, but that he can beat me when Niamh is in the house makes me even more determined to get her away from him. *Just leave,* my heart tells me. *Get out, while you can, before he does it again—or worse.* But there's another part of me, which has been subdued too long, that's growing louder all the time. *Andrew deserves to pay.*

When DS May came to the hospital, I almost told her everything about my life—my husband's abuse, my son's death, my fears for Niamh. There's something in the way she speaks to me that tells me she understands. But having experienced the force of Andrew's anger, I can't take the risk of his beating me again. Andrew needs to be seen for what he is. Until then, I have to let him believe he's won.

I'm not sure how many people believe I've fallen. A psychologist comes to the ward, under the impression I have a drinking problem. I wonder if that was prompted by Andrew, too—another seed of my intended destruction sown, while my husband waits to reap his rewards.

When Andrew comes to the hospital, my body physically

recoils at the sight of him, bile rising in my throat, so that it's all I can do to stop myself from throwing up.

"Say anything to the police, and I'll do worse," he whispers after DS May leaves us together. "You'll never walk again, Elise. Your legs . . ." He casts his eyes down my body. "Do you know what it would take to damage ligaments, snap bones? How easy it would be to make it look like an accident?" But he doesn't have to tell me. I already know what he's capable of.

Standing at the foot of my bed, he tells me. "I've contacted the rental agency."

I feel my eyes widen with shock.

"I told them you'd had a change of heart. Oh, and I said you felt bad about letting them down and not to worry about refunding your money." He even fakes a chuckle. "I explained that I was your doctor as well as your husband, and that you'd had a repeat of a psychotic episode. To be honest, I think they were relieved I'd told them. They think I've saved them a whole load of problems."

At his smug smile, I see what I haven't seen before. In Andrew's warped, twisted mind, he believes his own lies.

Left alone, I lie on my side, gazing out of the window over the rooftops, broken here and there by branches of trees wearing the pale green of spring. Before long, the first swallows will arrive, their dainty shapes carving graceful arcs across the sky. But right now, it's hard to find any beauty in my life. At this moment, I'd give everything I have, trade our big country house for a two-bedroom semi on a housing estate, if I could get away from him.

If it was just Andrew and me, I'd kill him. If I had to spend the rest of my life inside, so be it. It couldn't be any worse than living with him. But I can't even do that. Niamh needs at least one parent who cares about her well-being. It isn't my life I'm thinking about—not anymore. It's hers.

# Nicki

At my desk, I go through everything we have. Rather than solving anything, it seems the knot of unanswered questions grows ever more tangled. Carefully, I try to unravel the case, compiling a list of credible suspects to discuss with the DI.

"The first is Andrew Buckley, sir. His cast-iron reputation as a GP has been shot to pieces now that I know what he's done to his wife. If he were pushed, it's easy to believe that he could kill."

The DI frowns. "We need a motive, May. Do you have one?"

"There is a link with Hollie—as you know, she was in love with his son, Dylan. But from what Dr. Buckley said, it was Hollie ending it that triggered Dylan to take his own life."

"Go on."

"It's possible Hollie found out about Dr. Buckley's involvement with Stephanie and tried to protect her father. Maybe she challenged Andrew. Maybe he lost his temper." Looking at him, I shrug.

"Too many maybes." He shakes his head. "We need something more concrete."

I know he's right. "There's James Hampton, though I'm not sure he could kill anyone. But you couldn't imagine him buying into child porn, either. He doesn't seem the type."

The DI's silent for a moment. "Anyone else?"

"Only two more credible suspects. The first is Mason. What if Hollie realized he was blackmailing her father? She could have gone to see him and threatened to expose him to the police. Mason clearly has no scruples. Maybe he arranged to meet her in the Penns' garden, knowing that they were away, so the two of them could talk without being observed by any of the villagers. When she refused to be quiet, maybe he killed her, then pushed her body into the pool, where it lay submerged under leaves until we found it."

This time, the DI looks thoughtful. "We really do need to talk to Mason. You said you had one more?"

"Yes." I watch him closely. "Elise Buckley."

The DI looks surprised. "I wasn't expecting you to say that. Why?"

"She and Hollie were often seen together in the churchyard. It may just be because Dylan's buried there and they were both drawn to his grave . . ." I hesitate.

"But?" The DI's watching me.

"I'm not sure, sir. Not yet. I think Hollie knew something about Elise. Or maybe her husband. Elise is fiercely protective of her family."

"You've only just got through telling me he abuses her." The DI frowns.

"I know. But that's the point, sir. The behavior of abused women can't be understood the way most relationships can. I would imagine that until now, Elise has normalized her abusive relationship with her husband—it's what happens. So far, she's kept his dirty little secret about what he does to her. Who knows what else she isn't saying?"

"That doesn't make any sense," he says firmly.

"Oh, but it does." I stare at him, then drop the pretense. "People normalize dysfunction all the time. I was in an abusive relationship, sir. For five years. My husband used to regularly beat me when he was drunk or if something didn't go his way. I never told anyone. I had this misguided loyalty to him—but also, I was scared of being without him. That relationship came to define who I was. He'd completely suckered me in, then undermined me constantly, destroying my self-esteem, until I didn't believe I was capable of surviving on my own."

"I had no idea," he says quietly.

"I don't shout about it." I give him a warning look. "I'm only telling you because I understand how these relationships work. Right now, I don't suppose Elise can see a way out."

"Are you planning to talk to her again?"

"I'll try. I'm going to suggest she calls a domestic abuse hotline. There are several and if she seriously wants help, they're good. But . . ." I hesitate. "If Hollie knew something that threatened the Buckleys, I do wonder what Elise might have been capable of. Her husband's assessment of her is that she's fragile and unstable. But I don't think she is. I think she's desperate, too. To be perfectly honest, I'm not inclined to believe a word Andrew Buckley says." I give the DI a moment. "I suppose the missing piece in all this is Philip Mason."

He nods. "Bloody tangled web, isn't it?"

I nod. "You could say."

"What about the connection between Hampton and Calder? Or Buckley?"

"We have nothing, sir. Maybe forensics will come up with something from Mason's house. Shouldn't we have a report soon?"

Getting up, he nods. "I'll chase them up. In fact, I'll do that right now. I'll let you know what they say."

Before I leave the office late that afternoon, I call the practice where Andrew Buckley works, saying I need to speak to him.

When they tell me he's busy with patients until at least seven, I tell them I'll call back tomorrow. But knowing he's occupied for a couple of hours gives me a window to go and see Elise.

When I get to the hospital this time, she's sitting up. Even though she's alone, she doesn't look pleased to see me. Pulling up a chair, I sit down near the end of her bed. "How are you feeling today?"

"Sore." Her words bear more of her usual no-nonsense manner. "You shouldn't be here. If Andrew sees you, he'll be furious."

"He's with patients until seven. I checked with his practice. Is that how he was yesterday when I left here? Furious?" When she nods, I add, "I know how it feels."

Her eyes glisten as she turns away. "So you said."

"Look . . ." I pause. "I haven't come here on police business. I've come here as another woman who knows what it's like to be physically abused." I watch her take in my words before asking quietly, "How are you?"

Shaking her head, she sighs. "Honestly? You have no idea. I'd found a house to move into. I paid the deposit and three months' rent out of my savings. When he found out, he went ballistic. That was the night I ended up in here. He constantly threatens me. He thinks he can bring me down, just like that. But I have to try to be strong for Niamh."

I frown. "He can't do that, Elise—bring you down. What does he mean?"

"Oh," she says softly, "he can. If he wants to, in a few words he can bring the mighty weight of the medical profession crashing down on me. He's told me he'll get me declared insane, an unfit mother. I'll lose my job, my daughter . . ." As she says *daughter*, her voice cracks.

"It's a bluff, Elise," I tell her quietly. "He doesn't fool anyone. The police know what he's capable of. I can't tell you much, but we're watching him."

"Really?" There's a glimmer of hope in her eyes.

"How did he find out about your moving out?"

Her eyes are troubled. "Niamh told him. I don't really understand why."

I frown. "She's probably just as frightened of him as you are. She probably thought it would be worse if he found out later."

"I know." Elise nods. "That's what I thought. I have to get her away from him. It's terrible that she knows what he's doing to me. I need to get both of us away. But I don't know how."

Her distress is obvious. Getting out my phone, I bring up the number I found earlier. "If I gave you someone to talk to, would you call them?"

I wait for her to nod. "I'll text the number to your mobile—if that's safe?" When she nods, I add, "Why don't you call them before you leave here? You never know—they may be able to help."

"I doubt it." She sounds defeated.

"Elise." I wait for her to look at me. "For Niamh's sake—you have to try."

As I walk back to my car, I have a flashback to the lowest point in my marriage, when my husband's abuse had been daily. The future had been utterly bleak, without hope. I can remember the feeling like it was yesterday, just as I remember wishing with all my heart that he was dead. At one point I'd imagined killing him. It wouldn't have taken much at that point to push me over the edge.

# 24

# Elise

From the hospital, I call a taxi, clutching a bag of newly pre-scribed painkillers, hiding my swollen face from gawping eyes behind dark glasses and a large scarf. It's midday by the time I get home. The first thing I do is pour myself a vodka, taking it upstairs with me. In my own bedroom, in the full-length mir-ror in daylight, the bruising looks uglier than ever. Taking a mouthful of vodka, I start applying my heaviest makeup, trying to hide the worst of it.

Even when it's done, there's a bluish pallor through the thick layer of tan, but it's enough for now, and there are other mat-ters to attend to. Firstly, the rent Andrew told the estate agent that they could keep, which I want back. When I call them, they're reticent, until I explain that it was my signature on the rental agreement and that they had no authority to act on what anyone else told them. In the end, I have to kick up a fuss, threatening them with legal action until eventually they refund it all, but they ask me not to contact them again. After calling them fascist bigots, I hang up.

Composing myself, my next call is to the airline I work for, to whom Andrew has also spoken. Deliberately and patiently, they tell me that my doctor has suggested a referral for mental health problems and that I've been suspended from flying duties. Managing to keep my calm, I tell them that my doctor is my abusive husband whom I'm about to leave; who has an axe to grind and that I'll contact them as soon as I have a second opinion. After hanging up, I drink the rest of the vodka before hurling my glass at the wall.

I know only one person who understands what I'm going through—DS May. My fingers hesitate on my phone as I think about calling her, but then I remember the help line number she sent me. It's a lifeline I need, rather than a help line, but back downstairs, I call the number anyway, the knot in my stomach tightening as I wait for someone to answer. They're my only hope.

"Hello?" I'm reminded of the woman in the market in Marrakech, the stone she gave me. Kindness, again. It astonishes me how much can be conveyed in a single word.

Tears erupt, flowing down my face, so that I can't speak. Eventually they slow enough for me to mumble, "Please. Help me."

An hour later, after the call is over, I'm drained of emotion, but calmer. When I get up to look in the mirror, I gently feel my face, where my tears have carved their way through my makeup, exposing a lattice of bruising underneath. Going upstairs, I remove the rest of my makeup, flinching as the bruising comes into full view. I'd wanted to protect Niamh from it, but in order for her to understand, I need her to see the full force of what her father's done.

Then I do what the woman on the help line told me to do. I call the police—more specifically, DS May.

"It's Elise Buckley. I want to report an instance of domestic abuse." My voice is shaky. I can't do anything to stop it, but it isn't because I'm having second thoughts. I'm more sure than I've ever been.

"OK. Have you spoken to the help line number I gave you?"

"Yes."

"Good. So they've run through what you can expect. Elise, I'm going to ask Sergeant Collins to come over and take a statement from you. She'll have someone with her. They'll take you through what happens from here." She pauses. "It isn't easy, Elise, but this is important. You've taken the first step now. Keep strong."

Like the woman on the help line, I'm aware of the kindness in her voice, kindness that all of a sudden has become more impossible to bear than pain. I manage to say, "Thank you," before hanging up, doubling over as I try to stifle my sobs.

While I wait for Sergeant Collins, I make a mug of tea I don't drink, then pace around the kitchen until her car pulls up outside and two uniformed figures make their way toward the door.

Without waiting for a knock, I open it. "Mrs. Buckley? May we come in?" If Sergeant Collins is shocked by my appearance, she doesn't show it.

"Of course. Please." Leaving the door open, I hear one of them close it as I go into the kitchen. When I turn around to look at them, I lose my voice as the reality of what I'm about to do hits me full on.

Sergeant Collins nods toward the man with her. "This is Constable Emerson." Vaguely recognizing him, I nod, and she goes on. "Would you mind if I make us all a pot of tea?"

Realizing she's trying to inject normalcy into a situation that's anything but, I start toward the sink. "I'll put the kettle on."

"If you show him where the teabags are, Emerson will do it." She hesitates. "Let's sit down."

Nodding, I follow her to the kitchen table, pulling out a chair. She sits opposite me, waiting a moment before she says, "I understand your husband has assaulted you."

Years of habit kick in as I bite back the excuses I want to

make. *I fell down the stairs. We had a row and he lost his temper. It was just one of those things.* But thinking of Niamh, I know I can't do that anymore. "Yes."

"When did this assault take place?" Her voice is gentle, but there's steeliness behind it.

"Three days ago. I came back from hospital today."

"Apart from the obvious bruises on your face, did he hurt you anywhere else?"

"He punched me in the stomach." Words that sound light, belying the force he hit me with.

As Emerson joins us, carrying mugs of tea, she puts down her pen, her face sympathetic as she looks at me. "I hate to ask you this, but we need you to tell us what happened, including what was said leading up to his assault or what may have caused it."

Knowing this was coming, I nod. "I had found a cottage for Niamh and me to move to." Seeing Sergeant Collins lift her hand slightly, I pause.

"Niamh is your daughter, isn't she? How old is she?"

"She's fourteen. Andrew's behavior has got worse lately." I sigh, knowing I need to tell them about his affair with Stephanie, then about his other affairs, wondering how far back I should go.

"It's OK. There's no hurry. Take your time."

But I shake my head. There is. What if Andrew comes back? "It's complicated." I look at them both. "My husband was having an affair with Stephanie Hampton." From their faces, I remember the police already know. "Before her, he had other affairs. Anyway, since she died, he's been at home much more. His behavior's been getting increasingly aggressive. He uses foul language and thinks nothing of letting Niamh see his temper. She's frightened of him." My voice cracks slightly, my hands shaking as I take a sip of my tea. "I knew things couldn't go on the way they were. I found a cottage and paid three months' rent up front. When Niamh got home from school, I

told her. I thought she'd be pleased." I still don't fully understand why she reacted the way she did. "But she ran upstairs. I
found her sobbing on her bed. Then she told me she didn't
want to go."

Sergeant Collins is frowning. "Did she say why?"

I shake my head. "I know she's frightened of him. I don't
know if there are other reasons. When Andrew came in, she
told him. I was upstairs . . ." The same despair I'd felt when I
realized what was happening comes back. "He said he'd told
Niamh that he was going to have a chat with me about *my
naïve little plan*, as he put it. I told him he couldn't force me to
do anything, but he said he'd do whatever he liked. He wanted
me to stop dreaming up ludicrous ideas because he wouldn't let
me leave. In fact, he'd do anything to stop me." I pause. "I think
it was at that point I felt I was in danger. But I'd gone so far, I
couldn't back down and let him believe he'd won—again . . . I
suggested we should talk. I reminded him about his affairs. That
we didn't love each other."

"You actually said that to him?"

"Yes." I shrug. "But none of this is about love. It's about Andrew's need to control me. When I didn't say what he wanted
me to say, he started to hit me."

"I know it's hard . . ." Sergeant Collins's eyes don't leave
my face. "But we need an account of his assault. Where did it
happen?"

"In here. Over there . . ." I point toward the worktop near
the oven. "He slapped me across the face. Then he pushed me
into the corner and slapped me again. I think he must have
punched me here." I point to the swelling below my left eye. "I
remember his hands around my throat. I felt a blow to my
stomach. After that, I remember arriving in hospital. Andrew
was with me. He told the nurses that I'd had too much to drink
and fallen down the stairs. He also told them he had concerns
about my mental state—that he had for some time." I shake my

head, unable to keep the bitterness out of my voice. "While I was in hospital, he called the estate agent I'd used to rent the cottage. He told them I wouldn't be taking it and that they could keep the rent I'd paid in advance. When it was my money... Then he called the airline I work for and told them what he'd told the hospital staff. I'm suspended from flying duties. Basically, my employers now think I'm unstable."

"He's assaulted you before?"

I nod. "A number of times. If there's a pattern, I think it's to do with when he's under pressure of some kind. But there's an underlying current of abuse that never stops."

"Have you ever told anyone about what he does to you?"

"Until now, no. Andrew holds a winning hand. He's always said he has proof that I'm unreliable and unstable. He can bring me down." I stare at Sergeant Collins.

"Isn't that exactly what he's doing?" Her voice is insistent. "How much worse could it get?"

I shake my head. "You don't know my husband. He'll make you believe that my injuries are self-inflicted. That I make his life a misery, that I'm damaging Niamh. He'll even tell you..." I break off.

"What were you about to say?" Sergeant Collins looks at me.

I sigh shakily. "He'll tell you it was my fault our son died." A tear rolls down my cheek. "The trouble is, in many ways, he's right."

# Nicki

"There's no question her husband abuses her," Sarah Collins tells me. "It's complicated, though. He's completely undermined her in every respect. All much worse because he's a GP and everyone thinks he's God."

"Not around here they don't." Getting up, I walk over to the window, shaking my head. "It's always complicated. Are you going to pay him a visit?"

"We've given Elise the name of a bed-and-breakfast a few miles from here. She's packing a few things while she waits for Niamh to get back from school; she's going to let us know when they're on their way. After that, we'll go and talk to Dr. Buckley."

I nod. "I'll go with you. He knows Mason, and they're both suspects in Hollie's murder. We haven't ruled out a possible connection with Operation Rainbow, either."

Sarah stares at me. "You couldn't make it up, and all in such a small village." Her phone buzzes. "Collins." Holding her hand over the mouthpiece, she mouths *Elise Buckley* at me. Then she frowns. "Look, just stay put. We're on our way."

Ending the call, she turns to me. "We need to get over there.

Andrew Buckley's come home early. He's obviously got wind of something. She sounds terrified."

I'm already on my feet, pulling on my jacket as we walk. "I'll drive. Call Emerson and get him to join us. Tell him to bring someone with him." Outside, I break into a run. If he knows Elise has talked to us, I wouldn't like to say what Andrew Buckley is capable of. I drive as fast as I dare, while Sarah goes on talking.

"Elise did warn us that he'll be utterly convincing about how unstable she is. She said he'll tell us she has mental problems and that she was drunk when she fell down the stairs. He'll make it sound like it's completely her fault that it happened. She also said that he'll tell us it was her fault their son died."

"He'll what?" It's the first I've heard of that. "He can't. Their son took an overdose."

"I'm just telling you what Elise said earlier."

As we turn into the village, I slow down but only slightly. When we turn into the Buckleys' drive, I see both cars parked side by side. From the outside, it's the picture of a normal, well-to-do family home. But as we reach the back door, it's anything but. The sound of loud voices comes to me. I turn to Sarah. "Check that Emerson's on his way." Then I knock. "Dr. Buckley? Mrs. Buckley? It's DS May."

The shouting subsides. About half a minute later, Andrew Buckley opens the door, his features arranged into an air of artificial calm, his eyes filled with anger. "What is it, Detective Sergeant?"

"We'd like to come in. If you wouldn't mind . . ." I take another step toward the door, but he blocks it.

"As a matter of fact, I do mind." His eyes glint dangerously. "My wife is having some kind of breakdown. I'm trying my best to help her, but you lot turning up makes it all far worse."

From behind him, I hear Elise. "It's OK, Andrew. I can talk to them." Her voice is faint, thin, desperate.

He briefly turns to glance at her. "There is no need."

Just then, Emerson's car turns up. I wait for him and another uniformed officer to join us at the door. "We'd like to talk to you, Dr. Buckley. We can either do it here, or at the station. The choice is yours."

He glares at me, then suddenly flings the door open and stands back. As I pass him, he mutters, "You have no idea what's going on here."

Ignoring him, I go through to the kitchen. Elise's bruising has taken on a purple hue. I try to make eye contact, but she turns away.

"Now, what's all this about?" Trying to sound vaguely amiable, Andrew Buckley attempts to bluff his way out.

"We have concerns about your wife's safety," Sarah Collins says calmly.

"There's absolutely no need. There's been a misunderstanding, hasn't there, Elise? My wife has difficulty distinguishing between fantasy and reality, ladies." His patronizing tone makes my spine prickle. "Her problems started when our son died." He lowers his voice. "We're doing our best to overcome them."

"That isn't true." I know the courage it has taken for Elise to speak up. "There is no misunderstanding, Andrew. You did this." As she points to Elise's face, the blood drains from his. Then his eyes narrow.

"That is nonsense and you know it," he snarls. "You're deluded, Elise. I've tried to protect you, but you've forced me into this. You killed Dylan." Then he throws his hands up. "I can't do this anymore. I want a divorce."

I watch shock register on Elise's face; then she glances at me, terrified. But I've seen enough. I step forward. "Andrew Buckley, I am arresting you on suspicion of violently attacking your wife—"

But he interrupts me. "You can't arrest me. You don't have any proof I've done anything—"

But raising my voice, I talk over him. "You do not have to say anything but it may harm your defense if you do not mention when questioned something you later rely on in court. Anything you do say may be given in evidence." I nod toward Emerson, who comes forward and leads him away.

I look at Sarah. "You'd better go with them." Then I notice Elise is trembling. "I'll stay here. I'll let the DI know you're bringing him in."

As she goes outside, I walk over to where Elise is sitting. "I know it doesn't feel like it, but it's going to be OK."

But she shakes her head. "You don't know Andrew. He'll get me for this."

"Elise, he can't. At the very least, there are legal measures we can take to keep him away from you." I pause. "Is Niamh here?"

"She's upstairs." A look of horror washes over her face. "I have to protect her from this, but don't you see? Everything I do makes it worse."

"Your husband will be kept in overnight," I tell her. "I'm sure the hospital staff will confirm our doubts that your injuries were the result of a fall. They see this too often, Elise." I watch her. "So do we. Talk to Niamh, then try to get some rest. I'll call round tomorrow morning."

As I walk out to the car, I call the DI. "Sir, Collins and Emerson are bringing Andrew Buckley in. We've arrested him on suspicion of assaulting his wife. He denies it, of course, but he's guilty as hell."

"Right. I'm going to talk to him about Mason while he's there."

"I thought you might. I'll see you shortly, sir."

As I glance back at the house, Elise's battered face at the window reminds me of myself, again. But it reconfirms my belief that if Andrew Buckley is capable of doing that to his wife, he could have done far worse to Hollie.

# Nicki

When I get to the police station, Andrew Buckley's still in reception, demanding to call his lawyer.

"As soon as we've completed this paperwork, you can use the phone."

Emerson catches my eye.

"Everything alright?" I say breezily.

When Andrew Buckley spins around, there's a look of rage on his face. "No, Detective Sergeant. Everything is not alright. You've forced me to leave my unstable wife alone with my daughter. You have no idea what you're doing."

"Your wife and daughter manage perfectly well when you're working." I stare at him. "Sign the forms, and then you can call your lawyer." As I walk away, I hear him swear under his breath.

"He's digging himself a hole, sir," I say to the DI. "His behavior is classic of his type. He's all about control. Now that he doesn't have any, we're seeing the real Andrew Buckley. He's a nasty piece of work. But the problem is Elise. Even now, with him in here, she's terrified of him."

"We need to find out where he fits into this case. That's if he does . . ." The DI frowns. "I think we should level with him, now, while we've caught him on the hop. Tell him about Mason and Operation Rainbow. Watch his reaction."

"We already know Hollie had something against him. According to him, she made an appointment at the medical practice, then after warning him to stay away from Stephanie Hampton, accused him of touching her inappropriately. She wanted to cause him trouble. He said it's because Hollie found out about his affair with Stephanie, but maybe there could have been another reason. He's calling his lawyer, by the way. I'll let you know when they arrive."

As I walk back to reception to check how Emerson is faring, my phone buzzes. It's Elise Buckley. My first thought is that she needs to hear a familiar voice.

"How are you, Elise?"

"Niamh's just told me something. I don't know if it's relevant, but I thought I should tell you anyway." Elise sounds jittery.

My ears prick up. "What did she say?"

"You probably know that Hollie used to wander wherever she pleased and that Niamh was with her sometimes. She said that recently, they climbed into Phil Mason's place. Hollie knew a spot where the fence had weakened. Niamh said she tried to stop Hollie . . . I just thought you ought to know."

"Yes. Thank you."

Then she says, "I have to go."

After she hangs up, something about what she said niggles at me. But then Emerson calls me. "Buckley's lawyer is here. They're in the interview room. I said we'd give them ten minutes."

"OK." I hesitate. "Do me a favor. Elise Buckley. Do you have time to go over there?"

He looks unsure. "I have a stack of paperwork to write up. Is it important?"

"It's a hunch," I tell him. "That something's wrong. But only a hunch."

"Give me half an hour?" When I nod, he goes on. "Then I'll shoot over there."

"Thanks. Just check she's OK. Reassure her that we're keeping her husband in tonight."

Out of the corner of my eye, I see the DI coming down the corridor toward me. "Right. Let's do this. Are they in there?"

When I nod, he goes on.

"If he's involved, we need to nail him now." His face is grim. "From everything you've said, he's hiding something. I want to know what it is."

Andrew Buckley's lawyer is tall, with short black hair and an air of superiority. When we walk in, he stands up. "I'm Hamish McClure. On behalf of my client, I'd like to stress he strongly objects to being brought here under false pretenses."

"There is nothing remotely false about any of this." The DI speaks abruptly. "We will be recording this interview." He glances at McClure. "Start the tape, May."

While the DI gives the normal preamble for the tape and cautions Andrew Buckley, I watch the look of disdain on Buckley's face, knowing he believes himself to be above the law, but that's how people like him operate.

"Dr. Buckley, did you or did you not hit your wife three days ago?"

He folds his arms. "As I've stated before, my wife had too much to drink and fell as she was coming down the stairs."

"So presumably there's another explanation for the extent of her injuries. We've spoken to the hospital staff who looked after her. General consensus is that she was the subject of a vicious assault. Just to remind you, we have photos."

Reaching into a brown envelope, I pull out photos the hospital sent over.

Andrew Buckley looks furious. "Who took those? I didn't give them permission."

"We didn't need your permission. We had your wife's." I pause as McClure glances at them. "According to the doctor who admitted her, you tried to downplay what were clearly significant injuries. But you must have been worried enough to take her in. Did you realize you'd gone too far? Or did you think everyone would believe your story?"

"Objection." McClure interrupts. "You can't assume my client is guilty."

"I don't think there's any assumption being made. There was another injury to Mrs. Buckley's stomach. She was in considerable pain and they carried out a scan. There was no obvious damage and her pain subsided, fortunately."

"She could have fallen awkwardly. Pain like that isn't proof of anything." Andrew Buckley glares at me.

"No. But a fist-sized bruise is, Dr. Buckley." I pause for a moment. "She also told us that you canceled a rental agreement she'd recently signed. It was one you had no right to interfere with. You told the estate agent they could keep the rent she'd paid up front, then you called her employer and told them her mental state was questionable. Did you discuss any of this with your wife first?"

"Of course I didn't. She was in no fit state to make any decisions. It would have been highly irresponsible of me not to tell the airline she works for. I've talked to her about this in the past, but she continues to hide it from them."

I glance sideways at the DI, wondering if he realizes how typical of an abuser these acts are. "Hide what, exactly?"

"Her mental health problems." He almost sneers as he speaks. "She's very adept at pretending nothing's wrong, but you have to admit, she's all over the place. I've tried my hardest to take care of her, for Niamh's sake as well as Elise's, but she makes it impossible."

"Which is why you said you want a divorce." My voice is no-nonsense. "You think that's better for Niamh."

"She'll be better off with me, that's for sure."

I'm speechless for a moment at his arrogant assumption that a court will give him custody of Niamh. "You're assuming the court will agree with you."

He opens his mouth to say something, then changes his mind. The DI takes over. "Dr. Buckley, is it true you weren't happy about your daughter's friendship with Hollie Hampton?"

McClure butts in. "What does this have to do with Mrs. Buckley?"

"If you'll let me go on." The DI shows exemplary patience. "Answer the question."

"Hollie was unstable," he says brusquely. "She wasn't a good influence on Niamh."

"She went out with your son, didn't she? By all accounts, they were in love."

"Now look here," Andrew Buckley starts to bluster. "My son is dead. Leave him out of this."

But the DI frowns. "You told us that Hollie made an appointment to see you, with the express intention of causing you trouble. Is that correct?"

When Andrew Buckley nods, the DI says, "Would you like to tell us what happened?"

"She asked me to examine a lump in one of her breasts. She refused a chaperone, then after taking off her top, she started screaming. She accused me of touching her inappropriately."

"No one witnessed this?"

"No." There's a frown on Andrew Buckley's face.

"So it was your word against hers?" When Buckley nods, the DI says, "Everyone believed you, didn't they? No one doubted that you were in the right."

"It was obvious." Andrew Buckley looks angry again.

"To you, maybe." The DI pauses. "But there's the possibility, isn't there, that you did touch her? Or frighten her? No one can prove otherwise." As Andrew Buckley opens his mouth, the DI shoots him a warning look. "I understand you put the incident down to her discovering you were having an affair with her stepmother, Stephanie Hampton. Is that correct?"

"Absolutely. She said as much. Told me to stay away from her stepmother." He pauses. "Someone slashed my car tires a little while ago. It doesn't take much to work out who."

"You think Hollie did that?" The DI's eyes don't leave Buckley's face.

"For goodness' sake, there's hardly anyone else around here who'd do something like that."

"Do you have proof?" The DI asks the question deliberately.

"I don't need proof, Detective Inspector."

The DI leans forward. "Did you report it at the time?"

"No, but—"

The DI interrupts. "Apart from your affair with Mrs. Hampton, was there any other reason Hollie might have wanted to hurt you?"

"Objection." This time McClure is more forceful. "This has no bearing whatsoever on why my client is here."

"I think it does." The DI keeps his calm. "From what Dr. Buckley's just told us, it's clear he believes himself more credible than anyone else." He corrects himself. "No, infallible, I think the word is. I suggest that the same applies to everything he's said about Mrs. Buckley, though his account is no less subjective and no more credible than hers. As I was asking"—he pauses—"is there any other reason, Dr. Buckley, why Hollie Hampton might have wanted to cause you trouble?"

"Not that I'm aware of." His face gives nothing away.

"You've told us you don't think Hollie was a good influence on Niamh . . . Did you feel the same way about her relationship with your son?"

"My son is dead." Andrew Buckley's whisper is menacing.

"Life was very different before he died—for all of us. Including Hollie."

"You're saying his death was the reason for her difficult behavior?"

As the DI pauses, I add, "As well as your wife's? Sorry, sir, but this afternoon, Dr. Buckley made a point of saying that his wife's problems developed after their son's death."

As I watch him, Andrew Buckley swallows. Then he turns and mutters something to his lawyer. As McClure clears his throat, I can guess what's coming.

"My client is exhausted. He's had the worry of his wife's problems to deal with. I suggest we continue this conversation another time."

The DI nods. "Very well."

"Thank God." As Andrew Buckley stands up to leave, the DI gets up.

"Dr. Buckley, you're not going anywhere."

# Niamh

*I watch from upstairs as my father is taken off in the police car, running to the bathroom just in time before I'm sick. Getting the police here doesn't make things better. It didn't when Dylan died. It makes them worse.*

*When he speaks, my father undoes everything my mother says, before adding his lies. "Elise is unstable... She doesn't know what she's doing... I try to look after her... I don't know what else to do for her..." Then when he thinks no one's watching, he hits her.*

*Downstairs, my mother's shaky. When she looks at me, she's as frightened as I am. He'll come back. He always does. Each time, angrier than last time.*

*"I don't understand, Niamh. Why wouldn't you leave here with me?"*

*Shaking my head, I can't tell her that as long as he's alive, we'll never be free of him. It doesn't matter where we live. He'll find us. There's nowhere to go that's safe.*

*The only way for everything to be OK is to do what my father wants.*

*And he knows that.*

# Nicki

The next morning, before we continue questioning Andrew Buckley, there's something on my mind that I haven't been able to settle.

"Sir, do we know how long Andrew Buckley's affair with Stephanie Hampton went on?"

He frowns. "I don't know. Why d'you ask?"

"It may be nothing. But I want to check something out. I need to talk to James Hampton again."

In the interview room, James Hampton wears the resignation of a condemned man.

"I need to ask you about your wife's affair with Andrew Buckley." I watch as his face clouds over. "Can you recall when it started?"

"I don't know for sure, but something changed last summer. She was suddenly out much more. I knew she was busy with wedding flowers—I put it down to that. But she seemed brighter than she had in a long time. I put that down to her work, too. She loved what she did. Now I realize, she was with him."

"Can you narrow it down to a month?" I watch him closely,

knowing that if he says what I think he's going to say, there are huge implications for Andrew Buckley.

He tries to work it out. "My birthday's the first week in August. Everything was fine, then. The Buckleys even came to my birthday party. I remember catching Stephanie talking to him. It seemed harmless enough and I didn't think anything of it. But it was after that, she was different somehow."

"You're sure?"

He nods. Then he frowns. "A week later, I came in from the pub. I'd been having a drink with a couple of people. Buckley was one of them. Just before he left, he bought me a pint . . ." His laugh is hollow. "Then when I got home, his car was pulling out of our drive. When I went in, Stephanie said he'd called in to drop off some blood test results. I had no reason not to believe her. And by then, I had other things on my mind." His voice trails off.

By other things, I take it to mean his financial worries and his ongoing involvement with Mason, even before Andrew Buckley was seducing his wife.

After leaving him, I find Emerson. "Did you see Elise Buckley last night?"

He nods. "I called in an hour after I spoke to you. She was alright. Nervous, awkward . . . Didn't really want me there."

"OK. Thanks, anyway. I'll talk to her later."

Then I make a phone call that will tell me everything I need to know.

In contrast to James Hampton, Andrew Buckley's demeanor is one of outrage. When I walk in with the DI, he immediately gets up. "As soon as I'm out of here, I will be reporting this and all of you, for the appalling way I've been treated."

The DI stands there, an imposing figure as he stares across the table at him. "Sit down, Dr. Buckley. Before you go anywhere, we have more questions we need you to answer."

"I'm not saying a word until McClure gets here."

The DI folds his arms. "Fair enough. In that case, we'll wait."

An hour passes, in which I watch as Andrew Buckley starts to look like a caged animal. Experience tells me he's close to cracking. As the time approaches eleven fifteen, he gets up. "This is ridiculous," he snaps, just as the door opens and Mc-Clure comes in.

"Apologies for keeping you." Taking off his jacket, he sits down.

The DI shuffles the papers in front of him. "Right. Shall we get on with this? A question for you, Dr. Buckley. When did your affair with Stephanie Hampton begin?"

"I can't remember exactly."

"Well, give me a month. Spring? Summer?" I wouldn't mind betting he knows the exact date.

"September."

As the DI glances at me, I catch his eye. "So it must have been after that when Hollie made the appointment with you, where she caused such a song and dance?"

"It must have been." His eyes swivel between me and the DI.

"Dr. Buckley. You've told us that she asked you to stay away from her stepmother. Therefore, it stands to reason that you were already having the affair when Hollie came to see you."

Folding his arms, he glares at the DI. "I have no idea what you're getting at, Detective Inspector."

"Incidentally, that ties in with what James Hampton remembers." When the DI glances at me, I take over. "Though he thinks it probably started in August. Anyway, I called your practice this morning, Dr. Buckley. According to their records, the incident with Hollie took place on the thirtieth of May."

He blinks, just once. "Then they've made a mistake."

"I hardly think so. I mean, the practice manager remembered it very well. I spoke to her this morning—and it would be negligent, wouldn't it, to make a mistake recording something like that?"

When he doesn't respond, the DI leans forward. "I don't think there's any doubt that Hollie had an axe to grind, but it wasn't about your affair with Stephanie Hampton. So my question is, what was it about?"

Rigid, Andrew Buckley leans back in his chair, his arms still folded. "I'd like a moment with my lawyer."

Outside the interview room, I glance at the DI. "Nice work, May."

"Thank you, sir." I frown. "But we still don't know what Hollie had against him. There's something he's definitely keeping from us."

The DI nods. "When we go back in, I'll ask him about Mason."

Back in the interview room, Andrew Buckley catches my eye, holding my gaze too long before looking away.

"Dr. Buckley, I understand you often drink in the village pub with one or two other villagers. Anyone in particular?" The DI gets straight to the point.

"Not really. There are a number of locals who I regularly see in there. James Hampton being one, as you already know."

"Julian Calder?" The DI's face is implacable. "Philip Mason?"

As Andrew Buckley nods, his eyes narrow slightly. "As I told you, Detective Inspector, there are a number of regulars in there."

The DI pauses, but only briefly. As he speaks, he scrutinizes Andrew Buckley's face. "Did you know that James Hampton was investing in a business that belongs to Philip Mason?"

"I'd heard some vague mention of it. Yes."

"What exactly did you hear?"

He shrugs. "It wasn't specific. Mason makes a lot of money. I don't know exactly how. He was trying to give Hampton a helping hand. It's obvious the man struggles." His brusque, patronizing manner does him no favors.

The DI frowns. "What did you know about the Hamptons' finances?"

"Nothing." He stares straight at us. "Stephanie didn't mention anything, if that's what you're asking, Detective Inspector."

And so it goes on. An hour later, we're none the wiser. On the subject of his relationship with Mason, Andrew Buckley refuses to be drawn, insisting on his story that they see each other only occasionally in the pub. When it comes to Hollie, other than declaring her emotionally unstable, he can supply no credible explanation for her behavior in the surgery.

"Maybe she blamed me in some way for what happened to Dylan," he says eventually. "She probably thought I should have been able to stop him. I can't think of any other explanation for what she did."

That afternoon, I drive over to see Elise Buckley. When she opens the door, she looks as though she hasn't slept.

"I really wish I hadn't started this." Overnight, her face seems to have grown gaunt, so that her eyes seem huge, desperate. "I've made everything so much worse."

"You haven't," I tell her, knowing her guilt stems from years of brainwashing by her husband. "And you haven't done anything wrong. This is all about your husband. You need to remember that."

But my words seem to go over her head. "Niamh's beside herself. She went to school, but she's worried that when she comes out, Andrew will be there waiting for her."

"Andrew won't be going anywhere fast," I tell her. "We're still interviewing him." I pause, watching as she wrings her hands. "Listen. You have to take action. If you don't, what are you saying to Niamh? That it's OK to be bullied and beaten by your husband? That you're supposed to stay put instead of leaving him? Imagine Niamh in a few years' time. Yes, it will be difficult, but if you act, you will be empowering her. You have the chance to show her you're strong. No one believes Andrew when he claims you're unstable. You're not going to lose your job. Anyway, he's already said in front of us that he wants a divorce. You need a good lawyer who understands coercive control and domestic abuse, so that you can get things set in motion as soon as possible."

Our conversation is interrupted by my phone buzzing with an unfamiliar number. "Excuse me a moment."

I turn away from Elise. "May." After listening with interest, I end the call. "I'm sorry. I have to make one call. I won't be a minute." Going outside, I put a call through to the DI.

"Sir? I've just heard from the estate agent who measured up Mason's house. Mason's been in touch—apparently he's asked the agent to meet him there later today."

# 25

# Elise

No one knows what someone else's marriage is like. Just as there are 256 shades of the color gray, there are as many permutations of the expectations we all have, of our ideas about what's right. But at the same time, most of us know what's wrong.

The thought reminds me of the headline in the magazine on one of my last flights. Only ten percent of people are good. Out of the ninety percent that aren't, I imagine most of them are ignorant rather than bad. But that's not the same as the percentage who know something's wrong and calculatedly do it anyway—like Andrew. And unless I do something to protect Niamh, it's the category where I belong, too.

Either I maintain a status quo where my daughter sees her mother verbally abused and periodically beaten by her father, or I leave. Most women would think me weak for staying this long. For them, the decision would be easy. They wouldn't understand that in so many ways, it's easier to stay, but they haven't lived for years with someone who's controlled their every move, crushed their self-esteem, made them believe they're worthless. It's why I love my job. Away from here, behind my uniform and mask of makeup, no one knows who I am.

While Niamh is at school, I start doing what I meant to do before Andrew's attack on me. I begin with my clothes, packing what I need, then carrying the cases downstairs, before going to Niamh's room. The bracelet I brought back from Morocco lies on her dressing table, as yet unworn, in front of a photo. Picking it up, I study it. It's an old photo, from two or three years ago, of herself, Hollie, and Dylan.

I don't even know if Niamh is grieving; whether she still misses her brother. I was too lost in my own pain to help her deal with hers; I didn't support her after he died. Maybe in spite of his behavior, she really does love her father; because like me, this is all she knows.

But when I start to pack some of her things, I suddenly work out why she refused to leave with me; why she told Andrew I'd rented the cottage. With blinding shock, I realize Andrew's got to her. She's heard him say it so many times that she believes his lies. Niamh thinks I was the one who killed Dylan.

After I receive a phone call telling me the address of a cottage where Niamh and I are booked in to stay for a while, the rest of the day seems interminable. Knowing we're leaving, I have no interest in anything here. In the end, I wander outside, but even the appearance of more roses, the hint of color on the wisteria that grows up the house, are meaningless to me. As I wait on tenterhooks for Niamh to come home, I'm terrified also that any minute, Andrew will turn up here.

Several times, I try to call DS May, needing to hear a reassuring voice, but it goes to voicemail. Finally, I hear the school bus slow down, then pull away, and relief washes over me as Niamh's slender figure walks up the drive. By the time she reaches the door, I have a lump in my throat at the prospect of what I have to tell her. None of this was what I wanted for her.

As she walks in, I swallow. "Hi."

Her eyes briefly flicker to me as she continues toward the stairs.

"Niamh? I need to talk to you." My hands are shaking as I take one of hers and lead her over to the table, feeling sick, even though I haven't been able to eat. Pulling out a chair for her to sit on, I perch on another. "We can't stay here, Niamh. The police have found us somewhere to stay for a while. It may only be for a few days. But your father and I can't be together. The police have kept him in. What he's done to me—to both of us, is a criminal offense."

"If he's being kept there, why do we have to leave here?" Her face is suddenly pinched.

"The police say we have to. We'll come back, I promise you. But I don't know how long the police will keep your father there. Until I've talked to a lawyer, we have to go somewhere else, where we'll be safe." I pause for a moment. "I've packed some of your things. Why don't you check that I have everything?"

# Niamh

*My mother thinks we can run away from him. I can see she thinks she's worked it all out, imagining us in a small cottage with pretty curtains and a front door my father doesn't have a key to. But he doesn't need one. If he wants to break in, a lock won't stop him. Nothing will.*

*I imagine my mother's picture of sunlight and peacefulness ripped down the middle by my father's cruel hands, before he tosses the pieces aside.*

*"We'll go somewhere safe, Niamh. Until I've talked to a lawyer."*

*He won't listen to lawyers. There isn't anywhere safe. When he gets out, he'll come and find us. And this time, he'll hurt her far worse than before. That's what she doesn't realize, but she doesn't watch, like I do, as each time, he hits her harder, for longer. Each time, her wounds take longer to heal. This time, she was unconscious when he'd finished. Next time, or the time after that, he'll kill her.*

*She can't stop him. The police won't, either. The only person who can do that is me.*

# Nicki

At Mason's house, as police from the surrounding area conceal themselves amongst the trees and shrubs along his driveway, then come in from the woods behind to cover the area where his helicopter lands, I wonder if he's already inside watching us. The time he arranged with Adam, the estate agent, is an hour away.

"I hope the bastard hasn't got wind of us," the DI mutters grimly. "We can't afford not to get him. Not now."

"No." Mason is potentially integral to more than one crime, but until we question him, we won't know. "Sir, there's a car coming."

He freezes briefly as he listens, then mutters into his radio. As we wait, the car gets closer; then a black BMW comes into sight, speeding up the drive, stopping sharply at the gate. Immediately, twenty or so police surround it. Through the tinted glass, I see the driver's head turning frantically, as he thinks about reversing before realizing the futility of even trying.

The DI pushes through the police, then knocks on the driver's window. After a pause, it's lowered.

I hear the DI's voice. "Philip Mason? Detective Inspector

Saunders, Chichester police. I am arresting you on suspicion of the possession and distribution of pornographic images. You do not have to say anything. But it may harm your defense if you do not mention when questioned something which you later rely on in court. Anything you do say may be given in evidence."

Mason's mocking laugh reaches my ears. "Porn isn't a crime, Detective Inspector. Now let me get on, please."

"You're right, Mr. Mason. But possession of pornographic images of children is. Out of the car."

Behind Mason's BMW, a police car pulls up. There's no struggle. Maintaining his dignity, Mason gets out of his car and stands in front of the DI. His face gives away nothing. A minute later, the police car drives him away.

"Check Mason's car, May, will you? Then we'd better get back to the station."

There's a briefcase in Mason's car and a few CDs in the glove compartment, all of which I remove. When I catch up to the DI, he's talking on his phone. After he's finished, he glances at what I'm holding.

"Check the discs as soon as we get back. They might be innocent, but I'll bet they're not."

As we drive back, something puzzles me. "He was taking quite a risk, wasn't he—coming back to the house, when he knows we're on to him?"

"Possibly." The DI stares ahead. "I imagine he doesn't know we've found his cellar." He shrugs. "He may or may not be connected with Hollie's murder, even if he is guilty as hell of a number of other crimes. If he was selling his house, he would have had to get the cellar cleared out at some point. He wouldn't have known we've done it for him." The DI's referring to forensics, who will have removed everything of interest to them. "I don't know—perhaps he genuinely has a buyer. Maybe he was running out of time and it was a risk he had to take."

*    *    *

Two hours later, after Mason's lawyer arrives, I join the DI in the interview room.

"I'm Detective Inspector Saunders. This is Detective Sergeant May. We'd like to question you about the contents of a cellar on your property, Mr. Mason."

Mason is cool as he looks at us. "I'm afraid I'm not sure what you're getting at, Detective Inspector. What contents of which cellar?"

"The L-shape of converted farm buildings, just in front of where you land your helicopter." As I speak, something flickers across his face.

"I know the buildings." His voice is calm, but he frowns. "But I don't keep anything in there. I was going to do them up as holiday rentals. But as you obviously know, I've decided to sell."

"As you're aware," I go on, "walls have been built leaving a space that's unaccounted for on the floor plan. The door is around the back. We found it." I pause, watching Mason's face. "You didn't leave a key with the estate agent, so we broke in. It was obvious from the floorboards that some had recently been replaced. When we lifted them, we found a staircase."

There's a look of incredulity on Mason's face. "This is news to me, Detective Sergeant. Did you find anything?"

"Enough of this charade." The DI's voice is full of contempt. "You know full well what was down there. We have witnesses, Mr. Mason, who will testify about the business you encourage people to invest in, before you blackmail them. James Hampton, for one."

As Mason visibly pales, the DI goes on. "We're currently matching your fingerprints with those we've found on various items of computer hardware found in your cellar. I'd say it's a matter of mere minutes before we have proof." The DI leans back, studying Mason. "While we're waiting, let's talk about Hollie Hampton."

When Mason looks visibly shocked, a horrifying thought occurs to me. What if he'd groomed Hollie? What if she was one of his models? She'd been noticeably more distressed shortly before she died, according to several of the villagers. "A word, sir?"

Nodding, the DI gets up. "We'll take a short break. I'm going to chase those fingerprints, and then we'll carry on."

Outside, once we're out of earshot, I tell the DI what just occurred to me.

He nods. "You're right. We can't ignore the possibility. We'll get her photo over to forensics and ask them to check it against Mason's images. In fact, do that now, while I talk to them. I'll see you back here in ten minutes."

Ten minutes later, when we reconvene outside the door of the interview room, the DI nods briefly when he sees me. "Mason's fingerprints are on everything. Let's break the news." He holds open the door for me.

"Right." He sits down. "As we expected, your fingerprints were everywhere in that cellar, Mason. You may as well tell us what went on and who else was involved."

Folding his arms, Mason sits back. "I have nothing to say."

"What about Hollie Hampton? Did you pay her? Or did she try to buy you off?"

As Mason frowns, I see what the DI's getting at. "She came to you, didn't she? She knew you were blackmailing her father. She offered you photographs in exchange for releasing him. But you wanted it all, didn't you? By killing Hollie, you kept her photos and continued to force her father to pay you."

"That's ludicrous." But after his earlier performance, it's impossible to know if Mason's look of shock is genuine.

"Is it? We know you persuaded people like James Hampton to invest in your porn business, then blackmailed them for even more money." The DI leans back. "Or do you have a different version of events?"

After glancing sideways at his lawyer, Mason starts speaking. "I admit to some of the photographs—but not all of them."

"They're on your premises, on your machines." The DI's voice is sharp. "That's fairly conclusive."

"Someone else was in on it." He shakes his head. "That's all I can tell you."

"For God's sake, Mason." The DI looks disgusted. "You're doing yourself no favors here. Unless you tell us who it is, you'll be charged with all of it."

But even then, Mason says nothing.

# 26

# Elise

Niamh grabs my arm. "You can't do this. You have to stop. He's going to kill you."

I stare at her, suddenly realizing I've completely misunderstood the way she's been thinking. As she stands in front of me, she's distraught, tears streaming down her face. As it sinks in that she believes her father is capable of killing me, I know a new level of despair. No child should have to carry a weight like that.

"Niamh . . . he won't, he can't . . ."

"He will," she sobs. "You know what he's like. He doesn't care what he does."

I've never seen her so emotional. It's as though everything she's bottled up inside for too long is erupting from her. I try to grab her hands. "Niamh. Stop. This isn't helping."

"Nor is leaving," she sobs. "It will make everything worse. You know it will. We have to stay."

As I stare at my daughter, I know she believes what she's saying, but I have no idea how to respond. "It may seem like that now, but it won't always feel like this. The last few days have been horrible—I know that. But once we're away from here, you'll feel different. Everything passes, Niamh. Everything."

As she calms slightly, I take a deep breath. "Whatever your father told you and everyone else, I didn't kill Dylan."

I hear her sharp intake of breath as her eyes look up at mine. "I know he took my pills. But I used to keep them hidden in the bedroom. I honestly don't recall leaving them out." It's true. I don't. But I'm not absolving myself of responsibility. I was too heavily medicated after his death to remember clearly.

A single sob escapes her. "It was an accident," I tell her gently. "One that should never have happened."

As tears pour down her face, Niamh stares at me. "You don't know, do you?"

I frown at her. "What are you talking about?"

"About what he told Dylan. It wasn't an accident—not the way everyone thinks." As words tumble out of her, more words than she's spoken in weeks, my blood runs cold. Because Niamh tells me she heard Andrew talking to Dylan shortly before he killed himself. That he told Dylan he was ashamed of him. That he would never be anyone Andrew could feel proud of. That it would be better for everyone if Dylan was dead.

My hatred of Andrew reaches new levels. I can't bear to think of what he's put Niamh through and what she's kept silently, painfully, to herself since before Dylan died. "You should have told me this a long time ago." Suddenly I pull off my wedding ring. "The police need to know everything."

"No." The fear is back in Niamh's eyes.

"Niamh. He pushed Dylan over the edge. It's the same emotional abuse he inflicts on us. It's why Dylan took an overdose. This is really important."

"The police can't know." Niamh's eyes are like a rabbit's caught in the headlights of a car. "Not ever."

"Why not?" I study her face. "What haven't you told me?"

"Nothing." She shakes her head, but the shutters have come down.

Getting up, I put the kettle on. I know she's lying. Giving Niamh space for a moment, I make two mugs of tea and take them over to her.

"Here." Passing her one of them, I sit down next to her. "Listen, Niamh. What you've just told me strengthens the case against your father. If the police have enough evidence, they'll be able to charge him."

But she shakes her head. "I won't talk to them."

"I understand," I say softly. She's terrified that if the police fail to charge him, Andrew will be even angrier when he comes after us. "But if you agree to let me, I'll talk to DS May. I'll tell her some of what you've said, but I'll also tell her how frightened of him you are. You've been through so much, Niamh. She'll understand." I pause. "It might even mean we can stay here."

As we sit there a little longer, I pray to God that Andrew doesn't get out, because Niamh's right, in a sense. There's no question it will be worse than the last time he beat me up. But I can't let fear stop me. We have to do this while the police are still holding him. When eventually she nods, I get my phone.

DS May arrives an hour later. As she comes into the kitchen, I notice her long hair isn't as tidy as usual and there are dark circles under her eyes. From what she's said, I guess this case reminds her of what's happened in her own life. It's taking its toll on all of us.

"Can I make you a cup of tea?"

She nods. "I'd love one. How are you both?"

"We're OK." I glance at Niamh, then back to DS May. "We've packed. But there's something you should know. It's a conversation Niamh overheard between Andrew and Dylan, just before he died."

DS May frowns. "Niamh? Can you tell me what he said?"

"She'd rather I tell you," I say, then repeat what Niamh told me earlier.

There's an expression of revulsion on DS May's face as she makes notes. "Where were you when he said this?" she asks Niamh gently.

"Upstairs." Niamh's face is blank.

"I take it he had no idea you overheard."

Niamh shakes her head, an anxious look on her face.

"You mustn't worry about him harming either of you. We have evidence from the hospital, statements from both of you—and now, this. Please let me know if you think of anything else—such as the number of workdays you've missed, Elise, when he's assaulted you in the past. I'm guessing he's kept your medical records clean to cover himself, but the airline you work for will have logged it. Do you have a phone number of anyone I can speak to there?"

Nodding, I get my phone, bringing up the number of my fleet manager. "She'll have a record of all my sick days." I pause. "How much longer will you hold Andrew? I think Niamh needs a little more time before we leave."

"At the moment, tonight." She hesitates. "You'll be OK if you want to stay here one more night—but if you do, I'd recommend you move out first thing tomorrow. He's on record stating he wants a divorce. If I were you, I'd see a lawyer tomorrow and start proceedings."

# Nicki

Even with mounting evidence against Andrew Buckley, I worry for Elise and Niamh. There is still a chance his lawyer could get him out.

When I tell the DI what Niamh said, he shakes his head in disbelief. "We're holding him tonight, on suspicion that he's connected to Mason's business, but in the absence of any evidence, no longer than that."

"I advised Elise Buckley that she was OK to stay in the house tonight, but suggested they move out tomorrow."

"I'd tell her to leave first thing."

I nod. "I already have. We don't want to risk him going back and having another go at her."

The DI frowns. "We need to talk to Buckley again. Press him on what Hollie Hampton had against him. We have to get it out of him."

"Is it worth talking to James Hampton again? Would Hollie have talked to him?"

"Maybe." The DI scratches his head. "Do you want to go and see him? Then when you come back, we'll talk to Buckley together."

*     *     *

As I drive to the custody center where James Hampton is being held, the sun breaks through the clouds. By the time I arrive, it's hot outside. In the distance, the sea is a pale shimmer, just about visible before it merges with the sky. Then I glance at the building, thinking of James Hampton, waiting in one of its soulless rooms for the next stage of his life to be decided for him—a life inside. One he's brought upon himself, thanks to his association with Mason.

When I reach the room we've been assigned, he's already waiting. When he sees me, there's a flicker of hope, as if somewhere he entertains the fantasy that this is all a mistake, that I've come to get him out of here. Pulling out a chair, I sit opposite him. "We've been talking to Andrew Buckley." A shadow crosses Hampton's face. "You must be aware of the incident when Hollie accused him of inappropriately touching her?"

When he nods, I go on. "He's adamant he didn't. I'm not sure we'll ever know whether he did or not. But . . ." I pause for a moment. "He said Hollie did it for revenge, because she found out about his affair with Stephanie. It was a perfectly reasonable, tidy explanation for her behavior—until we found out the affair hadn't started at that point. There must have been another reason she wanted to cause trouble for him. Do you have any idea what it was?"

"None." It's his daughter we're talking about, yet he shows absolutely no anger, no grief, no emotion whatsoever.

I frown. "Do you think it could have been connected to Dylan in some way? Did Hollie talk to you about Dylan?"

"Not really." He sighs. "I wasn't good that way. She was more likely to have talked to Stephanie." Instead of guilty, he looks uncomfortable.

"By all accounts, they were really in love, weren't they? Hollie and Dylan?"

He looks surprised. "I suppose they were."

I try to push him. "So what went wrong between them? I know Hollie broke it off with him, and he was heartbroken—"

But James Hampton interrupts. "That's not right. That isn't what happened. It was Dylan who broke it off. I didn't know what to do with Hollie after that. When he died, she went to pieces. I was really worried about her. For a while, I thought she was going to do what he'd done."

I stare at him, speechless. Then it comes back to me, that it was Andrew Buckley who told me Hollie messed Dylan up, not the other way around. "Andrew Buckley told me Hollie ended it. Can you think of any reason why he might have lied?"

"Buckley." As he says the word, hatred fills his eyes. "You can't believe anything that man says. If he lied, you can bet there was a reason for it."

"But you don't know what?"

Rage briefly illuminates his eyes. Then as he shakes his head, it's gone. His daughter is dead. So is his wife. It's as though James Hampton has decided his life is over, too.

"Buckley told me Hollie screwed up his son when she ended their relationship. But according to James Hampton, it was Dylan who called it off," I tell the DI. "It's a small detail, but it's another lie."

The DI looks at me sharply. "Unless Hampton's lying."

"I suppose. But why would he?"

He shakes his head. "Buckley's in the interview room with his lawyer. He's raging to get out of here. Are you ready?"

After being held overnight, Andrew Buckley isn't his usual groomed-looking self. When he sees us, he immediately gets up. "This better not have cost me my job," he says menacingly.

"Sit down, Dr. Buckley." The DI pulls out a chair. "Mr. Mc-Clure, I suggest you inform your client that the fastest way through this is for him to quickly and accurately answer our questions. Right." He glances at me.

I wait until there's quiet before addressing Andrew Buckley. "We have a witness who overheard a conversation you had with your son."

His eyes glint at me, and he interrupts. "My son's dead, Detective Sergeant. There's no mileage in this."

"Dr. Buckley, let me finish. You were heard using abusive language as you told him he'd never be anything you could be proud of. You told him you were ashamed of him and it would be better for everyone if he was dead. It wasn't long after that he killed himself." I pause, but before he can get a word in, I ask, "Why did you lie to us about Hollie ending the relationship with your son? It was Dylan who broke it off, wasn't it?"

"Look, this has absolutely no relevance to what's happening now."

"I beg to differ," the DI butts in. "What we're hearing is proof of a longstanding pattern of your emotional abuse of your family, not to mention your own unreliability. Go on, Detective Sergeant."

I continue. "You've already told us that it was Hollie who messed Dylan up. However, I have from a reliable source that after Dylan broke it off with her, Hollie was devastated."

"Then your source is incorrect," he says coldly.

"Just as your medical practice had incorrect records of the date Hollie came to see you? And the way your wife denies the problems you accuse her of?" I say pointedly. "Isn't that rather a lot of other people getting it wrong?"

When he doesn't speak, I go on. "Your wife and daughter are staying somewhere for a while. We'll be watching them closely. You are advised to keep away from them, Dr. Buckley. You are already facing charges of controlling and coercive behavior, as well as assault."

For once he's silent. The DI takes over. "I'd like to ask you about Philip Mason. He and James Hampton are involved in a business investment. Did either of them ever approach you?"

"I've told you before, I have no idea what you're talking about." His voice is icy.

The DI gets straight to the point. "Porn, Dr. Buckley, including pornographic images of children."

"And you think I'd get involved in something like that?" His voice is full of contempt.

"I'm merely asking. We've seized Mason's computers. If your name appears anywhere, it's only a matter of time before we find it."

"He's a tricky bastard." Outside the interview room, the DI looks irritated. "He could well be connected with Mason, but if he's used a false name, we might never know. Unless we come up with a good reason, we're going to have to let him go." He starts walking toward his office. "Someone has to know something. The question is who?"

"Someone who knew Hollie, who watches what goes on in the village . . ." Then it occurs to me. "There is someone, sir. Ida Jones. I'll go over and see her now."

"I appreciate your doing this," I say to Ida Jones as she shows me into her sitting room. "I couldn't think of anyone else to ask."

"I'm not sure I can help. I told you before what I know." Her face softens. "So what is it?"

"Do you know Philip Mason, Mrs. Jones?"

She nods. "I do. Can't say I think much of him. He's too charming. People like that are never what they seem."

"Like Dr. Buckley." His name slips out before I can stop it.

She frowns. "I wouldn't say he's charming. That man's a common bully."

"What do you know about him and his family?" Feeling myself frown, I watch her closely.

"He thinks the world of himself, doesn't he? I feel sorry for her, though." She means Elise. "She's a nice woman, but he rules that house. And that poor girl . . ."

"Niamh?"

Ida Jones nods. "Best thing for her was when young Hollie was her friend. Gave her a bit of normality in her life. Didn't last though, did it? That father of hers saw to that."

"What do you mean?"

Her face is sharp as she looks at me. "Didn't like her, did he? Or has he lied and told you how wonderful she was? She was wonderful, you know, just like her mother. Hollie should have been a film star."

It's the first time anyone's mentioned Hollie's birth mother. "You knew Hollie's mother?"

"Oh, yes. I knew Kathryn years ago, when she was a teenager. Never really grew up, that one. Beautiful, free-spirited girl, she was. No wonder James fell in love with her."

"They were happy together?"

"Happier than either of them realized." She hesitates. "You have to understand, Kathryn was driven. James, bless him, never was."

Her words surprise me. "He wrote a book and got it published. That hardly happens easily."

She gives me a knowing look. "That's right. But his agent was a friend of Kathryn's. That's how he got his first break. After that, when Kathryn died, it didn't go so well for him."

I hadn't realized. "When you say she was driven . . ." I hesitate for a moment. "Did that cause problems between them?"

Her eyes gaze into the distance. "Oh, I'll say. It was terrible for a while. But they got over it. It was before Hollie, but after she was born, they seemed to sort themselves out."

I pause, wondering what she's implying. "Kathryn killed herself, didn't she?"

Ida Jones looks sad. "Kathryn was too good for this world. There are people who take advantage of girls like that. And women were jealous of her looks. But she was kind, too. Wouldn't say a bad word about anyone."

I imagine an older version of Hollie, struggling to find her place in the world. Another tortured soul . . . "Was it the same for Hollie? Do you think people took advantage of her?"

Ida Jones shakes her head. "Maybe. She was less tolerant than her mother. But I think the hurt of losing her mum, then Dylan, was too much for Hollie." She frowns. "Why do you need to know all this?"

I level with her. "Mrs. Jones, I'm not sure how much I really know about anyone in this village. It's as though there's an unspoken secret they're all keeping."

"And you think I might know what it is." She nods.

There's a question I have to ask. "Did you know Dylan?"

"Yes," she says softly. "Him and Hollie . . . they were a real love story, those two. I was very sad after everything that happened."

"Can you tell me what you remember about that time?"

Her face is somber. "I used to see them all over the place—walking along the road, up at the churchyard. They never argued. All you saw was his arm around her shoulders, his head leaning down toward hers . . . He was taller, you see. They had the same dark hair." She pauses, remembering. "That's how it was whenever I saw them. At my time of life, it was a blessing to be reminded of how true love felt . . . they seemed to be everything love should be."

I feel myself frown as I listen to her. "So what went wrong?"

Her face clouds over. "I never really understood. I remember that suddenly, I kept seeing Hollie on her own, running along the road, all times of the day and night. Her face was always white. She looked desperate . . . One time, I was in my garden. I called out to her. She turned her head and saw me, but kept on running, as though she couldn't stop. She looked tortured."

"Do you remember seeing Dylan after they broke up?"

"Once." She sighs. "He was standing in the churchyard. His head was down and his hands were in his pockets. You could feel his unhappiness, but it was hardly surprising. His heart had been broken. I didn't talk to him. You can tell, can't you, when someone doesn't want to talk? Of course, after, I wished I had. But I left him alone, thinking he and Hollie must have had a big bust-up. I remember thinking it was odd that he seemed to be staring at the graves." Her forehead wrinkles into a frown. "Then a week later, they were digging his." Her eyes fill with tears. "After seeing him so full of life, I felt it was tragic. I suppose the village did close ranks, as you put it. I think they were protecting the memory of that beautiful couple rather than anything else. And you know what Dr. Buckley's like."

Rather than respond, I let her go on talking.

"I've never understood that household. Elise is a smart woman. She knows what he's up to and she seems to turn a blind eye. I know it's what women used to do, back in my day, but not now, Detective Sergeant. Modern women don't have to let men treat them so shabbily."

"I know what you mean." My eyes meet hers for a moment. "It might seem unbelievable, but it does happen. I know that for a fact." As she looks at me, taking in what I'm telling her, she's silent for a moment.

She looks up. "If you're asking what I think happened to Dylan and Hollie, I believe someone broke them up. It's only my opinion, but from the outside, it didn't look as though it was what either of them wanted. I never saw either of them with anyone else. I don't think there *was* anyone else. Anyway, maybe now, wherever they are, they're together again."

"Why would someone have broken them up?" But as I ask the question, I'm thinking of Niamh's account of the conversation she overheard between her father and Dylan; of Andrew Buckley's comment about how he was glad that Hollie wasn't in Niamh's life anymore. Had he felt that way about Dylan? Had he seen Hollie as a negative influence on his son and somehow forced them not to see each other? But that didn't make sense, either. They were spirited teenagers who wouldn't have let one of their parents stop them from seeing each other. Shaking my head, I know I'm missing something.

"There's someone else who sees what goes on around here. More than you think she might." Ida Jones looks at me. "Young Niamh."

# Niamh

*I lie awake that night, wondering if I'll ever sleep in this bed again, listening to the sounds of night through my cracked-open window. The distant car driving through the village, the hoot from a nearby owl, the sound of the breeze rustling the leaves.*

*All the time, I'm waiting, for the sound of his car on the drive, then his key in the door, his heavy footsteps as he comes upstairs, his muffled angry voice. I imagine him breaking in, slapping my mother's face, which still hasn't healed from the last time, shouting foul words at her, before glancing at me as though I don't exist. And if we're gone when he comes here, he'll search the countryside until he finds us.*

*My father didn't like Hollie coming here. Hollie's independent streak, her free-spiritedness, threatened his hold over me. Her way of questioning what my parents said, asking too many questions I couldn't answer; never accepting what everyone told her. Digging deeper until she found what she was looking for.*

*I remember her coming over to my house that evening. Fragile in her silver dress, her hair tangled. When she told me what she'd found, I didn't believe her. I remember her hands shaking as she pulled it from her pocket, handed it to me. A piece of paper that changed her world—and mine—forever.*

*It's early the next morning, when my mother packs our bags into her car, then locks the house. As we drive away, the countdown begins to my father's explosion of anger; to another moment that's coming closer.*

*I can't put off what I have to tell my mother. She should know why Dylan died. Then when she knows, she'll be able to understand why Hollie died, too.*

*I know I made Hollie a promise, but I really don't know how much longer I can keep it.*

# Nicki

The next morning as I drive to work, I'm thinking about what Ida Jones said, about someone forcing Dylan and Hollie to break up. As I pull into the car park, I already know what I want to do.

Inside, I head straight for the DI's office. When I knock on his door, he's talking on his phone. Beckoning me in, he gestures to me to wait. "Sorry about that, May. That was forensics. They're sending over a list of names in connection with Operation Rainbow."

"Have they checked for images of Hollie?"

"Nothing so far, but they're going through everything more thoroughly now. Ah, here it is."

While the DI prints off the email that's just arrived, I tell him what I've been thinking. "Sir, I want to question Andrew Buckley one more time."

He looks up sharply. "Why?"

"It was something Ida Jones said to me. She's convinced someone must have forced Hollie and Dylan to break up. She doesn't seem to have any idea why. She also said that Niamh may well know more than she's said so far."

The DI looks thoughtful. "That girl drip feeds information, doesn't she?"

I nod. "She's painfully shy—and damaged by her father. You know—" I break off, thinking. "There are a lot of people who are all too keen to hint at what other people know. James Hampton said I should talk to Andrew Buckley. Buckley doesn't give anything away and when he does speak, you can't believe a single word. Ida Jones hints that various things have happened— James Hampton and his first wife went through a rocky patch, but Hampton hasn't mentioned it to me, and until now, Ida Jones hadn't, either. Then there's this whole story around Hollie and Dylan, neither of whom are still alive to tell us what really happened."

The DI frowns. "Buckley left half an hour ago. We've warned him not to contact his wife. Maybe it's worth talking to her again—and Niamh."

I nod. "I was thinking the same. They should be on their way to the cottage by now. I'll check to see if they've arrived."

As I drive along the narrow road that carves its way through miles of downland pasture, the grass verges on either side burgeon with tall grasses and cow parsley; the landscape is painted in hues of verdant green. I pass a flock of sheep and newborn lambs, suddenly hankering after a much simpler life, like the one I imagine Chris Nelson has. He's the retired detective superintendent who runs Mitchelgrove Farm, where Elise and Niamh are staying.

The small cottage Chris lets out from time to time stands in its own garden, away from his farmhouse, affording its occupants privacy. But his background presence is a safety net. After a career of policing, Chris misses nothing. When I pull up outside his house, he wanders outside holding a mug of tea.

"Nicki . . . they arrived about an hour ago." As he nods toward the cottage, I make out Elise's car parked in front of it.

"Thanks for having them here. You look well, Chris."

"You're welcome. Always happy to help in the war against the underworld. I don't suppose it changes much." His face lightly tanned, he has the ease of a man who's comfortable in his own skin. "I've left them some supplies and I'll take them bread and milk tomorrow. They'll be fine for a few days."

"Her husband is a piece of work. He's hiding something— I'm sure of it. Everyone in this case seems to be hiding something. I bet you don't miss it."

He's relaxed as he nods. "Not really. There's the odd occasion, but I could never give this up." I follow his eyes across the patchwork of fields, some of them dotted with grazing animals, the motley assembly of barns. "One of those cases, is it?" His voice is more serious.

"You could say." I wonder how much the DI's told him about the porn ring. "One of those villages where everyone has a secret. I'd better go and talk to them."

"I heard," he says suddenly, just as I turn to walk away. "About you and Joe. I'm so sorry, Nicki. You deserve better."

I feel myself start. It isn't just his words that are unexpected. It's the sentiment. When you work long hours and live alone, you get used to there being no one who cares. "Thank you." But my voice is husky. I clear my throat. "I'll see you later."

As I walk across the yard, I'm conscious of the depth of the silence here. Untouched by even the most distant sound of traffic, the air has a purity, the colors around me a softness. Niamh's face appears fleetingly in one of the cottage windows before disappearing. I imagine that even here, she'll be constantly on edge, thinking it's only a matter of time before her father finds them.

Closing the garden gate behind me, I find the grass neatly mown, the flowerbeds carefully tended. When my knock on the door isn't answered, I push it open.

"Hello? Anyone home?"

Elise's face appears in a doorway, her anxious look quickly fading when she sees it's me. Her bruising is still an ugly purple red, her eyes haunted.

"I'm sorry, I didn't mean to startle you. Is everything OK?"

"As OK as it can be, in the circumstances." Like Niamh, she's clearly on edge, her voice sharp. "I'll make us a cup of tea—if I can find anything."

I know from the bitterness in her voice, from the way she opens cupboards, then closes them loudly as she looks for what she needs, that she resents having to come here. Eventually finding some mugs, she fills the kettle. "How long do we have to stay here?"

I'm evasive. At the moment, there are too many unknowns. "Probably a few days."

Her shoulders stiffen. "And Andrew?"

"He was released this morning. We will be bringing charges against him for assault and coercive behavior. He's been warned to stay away from you, but right now, we can't hold him any longer." I pause, knowing that for as long as he can, Andrew Buckley will continue to deny everything. "How's Niamh bearing up? I saw her face just now, in one of the windows."

"She didn't want to leave our home. Neither of us did." Elise's voice is tight.

Given the memories the house holds for both of them, I'm surprised. "But I thought you were set to move. You'd found somewhere, hadn't you?"

"That was different." She pours boiling water onto teabags, then puts the kettle down, fetching milk before hunting around for the sugar. "It doesn't look like there's any sugar," she says irritably.

"I don't take sugar." Taking the mug she passes me, I watch her nervous movements. "Shall we sit down?"

I follow her across to the small kitchen table, made of antique pine on ornately turned legs. Chris has furnished the cottage simply, creating an air of calm that Elise clearly needs.

"Do you have enough money to tide you over?" I imagine Andrew Buckley using whatever he can as a means of manipulation, including money. I've seen it happen many times.

She nods. "I stopped at the bank on the way here. Once Andrew knows we've gone, he'll probably empty the joint bank account. I transferred what I could into mine."

"Good." I pause, relieved that at least she has her own account; many women in marriages like hers don't. "Have you thought any more about talking to a lawyer?"

She sips her tea. "I'll have to find one. The only one I know of is Andrew's. That's hardly going to work." She raises her eyes to meet mine. "Maybe you can help me."

"I'll get some numbers for you." My voice is quiet. "You really should see someone as soon as—"

"You've already told me." She interrupts, her voice shrill as she talks over me, reminding me again of the strain she's under. "I'm sorry."

"You don't have to apologize." Reaching across the table, I touch her arm, a gesture of human comfort. "I know this is difficult for you. Andrew's been warned to stay away from you," I repeat. "But if he does come anywhere near, call the police immediately." I pause for a moment. "I know you have a lot on your mind right now, but there are a few things I wanted to ask you about. I had a conversation with Ida Jones. She was telling me about Hollie and Dylan, about how in love they were. She couldn't understand why they broke up. After, she said, neither of them was with anyone else. She said it was as though they'd been somehow forced apart. She had no idea why."

"I don't know what went wrong between them. Dylan told me it was over, but he didn't tell me the reason." Elise's face is blank. "I assumed their relationship had run its course. They were young. It was inevitable."

I think back to what Ida Jones said, about how they had something rare, that she felt blessed to witness it. "Your husband said that Hollie ended it, but James Hampton said it was Dylan. You're not sure?"

Her voice is cold. "Dylan wouldn't have confided anything in Andrew. Niamh told you what she heard her father saying to him, before he died. It was Andrew who tipped him over the edge. It wasn't Hollie."

I've no reason to disbelieve her. What she says makes perfect sense. Out of the corner of my eye, I'm distracted by a movement. Looking up, I see Niamh standing in the doorway.

For a moment, she doesn't move. "There was a letter." Her voice is thin, clear.

"What letter?" Elise's voice is sharp.

"Dylan wrote a letter to Hollie. I found it after he died."

"Did you give it to her?" My voice is gentle. When Niamh nods, I go on. "You read it, didn't you?" Again, she nods.

"What did the letter say?" Elise speaks harshly, but everything about her is brittle, as though she'll snap. "Why didn't you tell me?" Then I get it. She's frightened about how much Niamh knows.

As I study Niamh, suddenly I know the answer. She's protecting her mother from something; as the DI said, drip feeding information to us, on what she judges to be a need-to-know basis. Suddenly I know, with certainty, there's more.

Niamh goes on. "Dylan told Hollie he loved her—more than this world. He said she should never forget that." Her voice is surprisingly unemotional. But this isn't new to her. She's been sitting on it for two years. "But he said that if they were together, his father had told him he would destroy her. The only way to save her was to give her up."

I frown at her. "What did he mean by 'destroy her'?"

Niamh's eyes flicker over me. "Before she was with Dylan, Hollie was on drugs. Dylan helped her get off them." Her face is expressionless. "My father said he'd tell everyone—her school, her parents. Everyone."

I stare at her. "Dylan wrote that just before he died?"

Niamh nods. "It was the day before. He left it in his room. I went in there before the police got here and took it. He wouldn't have wanted anyone else to read it. Just Hollie."

"It's why you became friends, isn't it?" My heart twists as I look at her. "You were each other's links to Dylan. No one else could understand." I wonder how Hollie could have tolerated seeing Andrew Buckley, knowing what he'd said to Dylan—unless she'd been biding her time, while she planned a way of getting back at him.

Drifting over to the window, Niamh nods.

"Is there anything else we should know, Niamh?" But as she shakes her head, I know that even if there's more, she's told me all she's prepared to at this stage.

I turn to Elise again. "I have to get back to the office. I'll send you over some phone numbers of lawyers—or if you see Chris, you could always ask him. You can trust him," I emphasize, looking at both of them. "But if at any time you're worried, call us."

"Andrew Buckley found out that Hollie had been on drugs and threatened to expose her."

"Who told you this?" The DI frowns at me.

"Niamh did, sir. After her brother died, she found a letter he'd left for Hollie and took it upon herself to deliver it. It explains what seems like an odd bond between them."

"Bound by a secret that only the two of them knew . . ." The DI nods, deep in thought. "But the knowledge that she'd been taking drugs would hardly have ruined Hollie, would it? Unless Buckley convinced them it would. Was there anything else?"

"Elise Buckley told me that Dylan wouldn't have confided in his father. I believe her—yet Buckley told us that Hollie ended their relationship. Makes you wonder how he knew. I'd like to question Buckley again."

The DI taps his pen on the table. "And I'm going to request an investigation into his finances. If he's involved with Operation Rainbow, the chances are he'll have a tidy sum stashed away somewhere. Buckley clearly knows more than he's saying. There's a good chance his daughter may, too. But we'll start with him."

"We've only just let him go." I glance at the DI. "He isn't going to be exactly pleased to see us."

"Take Collins and Emerson with you. If he tries anything, arrest him."

As we reach Abingworth, the sky clouds over, so that underneath the trees, it darkens to a kind of half-light. In the Buckleys' driveway, I pull up next to Andrew Buckley's car, then turn to Emerson. "Do you want to stay here? I'll let you know if we need you." I look at Sarah. "Are we ready?"

Behind me, Emerson's already climbing out, standing beside the car to make his presence obvious. I look up and see Andrew Buckley watching us from the window. He opens the door before we reach it.

"Back so soon?" His eyes glint dangerously, and he nods toward Emerson. "Isn't your friend joining us?"

I ignore him. "We'd like to ask you a few questions. Could we come in?"

"Do I have a choice?" Making no attempt to hide his irritation, he stands back, holding the door wide open, then closes it behind us. "What is it this time?"

"Do you think we could sit down?"

"Be my guest." He gestures over-expansively toward the table.

When I pull out a chair, he sits opposite me. "I'd like to talk to you about your son."

He folds his arms. "Is there any point? I've told you all there is to know about my son. He has nothing to do with Hollie's death."

"You told us that Hollie left Dylan."

He frowns irritably. "What's your point?"

"James Hampton told us that Dylan broke it off with Hollie."

"He'll say anything; he isn't reliable." Andrew Buckley speaks quickly.

I ignore him. "Your wife said something interesting." I watch his eyes freeze. "She said that Dylan wouldn't have confided in you. So my question is, how are you so sure that's what happened?"

"You had to be there." But he's bluffing. "It was obvious. Elise will say anything. She's—"

I interrupt. "Unreliable, Dr. Buckley? Like James Hampton and everyone else who doesn't agree with you?" As I watch him, he looks less sure of himself. "There's also the letter."

"What letter?" he snaps.

"The letter Dylan wrote to Hollie, the day before he killed himself. Apparently he told her she meant the world to him. But you told Dylan that unless they broke up, you'd destroy her."

"That's ludicrous. Who told you this?" His face pales.

"It was Niamh who found the letter. Dylan must have told her about the drug habit Hollie had kicked. Brothers and sisters talk, Dr. Buckley. It was one thing in your locked-down family you couldn't control. But you found out, didn't you—and used it to blackmail Hollie and Dylan."

His manner subtly changes. "I meant no harm. I was doing what I thought was for the best—for my family. Hollie wasn't good for Dylan."

"So you keep saying. As if you cared . . . It would almost be believable if you hadn't been overheard shouting at your son."

His eyes narrow. "If you want to find out what really happened with Hollie, you're talking to the wrong person, Detective Sergeant. I suggest you talk to my wife—I'm assuming you know where she is?"

He looks at me, as if expecting me to take him seriously. At that moment, my phone buzzes and the DI's number flashes up on the screen. "Excuse me a moment." Getting up, I walk over to the window before answering. "Sir?"

"Are you still with Buckley?"

"Yes."

"Arrest him, May. We've found enough to implicate him in Operation Rainbow. He and Mason were in cahoots."

"You're sure, sir?"

"A million in a bank account set up under a false name that's been found amongst Mason's records. We've got him."

After all his lies and inconsistencies, an odd sense of relief fills me, that this evil man will be removed from circulation for a long time. I end the call and send a quick text to Emerson, who's still waiting outside by the car. As he walks toward the house, I turn around and start back toward the table, glancing at Sarah quickly before I stand opposite Andrew Buckley. "Dr. Buckley, I am arresting you on suspicion of the production and distribution of pornographic images of children. You do not have to say anything. But it may harm your defense if you do not mention when questioned something which you later rely on in court. Anything you do say may be given in evidence."

"You're making a mistake." The look he gives me makes my blood run cold, and I think of what Elise has put up with. "I'm calling my lawyer."

"You can call from the police station, Dr. Buckley."

"I'm not going."

"I'm afraid you don't have a choice." I glance toward Emerson, who's just come in. "Handcuff him. The DI wants us to take him in."

While Andrew Buckley is detained, I go to the DI's office. When I get there, the door is open, his back to me as he stands at the window.

"Sir?"

He immediately turns around. "I take it you've got him?"

I nod. "There was something he said while we were there.

He said we were talking to the wrong person—that we needed to talk to his wife."

"You have—several times." The DI sounds impatient. "Don't get drawn in by anything he says. We know he lies. In any case, she isn't a suspect. What motive could she possibly have?"

"I don't know, sir, but her behavior is erratic. That could be put down to the stress of her marriage, but she isn't the most stable of people." I pause. "It's not like she needs to work, either. Think about it for a moment. Elise has an unpredictable working pattern. Her family takes for granted she is where she says she is. She could put on that uniform and go anywhere, for all we know. She might go somewhere else, even meet someone, especially given her husband's series of affairs. Or she could just be hiding from her miserable marriage. We've never actually checked out her job."

"Then do it," the DI says quietly. "We need to rule her out. The next time her slippery husband tries to distract us, we'll know exactly where we stand."

We should have done it some time ago, but as the DI said, Elise has never been a suspect. When I check my notes, according to Elise, the day Hollie died, she flew to Barcelona. It takes me five minutes to get through to her manager.

There's a brief pause. "That's right. She was rostered on a flight to Barcelona that day. But hold on a moment . . . I need to check something." The phone goes quiet for a moment. "She was definitely rostered to go to Barcelona that day, but on that morning, she didn't turn up."

# 27

# Elise

In the farm cottage, Niamh and I are still in limbo waiting for one of the lawyers to get back to me when my mobile buzzes.

"Elise? It's DS May. I thought you'd want to know that we've arrested your husband. I'll let you know more in due course, but I wanted you to be the first to hear."

My heart lifts. "Does this mean we can go home?"

"I'm afraid not." DS May hesitates. "We're going to have to search your house. I'm sorry about all this." She pauses again. "I'll stop over later on and fill you in on everything."

As the call ends, I stare in disbelief at my phone, then turn to Niamh. "The police have arrested your father. That was DS May. She didn't say why."

"So we can go home?" Niamh looks hopeful.

"Not yet." I look at her. "The police have to search the house, apparently. She'll come by later to let us know what's happening."

The color drains from Niamh's face.

"What's wrong, Niamh?"

She shakes her head. "Nothing."

"Are you sure?"

She's silent. Then she says, "I have some of Dylan's stuff, that's all. They won't take it, will they?"

I frown at her, wondering how I hadn't come across it. "What kind of stuff?"

"Just things he wrote. Some of his drawings. Photos."

"It's your father's stuff they'll go through. I can't imagine the police will want to look through your things." I look at Niamh more closely, taking in her anxious look. "Are you alright?"

She nods, but before I can ask her more, my phone buzzes again with an unfamiliar number. "I need to get this. It could be one of the lawyers." I answer the call, frowning as I watch Niamh slip upstairs.

An hour on the phone to Alison Wantley, the divorce lawyer, leaves me fortified. That I have an idea of where I stand and what to expect going forward gives me new strength. But also, now that Andrew's being held by the police, Niamh and I no longer have to stay in hiding.

"You could go back to school tomorrow." I look at Niamh. "I have an appointment to see a lawyer in the morning. It won't be long before things can get back to normal." I'm trying to reassure her, but both of us know that normal doesn't exist anymore; that time is needed to undo the damage inflicted by Andrew.

She nods, then suddenly remembers something. "I haven't got any of my school stuff."

"I didn't even think about that." I hadn't packed her uniform or any of her books. "I'll call DS May. Hopefully, they'll let us collect it."

Later that afternoon, the farmer, Chris, raises a hand as we get in the car. As we drive home to Abingworth, I realize the weight of what was hanging over me. For a brief moment, I can almost pretend nothing's happened, but the feeling doesn't last. When we turn into the drive, several police cars are parked there, including a white van. When we walk in, a man carrying Andrew's computer passes us on his way out.

Niamh turns to me in horror. "They won't want mine, will they?"

"I don't know. I shouldn't think so. Your father never used it, did he?" Then Sergeant Collins comes toward us. "Mrs. Buckley? Niamh? The DS said you needed to pick up your school uniform. I'm really sorry about all this." She glances back toward the house. "Niamh? I'm afraid I need to go with you. Is that OK?" She speaks as if we have a choice, but I know we don't.

Coming here has brought back too many unpleasant memories. "I'll stay here." As I watch them disappear inside, it's as if I'm standing outside someone else's house. Several policemen go to and fro carrying what I imagine to be the contents of Andrew's desk. Then a light goes on upstairs, in our bedroom, where no doubt the police will be going through my and Andrew's clothes. All this, and I still don't know why, though I'm guessing DS May will explain when she comes to see us.

A few minutes later, Niamh comes back with Sergeant Collins, carrying an armful of clothes and her school bag. Without speaking, she climbs into the car.

"Let's go." Putting the car into reverse, I turn it around, not wanting to linger a moment longer than necessary. In the short time we've been away, an invisible line has been drawn between the past and the future, one we've crossed so that we can go forward. I can no more imagine living here than I can imagine being with Andrew. As we drive away, the realization hits me. I've no desire to ever come back.

The next morning I drive Niamh to school, then go to my meeting with Alison Wantley, who's going to start divorce proceedings. In the safety of her office, with a view onto a quiet street in the heart of Chichester, I start to tell her everything about my marriage. It's painful. It's also cathartic. After, I walk around the town center, doing a bit of shopping and looking in the windows of estate agents, before I drive back to the farm. For the first time in years, I feel a tentative sense of hope. I'd never loved living in Abingworth. I miss nothing about village life, nor have I any desire to bump into familiar faces. None of those people really care. Even Sophie hasn't contacted me. All these years of living there and I know no one will miss me, even slightly.

When I get back to the cottage, I start to tidy away the breakfast things, then go upstairs, throwing open windows, picking up Niamh's discarded clothes on the floor of her bedroom. Underneath them, I find an envelope.

# Niamh

When Dylan and Hollie fell in love, my father always knew he'd have to stop them. But he let it go on, waited, until their hearts grew closer, their love deeper, until they couldn't live without each other. Then he went to Dylan's room and told him. My father likes to watch people suffer.

I heard my father shout, Dylan's cries of pain. Later, when I found out what he'd done, I knew he might as well have given Dylan a loaded gun and told him to point it at his head.

Dylan was supposed to be the brilliant academic who'd have the same high-flying medical career as his father. Anything else—being the brilliant artist and musician he was—that was a failure in my father's eyes. But it was never about what Dylan wanted. My father only cared about my father.

The sun was shining the day he told Dylan the truth. It was the day he destroyed his son's dreams. Dylan couldn't be with Hollie. Then my father told him he wasn't good enough to be his son. Dylan's hopes and dreams, and then his future, were dismantled, piece by piece, by layer upon layer of my father's cruelty. Dylan didn't kill himself; my father destroyed him.

# Nicki

In the interview room, while he questions Andrew Buckley about his involvement with Operation Rainbow, the DI barely conceals his contempt. "You used the name Charles Harvey. It appears on Mason's computer several times, as well as on one of your bank accounts."

"It doesn't prove anything."

"Forensics are going through your computer as we speak. We'll see what we find before we decide that." He pauses for a moment. "How does an established GP get involved in child porn?" Clearly disgusted, he manages to keep his voice quiet. "You must have known you were jeopardizing everything you'd worked for."

When Andrew Buckley says nothing, I know the DI's thinking the same thing I am. It isn't people Buckley cares about. It's power.

"You will be held while we continue our investigations." As the DI gets up and walks out, I follow him and find Sarah Collins coming toward us.

"There was a message while you were out. Elise Buckley urgently wants to talk to you. She called about half an hour ago. She sounded tearful."

I glance at the DI. "I'll call her right away."

On my way back to my office, I get out my phone, switch it on, then call her. "Elise, it's DS May. Sorry I missed you earlier. Is everything OK?"

She sounds jittery. "I found something earlier. I think you should see it."

As I drive over to the farm, the toxic effect of being in close proximity to Andrew Buckley seems to hang over me, and I think about what I have to ask his wife. I thought I'd got the measure of Elise Buckley, but now I'm less sure.

When Elise opens the door, she looks flustered. "Come in. I'll get Niamh."

"In a moment." I hesitate. "I need to ask you something. It's probably nothing, but when we were asking your husband about Hollie, he said we were talking to the wrong person— that we needed to talk to you. Do you have any idea why he might have said that?"

"No." I watch her tense.

"There's no easy way to say this, so I'm just going to come out with it. You told us you were on a flight to Barcelona the day Hollie died. I checked with the airline, Elise. They said you didn't show."

I've never imagined Elise could have killed Hollie, but when her face turns white, suddenly I confront the fact that I've let my own experiences influence my perception of her. Maybe I've read her terribly wrong.

"It isn't what you think," she says at last. "If you must know, I had a hospital appointment. I found a lump. I couldn't let Andrew find out. He'd use it to wear me down. Another addition to his list of reasons why I'm an unsuitable mother . . . I've been back several times—scans, a biopsy. It's malignant, but they think they've caught it early enough. I'm waiting for a date for surgery."

It seems too much for one person to cope with—alone, keeping it from her family. "I wish I'd known." Then I frown at her. "But he couldn't use your illness to discredit you."

"You think Andrew wouldn't do that? You don't know my husband. He'd say I couldn't possibly look after Niamh if I'm about to have surgery and all the follow-up treatment—on top of everything else." She sighs. "He's right when he says I had a breakdown. He's kept it out of my medical records, so far . . . If you were to look, you'd find no record of it. He says that if he wanted to, he could tell the airline enough that I'd lose my job." For the first time, she looks directly at me. "Basically, my husband's been blackmailing me."

It might sound implausible, but I can all too easily imagine Andrew Buckley's exaggerated account of the problems his wife has, no doubt most of them caused by years of his abuse. Shaking her head, Elise changes the subject. "This is what I wanted to show you." She passes me an envelope.

Inside there's a single piece of paper. Taking it out, I unfold it, feeling a sense of disbelief as I read it. "Where did you find this?"

"Niamh had it. She has a collection of things that were Dylan's. It was among them."

"She knows you're showing me this?"

A new calm seems to have come over Elise. As she nods, I ask, "And she's here?"

Elise glances toward the door. "She's upstairs. I'll call her."

At last, I feel things begin to fall into place. This single piece of paper explains Dylan's death and Hollie's behavior, why Andrew Buckley had to force Hollie and Dylan to stay apart. It fits with Ida Jones's account of Kathryn and James Hampton's marriage. It explains Niamh's reticence, too, but she's still lied to us.

I glance at Elise. "You didn't know Hollie Hampton was Andrew's daughter?" When she shakes her head, I watch her closely, thinking of Niamh, keeping her secret all this time, trying to protect her mother.

As Niamh comes in, her expression is wary as she looks at me. "I should have shown you before." She glances at Elise.

"Yes, you should have. But I understand why you didn't. You were trying to protect your mother, weren't you? She knows everything now, Niamh." I pause, thinking not just of Niamh's secrets, but the way Elise kept her cancer diagnosis hidden. "It isn't always easy, but sometimes it's better for everyone to be honest."

"Did he kill Hollie?" Her voice is quiet.

"We're still not sure. Tell me . . ." I pause for a moment. "Where did you get this?"

"Hollie gave it to me." Her eyes don't leave mine.

"When?"

"A week before she died. She asked me to look after it for her."

I shake my head slowly. It explains why she was so angry with him; why she set him up at the surgery, why she was so tortured. "When she understood why Dylan ended their relationship, she must have been beside herself." As I pause, I figure it out. "But you knew, didn't you? Before Hollie did."

Her calm is eerie as she nods. "Dylan told me." She pauses. "Hollie said her mother didn't kill herself."

Had she suspected that Andrew had had a hand in Kathryn's death? Another secret added to so many, until the weight of them crushed her? I make a note to look up Kathryn's death. Frowning, I go on. "Do you know if she spoke to your father?"

Niamh shrugs. "She said she was going to. She said she wanted to hurt him really badly, like he'd hurt Dylan, then she wanted to kill him, not just because of Dylan but because he'd had an affair with her mother."

"Do you know if she talked about it to her father—to James?

He must have known about their affair, from the birth certificate."

Niamh's face is blank. "I don't think they talked about it. Hollie couldn't bear to see him upset."

So, Hollie kept silent, bottling her anguish, knowing James Hampton had been hurt too many times, through circumstances beyond his control; especially when Andrew Buckley had had an affair with his second wife as well as his first. For the first time I understand just how much James must hate Andrew Buckley. Little does he know, Buckley's time is running out.

# Niamh

*It was Dylan who told me that Hollie was our half-sister. My father told him. Brutally, enjoying his agony, Dylan confided in me later. "He's evil, Niamh. He doesn't care about any of us. His whole life is a lie. Get away from him as soon as you can."*

*Over the days that followed, I saw how Dylan suffered. His father had watched him fall in love with his half-sister, taunting him with cruel words, dragging him lower, twisting Dylan's life in his bare hands until the morning it snapped.*

*The night before, there was a dullness in Dylan's eyes. "There is no point anymore," he told me. "I love Hollie and I can't be with her."*

*"You'll love someone else," I tried to tell him. "There'll be another girl, Dylan."*

*But the light was dimming in his eyes, his life force dimming as I watched him. He already knew, there never would be anyone else.*

*The next morning, I remember the quiet in the kitchen. The sense of emptiness in the house, as if it knew Dylan had already gone. It was an hour later my mother tried to wake him. "Dylan, it's late. You need to get up."*

*He didn't reply. But time didn't matter where Dylan had gone. I sat downstairs, listening as she opened his door; when she cried out, I knew. There was no one to keep him here. When the greatest love is taken from you, there is nothing.*

# 28

# Elise

Over the days that follow, I discover the extent of what Niamh's kept from me. Putting it together with what she still keeps to herself, I edge closer to the truth. Whether Andrew will ever admit to killing Hollie is another matter, but the weight of evidence against him, his proven violence and aggression, his treatment of Dylan, all paint a clear picture.

Andrew's arrest allows me to reset my life. When forensics finish in our house, Niamh and I go back to sort through what we're taking with us, putting the rest in storage for Andrew until he's released. Pitched from limbo into a process of rapid adjustment, I gradually come to terms with a failed marriage and a husband who's a criminal.

But, coexisting with evil in this world, some people are good. In an uncertain life, Chris Nelson is an unlikely guardian angel, offering us his farm cottage for as long as we want it and giving Niamh a place to stay while I have my surgery. It's a breathing space, a gesture of kindness in an unkind world, one I accept gratefully. In our own time we'll work out how to move on.

When Andrew is charged for his part in Phil Mason's porn

business, he's jailed. But as far as Hollie's death is concerned, the evidence is circumstantial and the investigation into her murder remains unsolved. When my divorce comes through, I'll be leaving Andrew in the past. By the time he gets out of prison, Niamh will be an adult and able to make her own decision as to whether she wants him in her life. But his part in mine is over.

So that's what it's about now. Leaving the past behind. We're all human, with short lives and instincts we have limited control over, but in a changing world, surrounded by other short lives, it's the only thing any of us can do. Keep moving forward.

# Niamh

*No ending is ever perfect. Pain and sadness can never be atoned for. But just occasionally, there is a way.*

*For a while I thought my mother was having an affair. It was those mysterious phone calls, the shadows under her eyes, her secrecy about her cancer. But everyone in my family has a secret, just as everyone makes mistakes. After Dylan's death, my father's abuse, learning Hollie was my half-sister, I had to do something.*

*"I'll fucking kill him, Niamh," she sobbed the night she showed me her birth certificate. "I hate him. He killed Dylan. He killed your brother..." Her voice grew more high-pitched with every word, until she fled, distraught, into the darkness. Running from pain there was no escape from, toward a future that, like Dylan, she didn't want.*

*Everyone noticed Hollie was at breaking point, but only I was the holder of her secret, the one that had the power to ruin lives. We'd gone to the Penns' garden again. "There's no point, Hollie," I tried to tell her. "You don't know what he's like. He'll hurt you. He hurts everyone. Don't tell him. You don't want him in your life."*

*The wind had picked up, the sky a shade of yellow under clouds that blotted out the last of the sun. Under the cover of dusk, she ran across the grass. "I want him to suffer." Her voice was murderous. Then, stretching out her arms, she spun around in circles. "I want everyone to know. Even your mum."*

*"No." My cry was drowned by the sound of the wind, as I felt anger rip through me. I'd kept everything to myself, protecting my mother from what really happened. Growing up, I'd watched her suffer so many times at the hands of my father. And now Hollie had the power to make everything a million times worse. "It'll destroy my mother, Hollie."*

*"What about me?" Her face was pale under a sliver of the moon that had appeared.*

*"You can't change the past, Hollie. It's happened. You have to move on," I begged her.*

*But her eyes were wild, desperate, as she stared at me. "He's evil, Niamh . . . Look what he did to Dylan. We can't let him get away with it. He has to pay."*

*As she said that, I knew she was right. My father deserved to atone for his sins, for the cruelty inflicted on all of us. But an image of my mother's face came to me. She'd suffered too much already. "You can't hurt my mother," I said softly.*

*"God, Niamh . . . this isn't about your mother." Throwing her arms up in the air in an exaggerated show of frustration, Hollie turned her back on me and started walking away.*

*I felt rage explode in me, that Hollie didn't care about my mother or about me; that she had the power to destroy what remained of my family. "You don't understand!" I screamed, running at her, knocking her off her feet.*

*When she sat up, she rubbed her head. When she looked at her fingers, there was blood. "Shit, Niamh." But her voice was subdued. "We'd better go back."*

*We'd reached the hedge by the pool when her steps became uneven. Suddenly she lurched closer to the edge; then, feeling herself lose her balance, reached out for something to grasp onto. I heard the wind gusting through the trees, saw the wildness in her eyes as they met mine. I wanted to reach out and grab her hands, but something stopped me.*

*It happened in a split second. She didn't cry out as her head cracked against the side of the pool. Then her body hit the water, and in the dim light, I stood there as it floated for a moment, motionless, surrounded by leaves. Around me, I heard the wind picking up force. Glancing up, I saw the clouds racing past the moon. When I looked back down toward the pool, the leaves had closed over her. Hollie had gone.*

# Acknowledgments

It's hard to believe that this is my fifth psychological thriller! And I'm thrilled to be published by such a dedicated team, to whom I owe a huge thank you. Firstly, as always, to Alicia Condon, for your thoughtful and insightful editing. It is a joy to work with you: To Elizabeth Trout, Crystal McCoy, Carly Sommerstein, and everyone else involved in getting my books out there, I'm enormously grateful to all of you.

Huge thanks also to my superstar of an agent, Juliet Mushens, for everything you do for me and my books. You truly have changed my life.

And the biggest thank you to you, my readers, for buying my books, writing reviews, sharing them with other people, because it really makes a difference. I'm grateful to each and every one of you.

This isn't the first time I've written about abusive relationships and I hope I have done justice to the immense damage they cause, as well as the pain and suffering inflicted. For children from abusive households, there can be a whole host of problems: depression, anxiety, low self-esteem, to name but a few, with consequences that can last a lifetime. If in any way this book helps highlight what goes on, that can only be good.

Last, but by no means least, I want to say thank you to my wonderful family and my friends. To my sisters, Sarah, Anna and Freddie, to whom this book is dedicated. Thank you for your unending support. I'm lucky to have you. To my dad—my love of books definitely began in my childhood. To Georgie and Tom, for your endless encouragement. You mean the whole world to me. And to Martin, for being my partner in this great adventure.

# Connect with

## Visit us online at
### KensingtonBooks.com
to read more from your favorite authors, see books
by series, view reading group guides, and more.

for sneak peeks, chances to win books and prize packs,
and to share your thoughts with other readers.

**facebook.com/kensingtonpublishing**
**twitter.com/kensingtonbooks**

## *Tell us what you think!*
To share your thoughts, submit a review,
or sign up for our eNewsletters, please visit:
**KensingtonBooks.com/TellUs.**